PEDRO DE TORREROS

AND THE VOYAGE OF DESTINY

OTHER BOOKS IN THE CRIMSON CROSS SERIES

CRIMSON CROSS SERIES

PEDRO DE TORREROS

AND THE VOYAGE OF DESTINY

PETER MARSHALL AND **DAVID MANUEL**
AND **ANNA FISHEL**

B&H
PUBLISHING GROUP

Nashville, Tennessee

ACKNOWLEDGMENTS

The authors express their thanks to Don Zuris and the other staff members of the Museum of History and Science in Corpus Christi, Texas. The replicas of the Columbus ships: *Santa Maria, Pinta,* and *Niña,* and the excellent exhibits there provided invaluable research help. We also extend a special word of gratitude to Kay Brigham, whose beautiful translation of Columbus's *Book of Prophecies,* and her encouragement when we were writing *The Light and the Glory,* were a blessing from God.

THE CHARACTERS

PRINCIPALS

Pedro de Torreros: a fifteen-year-old orphan of the famed Franciscan monastery, La Rábida, who dreamed of going to sea all his life.

Don Cristobál Colón: the visionary missionary explorer, known in the English-speaking world as Christopher Columbus.

AT LA RÁBIDA

Father Juan Peréz: the deeply spiritual abbot of the monastery, a counselor to Columbus, and a father to Pedro ever since the boy had been sent to him to raise.

Father Antonio de Marchena: the wise and kindly friar who taught Pedro to read, write, and work with figures. But his greatest gift was teaching Pedro to think for himself.

Caballo: the monastery's old and amiable horse.

THE SAILORS

Juan De la Cosa: master and owner of the *Santa Maria*.

Peralonso Niño: the ship's pilot and Pedro's mentor and friend.

Emilio: another ship's grommet like Pedro.

Chachu: the ship's boatswain.

Marco Arias: the ship's helmsman.

Martín Alonso Pinzón: captain of the *Pinta*.

Vicente Yáñez Pinzón: Martín's brother, captain of the *Niña*.

THE INDIANS

Macu: the Arawak Indian who became Pedro's friend.

Liani: Macu's wife.

Guacanagari: the grand cacique, or chief, who aided Columbus and his men on Española.

1

A RESCUE

The stone—the only one he had left—was flat and smooth in his hand. Carefully he rubbed it, drew back his right arm, and flung it sidearm. *Skip, skip, skip*—the rock skimmed the surface of the warm river water and startled its target, a tan sandpiper pruning her white underbelly.

Perfect, thought Pedro proudly. The agile fifteen-year-old sat down on the edge of the dock and, dangling his bare feet in water up to his ankles, watched all the commotion. Tomorrow was a big day for the town of Palos. No, as Father Peréz had said, tomorrow was a big day for all of *Spain*! Pedro's dark eyes weren't about to miss any of the preparations going on today.

Located on the brush-lined estuary that mixed the Rio Tinto's fresh water with the salt of the Atlantic Ocean, Palos de la Frontera nuzzled the southwestern coast of Spain near the Andalusian Mountains. Just over six miles from the sea and a little over one mile north of La Rábida, the Franciscan monastery where Pedro lived, Palos was well-known for its ship-building and its experienced seamen.

Today the harbor buzzed with activity. The rigging lines flapped against the tall masts of the ships, while barefoot sailors yelled instructions to one another. Women, dressed in plain garments with thick belts, carried handwoven baskets of food on their heads for the sailors. A small group of children splashed one another and laughed in the lapping waves along the muddy riverbank. Pedro caught scents of freshly cut wood and tar mixed with sweat and river marsh.

The largest ship, a *nao* called the *Santa Maria*, was moored at the dock, while sailors rolled kegs of fresh water from the old well up the wide gangplank. The two smaller ships, outfitted yesterday, were caravels named *Pinta* and *Niña*. They floated lazily at anchor in the rippling estuary, their flags hanging limply, their sails furled, and their crow's nests empty for the moment.

1

As the river current hurried along toward the nearby ocean, it called the ships to join it on its journey, nudging them to pull on their anchors. Pedro could feel the same tug on his soul. He loved the sea, and he spent as much time as the Franciscan friars would permit down at the dock. When a vessel sailed into the harbor, Pedro always asked questions of the bronze sailors lugging smelly barrels of fish toward market. He understood that the fore-castle was at the bow or front of the ship and the poop deck or stern-castle was aft, at the back. He knew that a lateen sail, the mainsail of the *Niña*, was triangular in shape, and that yards were the poles that held up and spread the tops of the sails.

He also listened to the many Spanish merchants, who told stories full of mystery and intrigue about North Africa and spice bazaars and faraway people with slanted eyes. Pedro's dream was to sail in command of his very own ship. He would, too—one day.

All at once, a cascade of water exploded over him, and someone was yelling.

"Emilio, we can't lose that one," a voice boomed. "It's sinking!"

Pedro spotted a short, stocky boy about his own age, standing on the gangway leading from the dock up to the port side of the *Santa Maria*. He was peering down into the water.

Pedro looked, too. Nothing remained but an irregular pattern of bubbles and ripples.

"Chachu," the boy cried, "you know I can't swim! How am I supposed to get it?"

"I don't care!" the sailor bellowed over the side rail. "That pulley is part of our steering rig. *You* dropped it. *You* get it!"

Pedro pushed his black bangs, sticky from the noon heat, off his brow. He could swim, and his well-muscled shoulders proved that he did it often. Maybe he could help.

He jumped up. "I'll get it!" he hollered and plunged in.

The river water was warm near the surface, but Pedro quickly swam down through the colder water to the spot where the pulley should have landed. For nearly a minute, he groped blindly around the slimy bottom. No pulley.

Like a dolphin he popped back up to the surface for air. Taking a couple of big breaths, he flipped over and dived back down into the murky water. Suddenly his fingers hit one side of a blunt square object. He grabbed it and, holding it tightly with one hand, swam hard up to the surface with his other arm.

As he came out of the water, however, his head nearly hit the bottom of the ship, right under the gangway. Paddling to stay afloat with the heavy pulley, he gasped for air. His eyes, still blurred from the river water, slowly focused on what appeared to be a sheet of lead in the hull of the flagship at the waterline. Square iron nails had been pounded into the lead every few inches. Pedro had never seen anything like this.

From above, the muffled words reached Pedro's clogged ears. "Hello, down there! What is happening?"

"I've got it," he yelled, trying not to swallow any more water.

In a few moments, he had scrambled back up the rungs of the dock's ladder.

The young sailor named Emilio was waiting for him. "I'll take that," he hissed and, snatching the heavy pulley, he turned and stomped away.

Pedro shook his head to get the water out of his left ear and adjusted the twisted three-strand rope belt around his waist.

Just then, the faint sound of three church bells floated upriver with a sudden breeze. The bells of La Rábida!

Vespers!

Pedro knew he'd better get back quick, or Father Peréz, the head of the monastery, would not be happy. Missing evening prayer was forbidden, and Pedro didn't really care to scrub the chapel's stone floor again today.

As he started up the dirt path toward the monastery, the smell of fish mingled with the salty sea air. In the early afternoon sun, the river's deep broad mouth stretched as far as Pedro could see, a perfect harbor for Palos, downstream close to the mouth of the river. The red-tiled roofs and white adobe houses of the town appeared like a bright, colorful painting tinged with yellow and outlined in sky blue.

And then he saw another ship, anchored just downriver from the town dock, near the place where the Rio Tinto joined the Saltés before emptying into the ocean. The ship's sails fluttered in the soft warm summer breeze while she waited for the outgoing tide.

Pedro had heard the friars talking about that ship. Its passengers were Jewish exiles, being forced to leave Spain today. Condemned by the Spanish monarchs and the Church for not following the Church's teaching, they were being deported to the Mediterranean and the lands of Islam.

Squinting at the ship, Pedro was able to recognize the village's black-smith and his family, huddled together on the main deck. He spotted the traditional, pointed, cone-like hat the bearded man always wore when he did work at the abbey. The woman's dark blue mantel partially hid her face. The two young boys, who liked to play in the open cloister while their father was occupied, buried their faces in the folds of their mother's dress, as if they could make this all go away by not looking.

Pedro paused. Tiny gnats buzzed about his damp ears. He scrunched his bare toes in the hot sand and waved toward the ship. But they didn't see him, or at least no one waved back.

A yellow-tailed dragonfly landed on Pedro's arm and brought him back to reality. He dashed up the hill past the two bronze plaques at the monastery's entrance. Having polished them many times, he knew them well. The top one commemorated the order's founder, St. Francis of Assisi, Italy, 1209. The other recorded the monastery's title and founding: Monasterio de Santa María de La Rábida, 1261—some 231 years ago.

Slipping into the very back pew of the chapel, he sat down quietly next to another orphan, trying to make his well-proportioned body as small as possible. His chest was still thumping, as he tried to even out his breathing in time with the song.

> *To you do we send up our sighs,*
> *Mourning and weeping in this valley of tears.*
> *Turn then, most gracious advocate*
> *Your eyes of mercy toward us.*

The melody of the Latin chant, "Salve Regina," echoed around the brown stone walls, the many male voices blending as one.

Maybe, just maybe, Father Peréz hadn't noticed.

2

A SPECIAL GUEST

While most of the common rooms in the monastery were of good size, the one opening onto the south cloister was small. It was exactly right for a private meeting between the abbot and two or three friars, or for entertaining a special guest, as was the case tonight.

Pedro shoved open the panel door in the arched doorway with his foot and entered. He carried a tray with two pewter plates filled with tomatoes smothered with olive oil and fresh oregano. The friars of La Rábida were known for their olive oil, which they pressed after beating the olives off the trees with sticks, and then crushing them in stone mortars. The aroma of the oregano, fresh from their herb garden, wafted through the little room.

"Set them here, Pedro," directed Father Juan Peréz, abbot of La Rábida, his deep baritone voice filling the small room.

Franciscan hospitality was well-known. The long, narrow oak table in the middle of the room had been formally set for two long before Vespers. The scent of five flickering wax candles on the table would have drawn anyone into the sparsely decorated room. Other than the crucifix on one wall, the surroundings were whitewashed and plain.

For a moment the only sound was the clacking of Pedro's leather sandals across the red tile floor.

"You missed Vespers, lad." The words were direct but not harsh.

"Sí, Padre," Pedro sighed. He loved the abbot very much and didn't want to disappoint him.

"I take it you were at the river again."

Pedro looked at him, surprised.

"You're still damp," explained the elderly Franciscan with a smile.

"Yes, Father. The *Santa Maria*, the *Niña*, the *Pinta*—they're all leaving tomorrow! I wanted to watch—and lost track of the time." The words nearly ran together.

"How many times have I told you?" Father Peréz's wrinkled brow softened. The two deep-set brown eyes twinkled slightly.

"I ran back as soon as I heard the bells, but I didn't have time to dry. I'm sorry, Father." Placing the abbot's plate before him, the slim fifteen-year-old held his breath for a well-deserved reprimand.

Instead, the friar turned to his guest and chuckled. "I've understood for some time, Captain, that we're simply caretakers of this lad." He smoothed out his brown woolen robe and shook open the white napkin, folded neatly by his plate. "I feel certain God has something other than monastic life in store for him. In fact, it appears he was immersed in it today."

"Oh, Father, it was a sight to behold!" The words gushed out of Pedro's mouth like a waterfall. "There were sailors everywhere! I watched them roll water barrels up the plank. I even rescued a pulley that one of the sailors dropped in the river!"

The visitor removed his soft black velvet hat and put it on the chair beside him. Pedro knew this visitor from his frequent stays at the abbey over the past seven years. He was Cristobál Colón, captain of the *Santa Maria* and leader of the expedition that would be sailing on the morning tide. No one in Spain called him by his Italian or English names, Christoforo Colombo or Christopher Columbus, especially not Father Peréz, who had become his close friend.

"A pulley?" the captain asked.

"Yes, sir," replied Pedro, placing his plate before him. "It had something to do with the tiller."

"Yes, a vital part of our steering mechanism," responded the captain who spoke fluent Castilian Spanish, with a hint of an accent from his native Genoa in northern Italy. He looked carefully at the boy. "You recovered it from the bottom of the river?"

"Aye, sir, I can swim," said Pedro proudly. "The sailor who dropped it couldn't."

The captain said nothing, but his eyes narrowed as he studied Pedro's intelligent face. The captain was a tall man, well-built, with the ruddy complexion of a seasoned sailor. His once red hair was now almost white. Pedro was struck by his serene manner, and the confidence that seemed to radiate from him. The man's presence filled the room.

The abbot steered the conversation away from ships. "Let us bless the food, Cristobál."

Sensing it was time to be quiet, Pedro stepped back and waited as the padre prayed. Reds, yellows, and purples streamed in through the small transparent mosaic window behind him, making a pattern on the refectory table and coloring the dust particles in the early evening air.

"Able seamen are rare, Father Juan," murmured the captain, as he sampled the tomato salad. "I hope the lad will get his chance soon."

"You've been quite busy these past few months, Cristobál," the abbot observed with a smile. "It is good to see you again."

The captain dabbed the white napkin at some olive oil from the reddish gray stubble on his chin. "That I have, Father. We're outfitted at last. I can hardly believe it myself. Don't know that I'll sleep much tonight." His blue eyes sparkled with the delight of a dream come true.

"God has been good to you, my son."

"I'm grateful for all your help. And that of Father Antonio, too." The captain pushed back the ruffles at the end of each sleeve so they wouldn't touch the oil on his plate. "I shudder to think what would have happened had I never met you or the Pinzóns!"

"God has a way of placing the right people in our path to enable us to do what He has called us to do." The old monk smiled. He turned to the lad standing quietly by the window. "You may bring us the next dish, Pedro."

Pedro went quickly to the kitchen to get it. Down the corridor, the heavy oak door to the abbey's library was ajar, and he could smell the leather and the parchment of the ancient hand-lettered books it contained. Was Father Antonio at work? He glanced in. Several freshly rolled sheep-skin parchments on the friar's desk, coupled with his puncher and awl, indicated that the scribe had been working recently. The quill pen wasn't perched in its usual hold in the desk, and the inkhorn was full. Perhaps he was working on another of his special drawings.

Pedro smiled as he continued on his way. He had spent many hours in that room, at his own waxed table, learning to etch perfectly formed letters with a special metal pen.

Father Antonio had taught him to read. Him! Pedro de Torreros. A peasant! Before coming to the monastery eight years ago at the age of seven, Pedro had never met anyone who could read. And now using his imagination as he read, he had traveled through the treeless chalky plains of Cadiz, the famous wine country. With saber in hand, he had scaled a fortress wall on the coast of Italia, after sailing the mighty Mediterranean. He had even bumped along on a dappled mare across the Holy Roman Empire with Marco Polo, all the way from Venice to Cathay and back.

All because he could read.

He returned to the small refectory with freshly grilled halibut drenched with lemon and garlic. After serving the abbot and his guest, he stood quietly by the open window, as the two men ate and talked.

"Our prayers are with you, Cristobál. You know that." The padre dipped a bite of halibut in the lemon juice with his long fingers before eating it.

"Without prayer, I wouldn't be here." He paused. "I've believed in the enterprise to the Indies for such a long time, Father Juan," he said with a deep sigh, "such a long time."

The elderly priest smiled. "God has given you the spirit and the mind for the task. I know how long a journey it has already been for you."

Don Cristobál nodded. "I first got the idea we could sail *west* to the Indies almost ten years ago, Father, when I was living on the isle of Porto Santo, off the coast of Portugal. There were stories of unusual things washing onto shore, like carved sticks and black beans. I actually saw two corpses myself, which were clearly Orientals."

"That part always fascinates me," commented Father Peréz.

"Then, of course, there were Toscanelli's projection drawings of the Far East. His maps are a main pillar of my theory."

The old padre chuckled. "I fear the King of Portugal is going to sorely regret turning you down."

The flickering candles cast moving shadows in the corners of the room.

"These last seven years have been the hardest, I think," mused the captain. "Believing something that very few believe, and almost no one is willing to support, would be impossible without the certainty in one's heart that God Himself is behind it."

Pedro knew about the captain's great vision to find the gold and jewels and spices of Asia by sailing west around the globe, instead of proceeding south around the bottom tip of Africa, and then east as the Portuguese were attempting to do. He knew the urgency Cristobál must feel. The Portuguese captain, Bartholomew Diaz, had successfully gotten round Africa's Cape of Good Hope, a scant four years before.

Many times he had seen Don Cristobál in their library, pouring over maps and making calculations. He also knew that whenever the captain visited La Rábida, he never missed a service. Pedro had seen his eyes closed and his lips moving during the prayers. Sometimes the captain even wore the same habit as the monks.

A hint of shame about his tardiness for Vespers drifted through Pedro's conscience. He would try to do better from now on.

Pedro had seen with his own eyes how hard things had been for the captain. A few weeks back he had gone into town with Father Antonio, to buy cinnamon and pepper. A small ship had been moored at the dock, just returned from the Alexandria bazaar. Its captain, Martín Pinzón, and Don Cristóbal were about to enter the Tavern of the Rooster on the village square. Suddenly three boys darted out from behind a shop corner, their pants' pockets bulging with pebbles. They started pelting the two men, as fast as they could throw, and yelling at Cristóbal, "Go home, Genoese!" The wooden sign hanging above the tavern door was still creaking from missiles that had missed their mark, as Father Antonio had turned the monastery's horse and two-wheeled cart toward the harbor.

The abbot sipped some wine from his mug. "People can be cruel," he murmured.

The captain nodded. "I waited seven *years* for their Royal Highnesses, Ferdinand and Isabella, to be persuaded."

"God knows the timing, my son. He'll reward your patience."

Keeping silent, Pedro shifted his weight from one foot to the other.

"There's no question in my mind," the captain declared, "that the inspiration to sail west to Asia across the Great Sea came from God. I've lost count of the Scripture verses that have been given to me, to keep me going."

"Yes, but be warned, Cristóbal." The elderly Franciscan's manner seemed to change, as he gazed into the captain's eyes. His tone was more serious now. Pedro sometimes felt like the old padre knew things before they happened. He didn't understand this, but it seemed to be happening again, right now.

"The riches in Asia may indeed offer the possibility of funding another Crusade to win back the Holy Land from the Muslims. And I want to see that happen, as much as our Sovereigns do—in fact, as much as all of Europe."

"*And* pay for rebuilding Solomon's Temple in Jerusalem," Cristóbal interjected.

The abbot nodded. "And that, too." He took the last bite of fish and wiped his mouth. "But the Scriptures and history both teach that riches can corrupt. Love of money *is* the root of all evil. The path on which God is guiding you is a narrow one, my son. Do not turn away from it. He has called you to bear His Gospel around the world. Remain steadfast to that goal, and He will mightily bless you."

The padre folded his napkin and placed it beside his now empty pewter plate. "Speaking of Jerusalem," he said, "my old mind fails me sometimes, Cristobál. How long has it been since we gave you the Crimson Cross?"

3

THE LEGEND OF THE CRIMSON CROSS

Don Cristobál Colón withdrew an ancient red leather pouch from his cloak and placed it on the table. Opening it, he carefully brought out a silver cross, worked in fine, almost lace-like filigree, with four red gemstones at the end of each arm, and another at the cross's center.

Seeing Pedro staring at it, the abbot beckoned for him to come over for a closer look. "The rubies represent the five wounds of Christ," he explained to the lad. "It was brought home from the last Crusade two centuries ago, by one of our Castilian knights. On the voyage home, their ship encountered a great storm and began to take on water. The knight called on all of his men to pray. And he himself vowed that if God would save them, he would give this cross, which he had rescued in Jerusalem—his most valuable treasure, to the monastery as soon as he returned home." Father Juan paused and smiled at Pedro. "He kept his word."

Pedro was listening with rapt attention. So was the captain. But why, he wondered, did they give it to Don Cristobál after all those years?

When Father Juan resumed his story, it was as if he had read the boy's mind.

"The first abbot of La Rábida was still alive when the knight made his presentation. He asked the knight if he had any special request concerning it. The knight simply said that it was God's now, not his, and they were to do with it whatever God directed. For many years it was kept in a hallowed niche in the chapel. But when I became abbot I had a dream about the Cross. I seemed to hear the Lord say that it was about to go into His service. It was to become a special sign of God's blessing, reminding each person to whom it was given of their destiny as one of His servants."

"Father Juan," the captain softly interrupted, "you never told me about the dream."

11

"I didn't? I told you my mind was becoming forgetful."

He went on with his story. "There were three dreams, actually. In the second one, I saw that the cross was to be passed on, from one bearer to the next, as the Lord led. And in the third, I saw that the first bearer was to be a sea captain who had been given a great commission: to bear God's light west to heathen in undiscovered lands." He paused. "That dream came a year before I met my good friend here and first learned of his quest."

He turned fondly to the captain. "Was that eight years ago, or nine?"

"Eight, Father." He handed the cross to Pedro for closer inspection. The boy marveled at it, turning it this way and that, watching the silver gleam in the candlelight and the rubies catch fire.

"It was the most prized possession of this monastery," Father Peréz informed Pedro. "But when the Lord made it clear that it was to begin its journey, how could I object?" He shrugged and smiled.

Pedro returned the cross to Don Cristobál, who turned to the abbot. "You cannot imagine how this cross has blessed me, Father Juan," he said softly. "So many times, when I was waiting to hear from the Spanish sovereigns, it would be the only thing that gave me hope." He shook his head. "So many times . . . ," his voice trailed off.

"It was meant to be a sign of God's presence and encouragement, my son. It would seem it has done its job well." He paused. "And one day, He will show you to whom it is to go next."

They turned back to the bunch of fresh and sweet Ximenez grapes Pedro had brought them, and he withdrew to his place by the window. He did not want the evening to end, but it was twilight outside and would soon be dark.

Suddenly he blurted out, "Father, may I speak?"

"Why, yes, lad. What is it?"

Pedro took a deep breath, just as he had when he dove into the water. "Don Cristobál, I saw something today that puzzled me."

The captain raised a reddish-gray brow.

"There was a piece of lead on the *Santa Maria's* port side, about eight feet below the waterline. It had square nails holding it in place. Does she have a leak?"

"She did," replied the captain smiling. "That lead patch covers a fair-sized hole in her hull. It's been carefully packed, watertight." His eyes narrowed, as he scrutinized the boy. "You were down long enough to retrieve the pulley *and* note the patch with the square nails?"

Pedro nodded.

The captain turned to the abbot, his lips pursed. "Father Juan, this is going to be a long voyage. We must carry everything on board we might possibly need for repairs. Including a diver. I learned this afternoon that our diver, Manuel, who had arrived only yesterday from the north country has come down with a high fever; it may even be . . ." he shuddered, "the plague."

The abbot was alarmed.

"Don't worry; he has been isolated. But he obviously won't be making the voyage with us." He looked into the candlelight. "To go without a diver would be folly."

Suddenly everything grew strangely quiet. With thumb and forefinger, the captain rubbed the sides of his long aristocratic nose. Now he turned his gaze to Pedro, and his deep blue eyes seemed to pierce the very recesses of the boy's soul.

The captain turned to the abbot. "I could use this lad. Would you be willing to let him join me as an apprentice seaman?"

Pedro couldn't breathe. His entire world had shrunk into this small room for a moment that seemed to last forever.

Slowly a smile spread across the kindly face of Father Peréz. "Nothing in heaven or on earth would please him more." He paused. "But allow me to ask the Lord." And with that the old monk folded his hands and bowed his head.

When, a few moments later, he raised his head, there was a twinkle in his eyes. "God has granted his wish." He looked into Pedro's eyes. "Always remember, it is He whom you serve. And be obedient to each task you are assigned, as if He Himself assigned it."

Pedro nodded. "I will, Father," and then, grinning from ear to ear, he could not help himself but ran to the old padre and put his arms around him.

4

"LOOSE THE MAINSAILS!"

There was no sleeping for Pedro that night. He listened to the breathing of the other boys fast asleep and tried to make the dawn come sooner. Finally he got up, quietly made his cot, and pulled on his high-necked tunic and a pair of rough cloth pants. He gathered his winter coat, his other shirt, and a spare change of undergarments, then added to them two goose-quill pens, a flask of ink, and three precious parchments, for the captain had promised to teach him how to make maps.

With his entire earthly possessions now stowed in a small cloth bag, he slipped outside to watch for the first lightening of the eastern sky.

Gliding just above the surface of the river, barely discernible in the pre-dawn light, a pair of gray-and-white herring gulls were heading west, as he himself would be before the sun was high.

He realized that for all his excitement, there was a twinge of sadness in leaving La Rábida. It had been his home ever since he had come here as an orphan after losing both parents to the plague. That was eight years ago. The friars had treated him like a son. While the ways of the monastery had been new and different, he had felt safe here from the very beginning. Each day, from early morning to evening, the regular chanted services provided a rhythm to their shared life that brought with it a sense of security and belonging.

As he looked at the low stone buildings, visible now in the growing light, there was a lump in his throat. He would miss this place.

Summer was coming to an end, and the friars would soon be tilling their vegetable garden to prepare it for winter. Where would *he* be this winter? Would they come back? He didn't know.

No one knew.

He shivered, as dread crept in like winter fog along the river. Pedro knew there was no record of anyone sailing across the Ocean of Darkness before.

No one.

And he had never really sailed anywhere, except in his mind. Oh, he had longed for the sea and had dreamed about it, more times than he could count. He had talked with sailors and even once boarded a galleon at the dock. He had stood on the rocks at the coast and gazed at the far-off western horizon. But he had never actually been out there!

Yet now that he was actually going . . . his eyes fell to a tiny ant starting out to traverse the stone courtyard that led to the entrance to their chapel. That was him. Only the ocean was a hundred times larger than the courtyard. Or a thousand.

He tried to shake off the thoughts, but more came. He had heard the tales—they all had—of phantom islands, and pirates, and sea monsters that broke up ships like matchsticks and gobbled sailors as if they were sardines. And there were parts of the ocean that boiled and turned white men black.

"*Here* you are!" whispered a voice behind him, that made Pedro jump. It was Father Antonio. "I've been looking all over for you!" He motioned to the two-wheeled cart with the monastery's sleepy brown-and-white horse Caballo hitched to it. "Come on! Father Peréz and the Captain are already on their way."

The two-wheeled cart jostled, as Pedro and the scribe rounded the first bend and headed down the hill toward the village. Caballo shook his black mane; he did not appreciate being hurried this early in the morning, as Father Antonio clucked and slapped the reins on his back, urging him into a trot.

"You have your other blouse?"

"*Sí,* Father."

"And the parchments?"

"Yes, Father. All rolled up. My quills, too."

For a short while, they rode in silence. The hood of the friar's brown wool habit screened his round face. With his free hand, he reached in and rubbed his bald head.

"I shall pray for you, Pedro, every day. You can be sure of it." The old monk's words did not have their customary humor.

"*Gracias,* Father."

Father Antonio was one of Pedro's favorites at the abbey. He had become more than a teacher; he had become Pedro's friend. Under the friar's mentoring, Pedro had learned many things. He had begun to draw. With his quill pen, he had sketched the angular lines of the monastery and a few of its rooms and had just started the circular lines of human faces.

Would he forget the father's plump olive face, with its brown eyes and thin mouth framed with wrinkles? Would he remember those gnarled fingers, permanently bent from years of a life dedicated to writing in exquisite detail? He wished he could have drawn a picture of the father to carry with him.

If only he had known.

"Mind you, say your prayers like I taught you." The scribe's sigh was so loud, Pedro thought he'd never forget it.

"I shall, Padre."

"And keep your mouth clean," he added. "Sailors—they're a foul-mouthed lot."

Soon, the sounds of a boatswain's shrill whistle, much like a bird's call, wafted up the path. The commotion of people's voices hung over the red-tiled roofs on the adobe houses.

At the dock, a crowd had already gathered. They got out of the cart, and Father Antonio tethered Caballo in a spot where there was grass to munch. The elderly monk and the lad made their way through the throng.

The onlookers were mostly men in wool caps and coats, though there was the occasional woman's colorful headscarf or shawl. While many ships had sailed out of Palos to all corners of the known world, the *Santa Maria* at the dock, with the *Niña* and the *Pinta* waiting in the river, would be sailing into the unknown. Some said they would sail right off the world's edge. The world was round, of course, thought Pedro, so *that* wasn't going to happen. But no one had ever sailed west over the Ocean Sea as far as they could go.

Father Peréz was standing on the dock beside the captain in the early morning light. Soon he began to speak, strongly enough for everyone to hear.

"We have come to bless the journey on which these brave souls are about to embark, and to worship our Heavenly Father. Let us pray."

The Sacrament of Holy Communion was part of every Spaniard's life. It was fitting that their voyage would start with this. As Father Peréz spoke in Latin, Pedro understood every word. "This is my body broken for you . . ."

Truly, he thought, as the sun began appearing in the eastern sky, God was going to bless their journey.

When the service had concluded, Father Antonio took Pedro to the captain, who was next to the gangplank of the *Santa Maria*. He and Father Peréz were talking, with people crowded all around them.

"Ah, here's my new cabin boy!" exclaimed Don Cristóbal, who was dressed this morning in his most formal attire: a broad-shouldered, knee-length burgundy cloak heavily collared with fur. His crowned hat was tilted slightly to one side on top of his long curly hair. "Bid your farewells, lad, and stow your gear aboard."

Father Antonio rubbed his eyes, as Pedro kissed his left cheek. Father Peréz gruffly cleared his throat and gripped Pedro's right hand. "You can hear God in your heart, lad," he said with difficulty. "Obey Him as you go."

Pedro could feel the tears in his own eyes, as he turned and walked up the gangplank. Now he was followed by the captain, who turned and waved to the crowd. A great cheer went up. Don Cristobál Colón, the Genoese sea captain, now in command of an expedition of three ships for their Spanish Majesties, King Ferdinand of Castile and Queen Isabella of Aragon, was about to embark on the voyage of his dreams.

"Make ready to sail in the name of Jesus!" cried the Captain, his voice confident and strong. Aboard the *Niña* and the *Pinta,* the order was repeated, and the two caravels began to weigh anchor.

"Cast off all lines!" Don Cristobál called to his first mate, who echoed the order, fore and aft. In an instant the ropes securing the bow and stern to pilings were flung onto the dock. The *Santa Maria* was picked up by the ebbing tide and was soon gliding downriver, followed by the *Niña* and the *Pinta.*

Pedro watched the wings of a white crane beat, as the bird accompanied them. Now he could see La Rábida up on the hill on their port, or left side. The old monastery greeted their passing with the joyous ringing of all three of its bells. Then the ringing changed to a more familiar pattern. It was time for Lauds, the service of Morning Prayer. The haunting melody of the friars' first chant drifted to them across the water.

Hearing it, the Captain removed his cap, crossed himself, and kneeled on the deck. Those sailors who weren't working, followed his example. The board felt rough beneath Pedro's knee-length pants. The moments were filled with the silence of many prayers punctuated only by the sounds of three ships straining toward the sea.

At last, Don Cristobál issued the order everyone had been waiting for. "Loose the mainsails!"

With a thunder of canvas and wild rattling of the blocks, the sails on all three ships billowed out with the sea's breezes.

Proudly displaying huge red Crusader crosses on the front of their now taut sails, the three tiny vessels heeled over to port, picked up speed, and headed out into the open sea. Pedro could feel the bow of the *Santa Maria* rise as she lunged into her first ocean wave. Behind them the sun rose higher and transfused the sails with a magical glow.

A large flock of storm petrels soared upward in a tight circle, riding a rising current of air in the blue sky as they escorted the ships, their cries blending like a cathedral choir.

5

THE FIRST DAY

It seemed as if they were flying! With every bit of canvas stretched to catch the favorable northwest wind, the three little ships raised large white bow-waves, indicating that they were making close to their maximum speed. Sailors scrambled along the yardarms securing the lines. Even amidst all the commands and commotion, Pedro sensed that everyone on board the ships knew that this was a voyage of destiny.

Though heavier and slower than the *Pinta* and the *Niña*, the *Santa Maria* had more sails, which helped her to keep up with the others. In addition to her large mainsail, she had a square foresail, a lateen-rigged mizzen sail on the quarterdeck, a spritsail in the bow, and a small topsail above the mainsail.

The *Santa Maria* also had more decks. His first hour on board Pedro had quickly explored the flagship and found that toward the bow, the forecastle deck sheltered a sleeping area for the senior members of the crew. Toward the stern he had climbed a ladder to a sizable quarterdeck, at the back of which was the captain's cabin, covered by a small poop deck, or stern-castle, also accessed by a ladder.

The flagship led the tiny fleet, while behind her on either side sailed the *Pinta* and the *Niña*. The *Pinta* was a square-rigged vessel with a main deck and a half deck in the stern. She was commanded by Martín Pinzón, head of a well-known seafaring family in Palos. The *Niña*, commanded by his younger brother, Vicente, was a lateen-rig, with a half-deck in the stern and a tiny stern-castle on top. Neither had any cabins for the captains.

It was a glorious day at sea! The cloudless sky was azure blue, and the whitecaps on the tops of the waves sparkled like new-fallen snow. It was a day of delight for everyone. Everyone except Pedro.

By now, a few hours out of port, he was miserable. He was slumped down on the quarterdeck, near the ladder from the main deck, leaning against the storage netting hanging down from the starboard, or right side railing. The sailors stored extra sailcloth, blocks and buoys, and all kinds of other lumpy gear in the netting, but he leaned his back against it anyway. It scratched at his loose white blouse, but he was too weak to move any further.

Were the square wooden posts at this end of the quarterdeck moving, too? His heart sank deep into his queasy stomach again. Did everything on the ship have to move at the same time? The railings. The masts. Even the droplets of scummy water trickling across the deck toward his left hand.

He couldn't watch them. He couldn't watch anything. His first experience of life on the high seas was anything but pleasant. Rolling and pitching . . . pitching and rolling . . .

The fleet hadn't been on the open sea more than three hours, before the waves had grown so large that they were beginning to move the ship every which way. He had long dreamed of one day enjoying the life of a sailor. Except the dream was fast becoming a nightmare. Rolling and pitching . . . pitching and rolling . . .

"*Uhh*," Pedro moaned, as his stomach turned over again. There was no waking up from this nightmare, because he was already awake! "*Uhh*," he groaned louder, holding his stomach and curling up on his right side into a tiny ball. Maybe by some miracle of the Blessed Virgin Mary, he would fade away into nothingness and never return. Don't bother carrying him back to Palos; simply throw him overboard.

Oh no, he thought with increasing apprehension. Maybe he wouldn't die after all! Then he'd have to spend the rest of his natural life like this—sicker than he'd ever been in his entire life! "*Uhhhhh!*"

He'd heard about this sickness, caused by the unceasing motion of seagoing vessels driven by the winds in unison with the currents and swells. Now he was experiencing it. His eyes could barely focus on the mound of dingy thick hemp rope lying in front of him on the deck.

And now the breakfast he'd never had, was coming up inside of him. Groaning, he barely raised up over the port rail in time. He retched and heaved and brought up very little, finding that it did not help at all. He felt just as awful as he had before throwing up.

"*Uuhhh.*"

To make matters worse, no one else appeared to be afflicted. The high-pitched notes of the boatswain's whistle, apparently signaling various commands that the sailors understood, reminded Pedro of the river birds at home. The ship's master, Juan De la Cosa, stood right in front of him, shouting a continuous stream of orders down the open hatch to the helmsman below. Above him, sailors climbed the riggings like they were born to do it. Squinting up at them, Pedro couldn't tell whether it was the sun's glare or his thick head that prevented him from seeing anything but a blur.

"Try focusin' on the horizon a bit, lad," said a kind voice above him and somewhere to the left. "Sometimes it helps."

The lengthy shadow of a man's figure now blocked the sun. Pedro tried to lift his head, but it was too heavy.

"What day is it?" he whimpered, his head cradled in his arms.

"It's still Saturday," the silhouetted man replied.

Two bare feet had been plunked right in front of him. Pedro noticed that the left foot was missing its little toe. Light brown knee-length britches displayed wispy gray hair on the man's legs. With great effort Pedro lifted up his head to see that the sailor's plain sail-cloth shirt revealed a muscular chest glistening with sweat.

"I'm Peralonso Niño, the pilot. I'm in charge of setting our course and altering it, as need be." The man's tone was gentle. "Right now, though, ye'll be needin' to stay the course you're on. Ride it out. Ye'll get yer sea legs soon enough." His last words offered Pedro a faint glimmer of hope.

"Not soon enough for me," Pedro mumbled.

He was barely able to hold up the arm he was now using to shield both eyes from the glaze. The halo surrounding the ship's officer suddenly disappeared, when a few high white cumulous clouds masked the afternoon sun. Pedro felt a slight breeze and, with a sigh, leaned back once again against the ship's side.

"Breathe in, lad. Long and slow. The fresh air will help."

Pedro breathed. Once. Twice. Three times. Long, deep breaths. His lungs seemed to appreciate the air.

"Most of us have been through it, at least once." The pilot's stubby fingers scratched at his gray whiskered face. "Happened to me on my first trip. About yer age, too. Was leaving Cadiz for Gibraltar, as I recall. Didn't get an hour from port when it hit."

"How long were you sick?"

The pilot's broad smile had a gap in it, where his left eyetooth used to be. "Me thinks you might not want to know that right now, boy." And with that, the mariner turned and hopped down the ladder to the deck below.

For the next four watches, or sixteen hours, time seemed to stand still for Pedro. He lay moaning, except for times he lurched to the rail to be sick again. Dry heaves, since there was nothing left in him to regurgitate.

But as night came, the waves of nausea subsided like an ebbing tide, and Pedro began to believe he might live, after all.

By morning of the next day, he was definitely better. Weak as a kitten, but definitely better.

"Try some water, boy." It was Peralonzo, and he had an oaken bucket with him and a ladle. "Just a sip."

Pedro did as he was bidden. The boy's dry cracked lips didn't feel any better when they touched the water.

"Don't lick 'em, lad," the pilot warned. "That'll only make 'em worse."

"Aye, Lonso. That it will," exclaimed a firm voice. Out of nowhere appeared the captain, with smile wrinkles etching the sides of both eyes.

"Looks like he's comin' round, Cap'n."

Pedro tried to smile and nodded. The creaking and humming of the flagship didn't bother him at all this morning. But his backside was numb from sitting in one place all night. He rubbed the seat of his pants.

"Every grommet, or ship's boy, has certain duties, Pedro," Don Cristóbal informed him. "The other grommets have been pitching in for you, but it's time for you to start doing your share."

"Brought him this here red stocking cap, Cap'n. Thought it might help with that scarlet color growin' on his head."

Pedro fingered the wide part down the middle of his scalp. It hurt. *Really* hurt. He realized it must be badly sunburned. "*Gracias,* Señor Niño," Pedro replied, taking the cap.

"Call me Lonso, boy, like everyone else."

The captain looked down at the main deck. "Get him down there, Lonso. Might help steady him a bit. Emilio should be calling table soon. Tell the cook we're smooth enough in the water for a fire today. Lentils and rice for the lad. They should stay down better."

Food! The very thought of it, made Pedro's stomach crawl up into his parched throat.

"Aye, sir. I'll take 'im."

A short while later, Pedro sat beside the steps leading down to the hold or belly of the ship, quietly watching the activity around him. Black-crested white-feathered terns, still following the ship like little ghosts, were enjoying a feast of crumbs from the sailor in the crow's nest aloft.

Two sailors in striped shirts tended a fishing line near the ship's small boat, tied down under a canvas tarpaulin on the main deck. In the distance, Pedro could barely hear voices on the other two ships, one on the port side, and the other on the starboard side.

Now one of the grommets, Emilio, the same one who had dropped the pulley at the dock, was lighting up the charcoal in the little stove, a square cast-iron box with a tall back. The grommet offered a tight, sour smile to Pedro.

Suddenly the smells of burning charcoal and frying meat coupled themselves with a strange odor from the open hold below. A faint sense of the old nausea found its way into the newest grommet's stomach.

"Table, table, sir captain, and master, and good company!" Emilio's straight black hair draped down to his shoulders. His voice was high but carried easily across the three decks. "Table is ready, table is set; who don't come won't eat."

Within seconds, the crew swarmed down the ladder to the hold like black ants. Pedro could see Emilio set down a wooden dish of roasted stringy salt meat on a nearby table, along with a pan of cold lentil beans and a bowl of sticky brown rice and chopped up squash. Bronzed seamen were soon shoulder to shoulder, as sharp knives appeared in strong grips, ready to hack off slices from the slab of meat.

Loud chewing and belching sounds reached Pedro. The boy slunk back against the rail on the main deck and decided he wasn't ready to put any food down just yet.

By noon, everyone was finished. A mass of used wooden bowls cluttered a nearby barrel. Longing for a bit more sleep, Pedro remained seated against the railing. Sailors were a noisy lot.

Just then, a sharp kick on his left leg startled him so much that he shrank back with a loud "Ow!"

"Hard to sleep around here, ain't it?" It was Emilio. A piece of straw dangled from his mouth. His dark eyes were as thin as a cat on the prowl.

6

THE NEW GROMMET

Slowly Pedro gained his sea legs and began to learn about life at sea. There was much to learn. Once a cargo ship, the *Santa Maria* was a seaworthy vessel with five sails. He learned how to furl them in a storm and how to rig them for a tailwind, when she could approach her maximum speed of ten knots.

Her forty crewmen were the pick of Spain's seafaring population, a fact Pedro quickly came to appreciate. They were willing to show him how to do a thing—once. But he'd better be paying close attention, because they were not about to show him a second time. They referred to the *Santa Maria* as a "hundred tonner," which meant her hold, the dark storage area in the belly of the ship, was large enough to store a hundred barrels or "tons" of wine.

But she was hardly what one might call roomy. In fact, Pedro thought, walking on the main deck was like threading your way through a giant spider web, with ropes and rigging and chains hanging everywhere. Moreover, thick hemp ropes or halyards for hoisting or lowering sails were coiled around the banisters and blocks. The netting, against which Pedro had leaned when he was seasick, hung along both the port and starboard rails, bulging with stored gear: brooms, mops, buckets, fishing lines, sinkers, harpoons, even extra ratlines, the rope ladders that allowed the crew to scale the masts. Throughout the day sailors washed and scrubbed the curved deck, or caught up on their sleep wherever they could find time and space before their next watch. Pedro had to step with care, to avoid waking them.

Gradually he began to fit into the rhythm of life at sea, which actually was similar to life in the monastery. Each day followed a certain routine that gave the men a sense of security and connection with their homeland. The four-hour watches were like monastic services: they were always at the same time, and the sailors always completed certain chores before a particular watch had ended. At the changing of each watch, special prayers were said, and everyone was expected to observe them.

The entire schedule was set by the ship's clock, a half-hour glass or *ampoletta*. As the last grains of white sand ran out of the upper chamber, the grommet whose turn it was would turn it and sing out the appropriate prayer.

Turning the *ampoletta* was Pedro's first responsibility. Assigned by the ship's master to teach him, Emilio led the new grommet into the steerage, the shaded area right below the quarterdeck. There the helmsman steered the ship.

It was clear that Emilio wasn't happy with this assignment. The boys stepped over long timbers jutting out onto the deck. "These are for the crosses the Captain's gonna plant at the first landin' and others," Emilio grumbled. "He's watchin' over 'em like a hawk."

Then the two boys skirted around two snoring sailors sprawled out on some planks, catching up on their sleep after the dogwatch, the midnight to four o'clock shift.

"Marco here is the helmsman for this watch." Emilio crouched down to miss the low overhead wooden beams. He did not introduce Pedro. "Since he can't see where we're goin', he steers by the compass in that binnacle right there." Emilio pointed toward a large rectangular hooded box fastened with wooden pins and secured to the deck.

"Binnacle?"

Emilio swore. "Landlubbers don't belong at sea!" he declared. "The box, you idiot! It holds the compass!"

Looking out at the rush of the ocean below, Marco Arias, a dark old seaman whose thin greasy hair curled over the collar of his calico shirt, was seated in front of a large porthole in the stern. Through this opening, the giant square tiller was attached to the ship's rudder. The rudder was attached to the stern with iron pinions that fit snugly into iron loop-shaped sockets, enabling the helmsman to move the rudder from side to side and control the ship's direction. Marco gripped the smooth timber with both his hands. A wooden cane leaned against the stool on which he sat. One of his legs was missing just below the knee.

"Landlubbers always gawk," Emilio grumbled, flinging a stray rope out of his way as if it were a fly. "But he lost his leg, and that's that."

In front of the helmsman, the *ampoletta* swung lazily on an iron hook with each roll of the ship. The sand had almost run out.

"It's almost ready to be turned," Emilio said with a smirk. "Watch and learn, landlubber."

The moment the upper chamber was empty, he tapped it lightly, then turned the glass and attached its leather strap back to the hook. Then he stepped out into the open and sang the assigned song or ditty, as the sailors called it, loud and clear.

On deck, on deck,
Señor Mariners of the right side,
On deck in good time,
You of Señor Pilot's watch,
For it's already time;
Shake a leg!

"South by southwest. Nothin' to the north. Nothin' to the east," called up Marco to the master coming on watch on the quarterdeck, the deck at the stern of the ship, part of which was taken up by the captain's cabin.

"Aye, Señor Arias. South by southwest. Nothin' to the north. Nothin' to the east." The master repeated it, so the helmsman could be certain he had been heard correctly.

"Garcia," called the master to another grommet, "man the pump."

At the master's order, the ship's boy scurried toward the pump just outside the steerage, to see if the ship's hold had taken on more sea water during the night. Wooden sea vessels took on water through their seams. To correct this, each ship had a bilge pump located on its main deck—a long tube with a wooden plunger down the middle. When the plunger was pressed down, a leather flap valve allowed bilge water to enter it, and then sealed it when the plunger was lifted up, expelling the brown water out on the deck and over the side.

"Look alive durin' yer watch landlubber," Emilio grimaced. "The Captain don't take kindly to ye missin' yer duties."

A little later, the door to the Captain's cabin opened, and Don Cristóbal emerged. "She'll be a brilliant sea today, Pedro." Off the port side daybreak offered a horizontal kaleidoscope of orange, red, and blue. The sun was about to rise.

He motioned Pedro over to meet the ship's master. "Lad, this is Señor De la Cosa, my second in command."

"Yes, sir," replied Pedro, bowing slightly to the master, who was responsible for the managing of the ship, both in port and under sail. De la Cosa was a pig-tailed, salty looking merchant with jet-black eyebrows that almost met in the center. A giant green-and-black serpent was tattooed on his right forearm and visible under the ruffles of his muslin sleeves.

The man fixed Pedro with a cold stare. "It will be *Master* De la Cosa to you, young man," he growled. "I own this ship."

"That he does, boy," replied the Captain with a hint of resignation.

"I'd like to own a ship one day, too," Pedro declared, excited at the thought. "Maybe like this one."

"This one's the newest and the best," De la Cosa barked. "She's carried cargo all the way to Egypt."

"Lad," said Don Cristóbal, redirecting the conversation's course, "Father Pérez tells me you're good with figures."

"Aye, sir. I've learned about leagues and fathoms, and I know my knots and sails and can even box the compass."

"I'm sure you can, boy," the Captain chuckled. "Come into my cabin, and you can tell me all you know about navigating."

Pedro could almost feel De la Cosa's icy stare, as he ducked his head and followed the Captain through the low doorway.

From the moment Pedro stepped into the cabin, the young Castilian knew he wanted to be a captain more than anything else. One day he, too, would have a cabin like this all to himself.

To his left, a shiny enclosed pine hutch provided storage. Under the small window that opened to the quarterdeck, a rolled-up sheepskin sea chart and a well-worn leather-bound book covered the top of a rough wooden bench. On the next wall a set of dark maroon velvet curtains opened to the Captain's berth, situated right next to two slender closet doors. At the back, two stained-glass windows were partly opened to the sea. They colored the light, but the air still felt stuffy. Three large poplar trunks with curved lids were closed but not locked, holding secrets only the Captain knew.

"Young man, suppose you tell me what you know of dead reckoning."

The red cap Pedro had just pulled off his head was now being twisted into knots by nervous fingers. "Father Antonio told me it's the way a captain estimates where his ship will be if he maintains his course and speed, sir."

"He's right, lad." Strands of the Captain's thick almost white hair brushed the low ceiling. "There are three factors to consider: course, time, and speed. You already know how we determine time."

"Aye, sir. The *ampoletta*. One of my first duties."

"So it is." The Captain's straight-back chair scraped the plank floor, as he tucked it under his oak desk. "Let's start today with plotting our course. Fetch me that sea chart over there on the bench."

The Captain unrolled the wrinkled calf-skin vellum. He set a small silver mariner's compass and an inkwell to hold down one curling side, and a long wooden ruler from his desk drawer to hold down the other.

"You can see here," he said, pointing toward the right side of the map, "the coasts of Spain, Portugal, North Africa, and the Canary Islands."

The Captain's knotted fingers reminded Pedro of Father Antonio. Only someone who had spent many years writing or drawing maps or pictures would have such calluses, especially on his right middle finger.

"And here," the Captain's weathered finger traveled left across the drawing of the Atlantic. "Here are Cipangu and Cathay."

"They don't look that far away, sir," Pedro observed. The beat of his heart had slowed till it was almost normal, and he had stopped mangling his hat.

"Aye, lad, they aren't. And that's the beauty of our voyage; we're going to prove it." The Captain's tall frame nearly filled the cabin. "Our destination is a scant 2400 nautical miles away, lad. Barely 750 leagues."

With hands clasped behind his head, the Captain's whiskered face suddenly resembled that of a teacher with a very good question.

"Tell me, lad, where are we right now?"

Just as suddenly, Pedro felt like a student who might not have a good answer. He had no idea where they were right now. But he guessed: "If we're heading south by southwest, that would mean we're heading for the Canaries?" he ventured.

"Very good!" murmured the Captain, impressed. He unrolled another chart of larger scale, which had their course drawn on it: a line heading south by southwest, beginning at Spain and ending at the Canaries. "Now, if we're making, say, 150 miles a day, where would that put us?"

For a moment, Pedro panicked. Then he remembered what Father Antonio had shown him. Looking at the bottom of the map, he found its key in the left-hand corner: a scale showing distance in ten-league or 26.7-mile segments. "Do you have a pair of dividers?" he asked the Captain.

Without speaking, the latter opened the desk drawer and handed Pedro a two-legged brass instrument with sharpened points at the end of each leg. Pedro set the two points at either end of the ten-league scale, then with the dividers walked off fifteen segments down the course line. "I would say we are about here, sir."

"Bravo!" exclaimed Don Cristóbal. "You are within thirty miles of where I myself believe us to be!" He clapped Pedro on the back. "This is going to be an interesting voyage, my young friend, in more ways than you can imagine."

7

WESTWARD, HO!

After six days, the three ships had finally reached the Canary Islands off the coast of North Africa. Under Spanish rule, this tropical paradise of majestic castles and cobblestone streets offered excellent ports for Spanish seagoing vessels needing to restock supplies, repair broken rudders, or obtain new sails. Chachu, the boatswain, who answered to the ship's master, was in charge of stowing the cargo.

"Bring 'em in tight, mates. Look alive! We ain't got all day!" He was down in the hold, directing traffic. "No, not there! That's too far aft. Lug them up here, toward the bow."

Huge sweat beads dribbled down the back of Pedro's legs, and his muslin shirt looked like he'd gone swimming in it.

The boatswain fingered the gold hoop in his left ear. This job of refilling the water barrels, then toting and maneuvering the huge wooden casks into the dark hold was taking too long, and he was tired of fooling with it.

"We're keepin' her center of gravity low, so she don't list too far to either side," Chachu explained to anyone who happened to be listening. His long pigtail looked like rope yarn, as the man wiped the sweat off his brow. "You, there! Torreros! Stand fast!"

Pedro halted. "Aye, sir."

"You and Emilio, get that loose keg back up here!"

The two lads hurried to do so.

"Smell down here's enough to make me throw up the cheese from the morning market," Pedro offered, as they tugged the cask back into the aisle.

"Real sailors get used to it," Emilio snapped.

Just then, the edge of the cask slipped out of Pedro's sweaty grip and came down squarely on Emilio's big toe.

"*Fool!*" the grommet cried, grabbing his left foot.

"Emilio, I'm sorry," blurted out Pedro, meaning it.

The other grommet, still holding his aching foot, let out a string of curses, many of which Pedro did not understand, though there was no misunderstanding the intent of them.

When he had finally calmed down, Pedro ventured, "I don't know what I did before we left Spain to get you so mad at me. Maybe you can tell me."

"You exist, that's what," Emilio growled. "How much did ya pay the cap'n to take you on as his boy anyway?"

All of a sudden, Pedro understood. "Was that supposed to be your job?"

The scowl on Emilio's face confirmed Pedro's suspicion. "I thought so, till you came along."

"Let fall!" Señor Lonso ordered. Two dozen sailors balanced themselves on the ratlines up high above the flagship's decks. They were perched near the floating yards, wooden horizontal spars from which the four-square sails and the one lateen sail were suspended. Hanging in midair, the men had already loosened the lines that had held the tightly furled sails since their arrival. At Lonso's command the gathered canvas under their arms plummeted down toward the deck and billowed out with the northeast wind. *Niña*'s new sails looked especially smart today. Don Cristóbal had ordered her old lateen sails to be replaced with square ones on her main and foremasts.

With the Canaries now well to starboard and a bevy of white-plumed tropical birds to accompany them, the three ships were on their way, at last. It was Saturday, the eighth of September.

From the deck atop the forecastle, Don Cristóbal Colón, captain of the expedition, surveyed the ocean ahead of them. A thick halyard, straight and tight, ran through his calloused hands to balance this man who knew the sea so well.

The *Santa Maria* seemed a bit heavy in the water today, but the trade winds blowing the Captain's fleet across the ocean were strong, flapping his linen shirt and tossing his white hair.

"Señor De la Cosa, set the course! Westward, ho!"

"Aye, aye, Cap'n." De la Cosa leaned over the hatch and shouted below: "West, Señor Marco. Due west!" The master then plucked the slate off the bulkhead hook and took a piece of chalk to note their course.

"Coming starboard to due west," came Marco's reply. And as soon as it was accomplished, he added, "Steady, as she goes."

For a few seconds, the mainsail fluttered, then it ballooned out, taut. The *Santa Maria* surged forward, plunging her bow and raising her stern in the mighty waves of the vast Atlantic.

Sailors scurried up and down the ratlines making small adjustments to her rigging. Pedro had been squeamish his first time up. It was a long way down, and the roll of the ship swept anyone aloft through a far greater arc than those down on the deck.

But Pedro, young and fearless, soon learned how to balance himself, using his hands and toes. Today, perched on a ratline not far above the starboard rail, he could see the sea spreading out like a blue-green blanket on all sides, bordered only by the sky itself. As he watched the *Pinta* and the *Niña* plunging through the water in harmony with the flagship, he knew he belonged here. Calluses were growing on his hands and feet. The sea was becoming his world.

"Signal the other ships, Señor De la Cosa,"

Pedro knew the reason for this signaling. Most fleets would naturally draw apart, but the Captain used a special system to keep his ships together. One of the seamen would light an iron torch mounted on the stern and then wave some canvas over it to create smoke signals. These would alert the *Niña* and the *Pinta* to any change in course, or making or striking sail.

Suddenly a gust of wind flipped off Pedro's red cap. He scrambled down to rescue it from some netting on the quarterdeck, before it went over the side.

Seeing him, the Captain beckoned Pedro to join him on the quarterdeck. There he asked the pilot, "Señor Lonso, your best estimate, if you please."

"Aye, sir." Raised up on bare feet, the aged mariner clutched the rail and peered over the side. "I'd give her three knots, Captain, maybe four."

Pedro knew that a knot was one nautical mile per hour, which was slightly less than one mile per hour on land.

"She's not bubblin' much, sir," continued Lonso, "which is surprising, given all this wind. It's as if something's holding her back."

"I agree, my friend. Something's wrong. Note it in your log. We'll have to figure it out, soon enough."

The Captain turned to his cabin boy. "The most important factor in dead reckoning is judging how much speed your ship is making through the water. You look at the bow wave, the bubbles floating past and the wake she's leaving behind. You must develop a sailor's eye for these things."

"How often do we estimate our speed, sir?"

Don Cristobál smiled. "A good question, lad. You remind me of myself thirty years ago, always full of questions." And then he answered it. "We take at least one sighting each watch, and record each estimate in two notebooks. The officer of the watch keeps one; I keep the other."

Pedro got it. "And at the end of each day, you figure out the average speed for that day and record it on your dead-reckoning chart."

"Aye, that's the idea," Cristobál replied with obvious pleasure at Pedro's response.

The following day, however, their progress had slowed even more. The *Santa Maria* was now plodding through the water, as if she were an overloaded cart, nearly stuck in the Rio Tinto's muddy bank, and the other two ships had to take in sail, to keep from running away from her.

The Captain's tension hovered over the quarterdeck like a thundercloud. "Señor De la Cosa!" His words rang out over the *Santa Maria's* three decks. Every mariner who wasn't asleep looked up, wide-eyed. "She's nose-diving! Taking water over her bow! I want to know why!"

The master called the first mate and the boatswain's mate, and the three of them went below. In a few moments they returned, shame-faced.

"The water casks were stowed too far forward," De la Cosa explained, angry at being publicly singled out. "I'm having the men move them now."

"Who is responsible?" demanded the Captain, the veins in his neck quite visible.

"Chachu."

"No, by heaven, he is not!" Don Cristobál snapped back. "This happened on your watch, Señor De la Cosa. *You* are responsible. Do not let it happen again!"

Pedro could see the look of hatred that the master shot at the expedition's captain. For the first time since they'd set sail, he felt a sense of alarm. The two chief authorities on board the flagship were at odds. Pedro quickly learned the lesson: No matter who was at fault, the over-all responsibility was borne by the officer on watch. De la Cosa was responsible, even though Chachu had given the wrong orders.

It grew strangely quiet aboard the *Santa Maria*. For the next two turns of the *ampoletta*, the only sounds on the vessel were the scraping of moving water kegs down in the hold. Even the storm petrels above had ceased their endless twittering.

Knowing looks passed between the sailors. They were as uneasy as he was. But there was something more, Pedro realized, as he looked behind them. They had now sailed completely out of sight of land, on a course no one had ever followed before.

8

A SAILOR'S LIFE

With the *Santa Maria*'s balance restored, she was once again coursing over the bounding main like a beagle after a rabbit. The next ten days sped by. Under fair skies, flying fish frequently raced with them, their winglike fins and strong tails lofting them through the air, sometimes for the entire length of the ship.

Each evening, one of the sailors would retrieve a plumwood recorder, no bigger than his hand, from his pants pocket and fill the air with rich tunes. A second might pull out a wooden flute to add a higher pitch.

After dark, the sky presented another sea, this one full of sparkling stars poking holes in the night. On this particular night, the three ships had already drawn together as usual for safety.

"Pedro, can ye find the Pole Star?" Across the darkness, Lonso's voice sounded raspy from a long day. The mariner had just finished another tune on his recorder and was slipping it into his back pocket.

Pedro quickly found the seven constellations known as Ursa Major, the Great Bear. To him, it looked more like a pan with a handle, than a bear. The outer rim of the pan always pointed to the Pole Star, which was right over the North Pole. He pointed to it. "There!"

Lonso nodded. "Good, lad. If you ever lose your compass, you can always set your course at night by that star. She's the only one who never moves."

Pedro slumped down beside the old seaman, next to a scratched-up chest covered by a bundle of fish netting left over from the day's fishing. Lonso tied the loose leather strings from his hooded smock into a knot at his neck, a sign he was ready to sleep until the next watch.

Pedro looked over at him. The gray whiskered ship's pilot was becoming Pedro's friend. Lonso reminded him more and more of his grandfather. Tight gray ringlets of hair . . . a missing tooth . . . and dark brown eyes that offered the wisdom of age.

"God's in His heaven tonight, to be sure, boy. Think I'll pray a bit and get some shut-eye." And with that, his eyes closed and his shoulders relaxed. Soon his rhythmic breathing joined the chorus of the other loud snorers about the ship.

The day before, Pedro had retrieved his parchment, his quill pen, and ink from his belongings stowed behind one of the chests in the Captain's cabin. He had already copied a world map like the Captain's. Now, snuggled in the forecastle beside a group of sailors playing a quiet game of cards in the lamp's light, he wanted to sketch his grandfather.

But while his heart remembered the closeness and love he felt for his grandfather, his mind could barely recollect his face. What would Father Antonio have told him to do?

"Use what you can see," the padre would have said. Pedro's quill pen scratched out his wizened old friend, Señor Lonso—the nose, the eyes, the strong wise hands that knew a life on the high sea and a life of prayer.

That was another thing. Pedro had discovered Lonso praying more than once. "Just talkin' with the Master Mariner," he would say. "And listening to Him."

Listening to Him? Pedro had spent the last half of his young life with men who prayed almost constantly. He had often prayed with them, in their daily services. But none of them had ever mentioned hearing God's reply to their prayers. Even their abbot seemed to hear God mainly through his dreams.

He wondered if he, too, like Lonso, could hear God in his heart. It was a weighty thought, weighty enough to put him, too, fast asleep.

A few hours later, Emilio's high-pitched morning ditty jolted him awake.

> *One glass is gone*
> *And the second floweth.*
> *More shall run down*
> *If my God willeth.*

"Table!" shortly came the cry. It was time for breakfast.

"These weevils ain't goin' anywhere exceptin' in yer stomach." The helmsman, Marco, tapped his hardtack biscuit against a peeling wooden beam before dunking it in a mug of dark water. "Water's gettin' a bit ripe, too," he slurped, wiping his mouth with the sleeve of the same filthy calico shirt he'd been wearing the entire trip.

Hardtack was made from flour, water, and salt thickened to a paste, pressed to look like a huge cracker, and slow-baked so hard that it would last for years. The morning watch had eagerly crowded around the huge flat straw basket of breakfast—sea biscuits and cheese and a pan of olive oil to moisten the biscuit, plunked on the deck. Unwashed fingers grabbed the morning's fare. So did Pedro. Be late and be sorry; there'd be nothing left.

In the midst of the commotion, however, Pedro didn't hear the scratching at the bottom of the wooden keg still housing used dishes. Suddenly, a rash of nasty cockroaches streamed over the barrel's rim and down its side. Startled, the boy jumped out of their way, but not before his bare right foot had provided a hill for them to skitter over.

"Off, you varmints," he cried, flinging his foot high in the air and slinging off the last few scratching at his skin.

The group of sailors swigging their drinks, laughed.

"The insects are gettin' worse," observed Emilio. "Ain't goin' to git better, so you best get used to 'em." The grommet's words weren't as harsh today. "We'll have to mix wine in with all our water soon."

"Why?" Pedro wiped his nose with one sleeve. Every sailor knew how valuable fresh water was to a sea voyage. It was one of the reasons no one bathed except for short swims in the sea. They couldn't waste any of the precious commodity, especially if it didn't rain.

"The wine kills what little bugs live in the water. Keeps it from getting any worse than it already is."

"Surely, it will rain soon," commented Pedro.

"Don't bet on it," Emilio replied, draining the final contents of an earthenware mug. "Water goes bad, no matter what you do to it. Stinks so bad, you have to hold your nose to drink it. But it beats the other thing that could happen."

Pedro wrinkled his brow. "What other thing?"

"Runnin' out. And if we don't see land soon . . ."

"Then what?" It was every sailor's worst nightmare: no water.

"Your tongue turns black, your limbs go numb." Emilio stuck out his tongue. "You lose yer sight. Not many days till ye die. Before that happens, though, you go mad with thirst. You start drinking seawater, even though you know it'll kill you. And it does." He paused and shuddered. "Ain't somethin' I care to experience."

A short while later, Pedro knocked at the Captain's door. "Sir, may I ask you a question?"

The right page in the Captain's leather bound logbook was half full of his beautiful Spanish calligraphy. Tucking his quill pen safely in its holder, Cristóbal closed the binder to reveal his world map right underneath.

Pedro tried not to bother the Captain, but something had puzzled him since they had left the Canaries.

"Yes, lad."

"Why did we drop down to the Canaries instead of going west to the Azores off the coast of Portugal after we left Spain?"

Pedro could hear the voices of sailors yelling back and forth to one another across the halyards. The Captain remained silent.

At last Cristobál replied. "Because God has shown me a secret, lad. A secret that will take us all the way to Asia. Would you like to see where we are now?"

"Aye, sir." Pedro stepped to the left side of the Captain's straight-back chair.

With one broad sweep, the Captain smoothed out the wrinkled map, the one he had let Pedro copy for his first project.

"Can you see these points I've placed along the map?" Cristobál's right index finger showed Pedro where to look.

The young apprentice squinted. Lo and behold, tiny pin pricks in the paper created a line between Spain and the Canaries. Another series of small holes formed a second line from the Canaries into the Atlantic. Each hole had a date neatly written in black ink right above it.

"Today is Friday, September 19," the Captain began, "and our course remains due west."

He laid the edge of his wooden ruler squarely on the last point and parallel to the nearest latitude line on the chart. "By my reckoning, we've made nine leagues since the last point." He then pricked a new point at the nine-league mark and penned in the date. This is called 'making point.'"

"Aye, sir, I've heard you and Señor Lonso talk about this," Pedro replied.

"Every good captain consults with his pilot and master about their ship's course, Pedro, which means you must always look for able officers to sail with you.

"So, how far did we actually sail yesterday?" the Captain asked, rubbing his chin, where a bushy reddish beard was now growing. He waited for an answer.

Pedro was glad he had learned to multiply. One Italian league equaled 2.67 nautical miles. This one was easy. They had traveled a little over twenty-four nautical miles yesterday. "Twenty-four, sir."

"Right you are, boy. Now, take my dishes down to the barrel. I'd venture to say it's about time to change the *ampoletta*."

"Aye, sir. It's my watch today, sir. I'm right on it." Pedro scooped up the wooden bowls and mug and started for the rectangular door, still ajar. That same nasty odor from way down in the hold crossed the threshold.

"You know what, sir?"

"Yes, Pedro?" The vellum crinkled as the Captain furled the map up into a neat roll around its metal cylinder.

"I'm glad we have the *ampoletta*, sir. It gives us a rhythm. And with all the religious ditties, it helps me stay connected to La Rábida. I rather miss them, you know?"

"Aye, lad. It's the lot of a sailor's life—to miss home." He suddenly seemed far, faraway. "And you're right. The half-hourglass does help us stay connected, just like our own hearts long to be connected to God. We have to listen."

"Sir?"

"As a captain, you must listen to your ship, lad. She will tell you a lot about herself. The same is true of God. If you listen, He'll reveal things you wouldn't otherwise know. I know because He gave me this vision. We will find the continent to the west because God has told me so.

"Now go, so you won't be late."

As the rusting hinges rattled behind him, Pedro stopped at the rail to gaze at the immense sea stretching as far as he could see. God had created this sea, because it almost sang His glory. God had created the dry land as well. But, just what was God like, this God that Cristobál spoke about? Pedro felt a sense of awe about this man, who held such a strong belief that he could actually hear God's voice. Pedro had never met anyone quite like Don Cristobál Colón.

9

A SEA OF TROUBLE

It was almost the end of September and there was still no sight of land. Instead, the sight of something else was causing the men on each ship to worry. Sailors crowded at the rails or hung off the ratlines, staring out at a vast carpet of yellow and green seaweed that stretched out in every direction in the gray morning haze, as far as the eye could see.

Moreover, the great Ocean Sea was still—eerily quiet—as if the seaweed had strangled the life from it. No cawing petrels circling the ship and diving for plankton in the vessel's wake. No dolphins preceded them; no flying fish leaped alongside of them. Nothing moved, except for the sailors trying to find the bottom with the fathom line.

"Put your backs into it, gents!" Señor Lonso directed from the *Santa Maria*'s steerage. The muscles in the two sailors' forearms were bulging, as off the ship's stern a heavy hemp line with lead weights attached to it at intervals plunged into the water. As each weight disappeared below the surface, the line got heavier and heavier. The men's loud grunts helped them keep the line tight in the block or pulley system through which it ran.

"No bottom yet, sir," one of them announced, the strain in his voice clear.

"How far down is the line?"

"Fifty fathoms. As far as she'll go."

With arms folded across his chest, the concerned pilot reported to the Captain, who was standing on the main deck. "No bottom, sir."

"Captain?" A male voice from the *Pinta* echoed across the seaweed swamp. Pedro recognized the voice of Martín Alonso Pinzón, its captain. "Have you sounded completely?"

"That we have, Captain," replied Don Cristobál Colón. "This is very strange indeed." His reply was almost lost in the banging of the lead weights being hauled back aboard the *Santa Maria*.

43

"We must find open water, sir, and soon!" Pinzón's voice reflected the rising concern that every sailor within earshot was feeling, including Pedro. What if they got stuck here? What if they never found their way out?

"Captain, what do you make of all this?" This voice came from the port side. It was Martín Pinsón's brother Vicente, captain of the *Niña*.

Don Cristobál slowly shook his head, his shoulders visibly slumped and his sigh loud enough to be heard. He had no answer. Pedro's hopes had been dashed, too. The first sight of the seaweed had been encouraging, a clear indication that they were nearing land. All three ships had buzzed with excitement at the possibility. Except the ocean remained bottomless, and the seaweed was attached to . . . nothing.

"Sir," Pedro asked the *Santa Maria*'s captain, "the water itself looks clear and blue, but the smell . . . " he grimaced and pinched his nose shut.

"Aye, lad," nodded the Captain.

"Should there not be land about—somewhere?"

"You heard them sounding, boy. There's no bottom." He sighed again. "We are in God's hands now. Until He sees fit to move us, we will stay exactly where we are."

An hour passed.

Another.

Then slowly, out of nowhere a gentle breeze came up, luffing the ship's slack sails. With an air of authority, the Captain inhaled a breath so deep it moved the linen ruffles on his open-necked shirt. "Keep a straight course, gentlemen!" he shouted through cupped hands. "We shall soon sail out of this mess, through it and due west."

"Our mileage, sir!" cried the younger Pinzón, who took his command as seriously as Don Cristobál himself. "The *Niña* reckons 440 leagues from the Canary Islands."

"And ours, sir!" Wearing his blue jacket, the older Pinzón was a proud man, who knew his family was important to the community and made sure everyone else remembered it, too. "The *Pinta* reckons 420. What is your reckoning, Captain?"

For just a moment, Pedro caught a hesitation in the Captain's expression. The squint lines etched at the corners of the Captain's clear blue eyes deepened as he glanced quickly toward Lonso, whose jaw seemed to be set in Mediterranean stone. With pursed lips, Cristobál finally called across the water, "You're both off, gentlemen. We're presently at no more than 400 leagues."

"Sir, I beg to disagree!" Martín Pinzón's thick Castilian reply was punctuated by a crispness in tone. "I believe the *Pinta*'s reckoning is accurate."

"No, Captain, I don't believe it is." Don Cristobál spoke sharply now. "Nor do I wish to delay matters by beating wind over this. We shall settle on a reckoning of 400 leagues."

Later that morning Pedro was in a hurry. Scrubbing the deck of a ship with a holystone, the sandstone used for scouring, was no more holy than scrubbing the chapel's floor at La Rábida. The faster he could get through with this chore, the better. Besides, he was growing calluses on his wet knees from doing this on a regular basis. Real captains have calluses on their fingers, he thought, not their knees.

What Pedro really wanted to do was grab his satchel and pen and draw this mysterious picture now surrounding them, a sketch he could show both Father Peréz and Father Antonio, a picture of what the Dead Sea must look like.

Crouched just under the Captain's small window on the quarterdeck, Pedro knelt on all fours. The murky seawater slopped over the sides of the bucket onto the old scarred planks, creating small rivers and lakes that quickly flowed into various pools. He couldn't do anything else until he had completed this chore. He bit his top lip and squared his jaw. He'd finish it before the next *ampoletta*, or his name wasn't Pedro de Torreros.

As he worked, voices inside the Captain's cabin, once muffled, grew louder. Pedro's ears perked up.

"Sir, Vicente Pinzón's estimate of our distance is accurate. By my log, we've sailed nearly 440 leagues."

"I've given the order, Señor De la Cosa. We sail by my reckoning and mine alone." The Captain's tone sounded final.

"But Captain, . . . "

"You're dismissed, sir."

The cabin door slammed shut as De la Cosa ducked out and stormed across the deck, his serpent tattoo clearly visible under the rolled-up sleeve of his muslin shirt. After he disappeared, Pedro could hear his grumbling through the overhead beams of the steerage compartment right below him.

"Sir?" came a third voice through the open porthole to the Captain's cabin. "What little wind we had, has died away. We are once again becalmed."

Pedro jammed his hand back in the bucket. This was going to alarm the men more than the seaweed, he thought.

"Lonso, I can only harness the wind; I can't create it."

"Aye, sir. Only God can do that."

"And it's God we will have to trust."

"And the men, sir? What shall I tell them?"

Pedro scooted over to a dry patch of deck and scrubbed some more.

"The air will freshen, soon enough. We *have* had wind today; we'll get more tomorrow."

Looking around, Lonso lowered his voice. "Captain, my reckoning agrees with De la Cosa's. We're farther away from Spain than you're telling them. Be careful."

Pedro's heart was thumping so hard, it felt like he'd just run all the way to Palos. The odor from the seaweed smelled like rotten eggs, and it mingled with the stench of their own rotting food, coming up from the hold. It seemed to make the tension aboard each ship worse, as the men imagined sitting here day after day, with the drinking water progressively rationed out in smaller amounts, until they were down to only a few drops apiece per day, which would drive them mad with thirst.

10

MORE TROUBLE

A slight breeze at their sterns enabled the three Spanish vessels to creep out of the gulfweed and make their way slowly west. But they were making no more than two or three knots, and so, other than their routine chores, there was little to keep the men busy.

They repaired split blocks and broken pulleys. They mended torn sailcloth. They scrubbed down the sides and hulls above the waterline. And trolled for dolphins—anything to eat other than wormy meat and moldy cheese.

Aloft in the crow's nest, the lookout scanned the horizon for some sign of birds, like the ones that had abandoned them over a week ago. Or failing that, at least a glimpse of rain clouds. A real rain would be a marvelous blessing. With sail canvas they might be able to catch enough to sweeten their rancid drinking water. But in all directions, the heavens were dry.

On the main deck below the lookout, some of his off-duty mates played cards, while another serenaded them with a Jew's harp. But mostly they grumbled.

One evening at sundown, Pedro hoisted himself up onto the lowest ratline. He and Emilio were climbing up to pass the time and survey the scenery. Everything, from the sails to the waves to the sky itself, glistened like gold in the waning sun.

"The Captain says we've sailed more than five hundred leagues," Pedro commented, as the thick rope he was holding made crisscross marks on his hands. Clinging to one of the lines up near the square sail, he leaned way back, far enough to feel a breeze in his hair and catch the invisible wind with his hand. "We're two thirds of the way there."

"If ye believe that, I've got some swamp land to sell ye, when we get home," Emilio quipped, climbing up to the next rope rung, and then added, "*If* we get home." He shook his head in disgust. "That land the *Pinta* thought they saw a few days ago was nothing more than a phantom."

"Maybe," Pedro replied, maneuvering his way across the floating ropes to the other side of the sail. "But the Captain says he doesn't want to waste time tacking around, looking for the odd island. He's headed for the mainland."

Pedro had finally gotten his real sea legs. He no longer noticed the motion of the ship and could spend long hours in the sun, without getting burned. His body was bronzed and fit now, and he could climb the ratlines with Emilio or any of the men. Though he seldom thought of it, he had become an honest-to-goodness man of the high seas.

"I'll wager all my *maravedis* from this trip, we run out of water." Emilio stuck his tongue through the space between his two front teeth. "Chachu says we're runnin' low."

Pedro shrugged. He had heard the rumors about the supply, but he wasn't ready to doubt the Captain, at least not yet. He snatched another line hanging beside him. "Say, Emilio. How much *are* you getting paid, anyway?"

"Same as the other grommets; 666 *maravedis* a month."

Pedro was getting paid, too, but he'd always been afraid to ask how much. The reality struck him like a lightning bolt. At 666 *maravedis* a month, for three months, that was—Holy Saints! Nearly 2,000 *maravedis*! That was more money than he'd ever *seen*, much less ever had!

Now, if they happened to be gone another three months . . .

"How 'bout you, cabin boy?" Emilio could still get a bit testy, though their relationship had definitely improved. He dangled like a monkey from the ropes. "Ye're makin' the same, ain't ya?"

"Of course! Same as everybody!" Pedro retorted, his head still reeling with thoughts of how rich he was going to be.

Later, just after evening prayer, the smell of smoke from the freshly extinguished galley fogon still hovered in the air. Pedro was squatting beside the capstan, a spool-shaped cylinder mounted on a spindle holding the anchor rope in the steerage. Suddenly, he heard voices wafting up the nearby steps from the hold.

"I've checked the water kegs, Chachu. We don't have enough to get us home, even if we turned about, right now."

"I told you, mate. That Genoan is mad."

"And I tell *ye*, he's deliberately underestimating our distance. We're a lot further from home than he's tellin' us."

Pedro would recognize that salty voice anywhere. It was De la Cosa! The boy scrunched his lanky frame into a ball, so the men wouldn't spot him.

"I'm in this for my share of the riches we find in the Indies, as much as anybody is," a third voice snarled, "but he's trying to make himself a great lord at our expense! At this rate, even our rotting food will give out 'fore we can sail home." There was no mistaking this crusty voice. It was Marco!

Pedro strained to hear the conversation, now moving away toward the bow. Still crouching, he carefully peered around the wooden cylinder.

"Ye know, mates, I see 'im up there on the poop deck watchin' the stars every night. Wouldn't be nothin' to heave him overboard and say it was an accident."

Pedro was stunned. They were talking mutiny! He felt as if an Arctic breeze, far colder than the sea winds at night, had blown down to the 28th parallel. As soon as the coast was clear, he pulled the hood of his gray jacket over his head, sought out Lonso, and told him what he'd overheard.

"Ships have a tendency to bring out the worst in people," Lonso told him. "Everyone gripes on the high seas, especially when they can't see land. They grumble, to let out their frustration." The mariner returned his pilot's slate to its peg beside the chalk at the bulkhead and arranged the rigging banging against the lateen mast on the quarterdeck. "It's hard to hide things on a ship like this, lad. But rest assured; the Captain knows."

With the Captain's window open and Don Cristóbal inside his cabin, Pedro spoke in a whisper. "But Lonso, they think the Captain's shortening the distances on the log."

"What do you think, boy?"

"I don't know what to think," Pedro muttered, stuffing both hands, now chilly from the October night air, deep into the pockets of his jacket. "We haven't seen land for three weeks, and we're running low on what little bad water we've got. We've hardly any wind to speak of, and we don't know if we'll ever find land, let alone Asia." He looked up at Lonso. "How far have we really come?"

The pilot didn't answer. He was resting against one of the square wooden posts dividing the upper and lower decks. Instead, he pulled out a worn and tattered handkerchief and wiped off his recorder.

"Lonso," Pedro persisted, "the Captain told me God had shown him a secret—a secret that would get us to Asia."

Lonso raised a brow, as he fingered his recorder. "And have ye figured it out?"

Grateful for the reply, Pedro hunkered down beside the aged mariner. "I'm not sure . . . but I think it's got something to do with the winds. Am I right?"

The gleam in Lonso's dark eyes gave him away. "Ye're thinkin' right. It is indeed the secret of the winds."

"The trade winds?" he asked, referring to the winds that blew from the northeast, just above the equator.

"Aye, lad. The trade winds."

"By dropping south, down to the Canaries, instead of sailing due west from Spain, we avoid sailing directly into the prevailing westerlies. Instead, we pick up a following wind, off our starboard quarter, and it carries us all the way to Asia. Is that it?"

A slow smile spread across Lonso's face. "*Sí. If* God provides the wind."

"Will He?"

Lonso chuckled. "I do not think He would have brought us this far, only to abandon us."

Now that the old mariner was talking, Pedro thought he would try one more time to find out about the distance they'd come. "I heard you and the Captain talking, Lonso. You told him your log agrees with the Pinzóns."

The smile left Lonso's face. "Do not tell one soul what you know, boy!" Lonso's voice was sterner than Pedro had ever heard it. "And that's an order!"

And with that, he raised his recorder to his lips. Its smooth notes lent a sense of the ordinary to the surrounding atmosphere. Yet tonight was far from ordinary, Pedro thought. He would never betray the Captain or his friend, Lonso. But they needed a miracle. Soon.

11

CAPTAINS CONFERENCE

At sea longer than they had ever been before, the men were now getting on one another's nerves and were about as friendly as tomcats in a sack. Tempers flared over the least little thing. What might have been meant as a joke was taken as an out-and-out insult. Ugly hand gestures and shifting eyes were common. Some even failed to salute the Captain now. And when he stepped out of his cabin and went to any of the three decks, the only sounds were the rhythmic slapping of halyards and lines, coupled with the continuous creaking of the ship's hull.

"We'll have to tack against the headwind to get back," Emilio complained to the other grommets, as he yanked up the plunger on the bilge pump to suck out the smelly water from the ship's hull.

Emilio huffed and pumped some more. "Sailing home in this wind, tacking back and forth, will take forever. We don't have enough drinking water. What's more, who knows when a monster will come up from the deep and swallow us all? I say, we forget trying to find the Indies, and go home now."

The others agreed with animated enthusiasm.

"He's going to take us all straight down," one complained as he shook a drowned cockroach off his left foot.

"We'll be a ghost ship before long!" another shouted.

Pedro's confidence had dwindled to almost nothing. Worry consumed every thought. He couldn't swab the deck or carry supper to the Captain without feeling the tension. He couldn't sketch pictures or gaze at the twinkling stars, because if the silence didn't get to him, his own internal turmoil certainly would. The terrible thing was, he was beginning to agree with Emilio and the others.

Worse, he was beginning to miss Palos and La Rábida, more than he ever thought possible! Where were the chirps of the brown tree crickets or the trills of the red-winged nightingales? At sea, no dogs barked in the distance, and no dragonflies tickled your arms. Pedro had not scrunched his toes in the hot sand in weeks, or handed Caballo an extra handful of feed when the friars weren't looking. While prayer time on the ship was regular, the boisterous and frequently off-key singing of the sailors was nothing compared with the melodious tonal music of the padres' plainsong.

What had been a life-long dream to Pedro—adventure at sea—was becoming a nightmare.

At sunset that evening, Emilio sang the regular ditty, as all hands gathered for evening prayers. The grommet led them in the "*Salvé Regina.*" Tonight, the words held a special sad meaning for Pedro, as he crimped his red woolen sailor's cap with both hands and bowed his head. If people could talk to God, he hoped God would really hear them, tonight of all nights.

> *Hail, holy queen, mother of mercy . . .*
> *To you do we send up our sighs, mourning and*
> *weeping in this valley of tears.*
> *Then turn, most gracious advocate,*
> *Your eyes of mercy toward us . . .*

"Yo! *Santa Maria!*" Evensong had just ended, when the pilot from the *Niña*, already in her normal evening position on the port side of the flagship, shouted across the water. "Captain Vicente Pinzón requests a meeting!"

"Aye, *Santa Maria!*" A shrill whistle from the *Pinta* gave its notice, as well. "Captain Martín Pinzón requests a meeting!"

In a few moments, Chachu's shrill whistle signaled the reply. Don Cristobál would see them in his quarters on the hour *ampoletta.* The date recorded in the ship's log was October 9, 1492.

"Do you need me, sir?" Pedro's left hand held onto the cabin's peeling doorframe. "Wind's still down. They'll be boarding soon."

"I'll need that chart over there, lad." Don Cristobál closed his journal and placed it in his desk drawer. "And my dress jacket in the closet."

The Captain gave a shaky smile and quietly got up from his chair. A golden hue from the evening's rapidly setting sun filtered through the transparent windows aft, latched open at the bottom. The Captain's tall frame almost filled the tiny cabin tonight. He gazed out the windows in a silence broken only by the lapping waves behind them and the familiar hollow sounds of the hold.

Pedro smoothed the curling edges of the animal-skin map with his hands and secured their edges with the Captain's compass and the inkhorn supplying his quill pen. He could only imagine what the Captain must be thinking. The captains of their sister ships had requested a meeting.

No, *demanded* a meeting. This had never happened before, and it was no easy task to hold a meeting at sea. Unlashing and lowering the heavy ships' boats and rowing men from two ships to board a third was both difficult and dangerous. Though the wind might be soft, it was variable. Anything could happen.

"Here you are, sir." Pedro placed the Captain's scarlet wool jacket over his shoulders.

"Good. Now bring three mugs, lad, and the wine," he ordered, as he fitted a brass button through its buttonhole. "And stay close, in case I need something else."

"Aye, sir."

Don Cristobál tugged the jacket snugly into place beneath his belt and ran the fingers of his right hand through the strands of curly white hair that had fallen onto his lined brow. His blue eyes almost looked glazed, like the blue sea in the glare of a late afternoon sun.

Leaving the door ajar, Pedro stepped outside. De la Cosa was there, pacing the quarterdeck like a hunting dog, obviously angry because the Captain had not invited him to the meeting, too. After all, this was his ship.

Before the hour, the other two ships' boats had been tied to the flagship, and Chachu's whistle had announced the arrival of the guests. Martín Pinzón boarded first and waited amidships for his brother. High above him, at the peak of the mizzenmast, the flag of the Spanish sovereigns with its reds and golds slept.

The silence on all three ships was so loud, it was almost deafening. Sailors jammed the wooden rails on every deck, fore and aft. They hung off the ratlines and crawled up to the crows' nests to watch. Some were suspended off the bowsprits, the spar projecting off each bow. Others dangled their bare feet off rectangular wooden seats swinging on thick hemp ropes and pulleys attached to the ships' sides.

No one said a word.

Within a few minutes, the two men climbed the ladder to the quarterdeck to join the Captain in his cabin.

Pedro sank back into the shadow of the back corner, next to one of the Captain's leather trunks and a slatted wooden chair. The two brothers quickly saluted and slipped off their brown wool caps, but neither sat down. In fact, no one sat down.

"Captain," began Martín Pinzón, coming right to the point, "if your calculations about the circumference of the earth are correct, then according to our reckoning, we should have reached Asia by now." He paused. "Something's wrong."

"The men are no longer nervous," his young brother Vicente blurted out. "They are *fearful*, Don Cristobál. It's been thirty-one days since we left the Canaries. *Thirty-one days!*"

The younger Pinzón looked at his brother and Cristobál. He, too, was a skilled mariner, but his jet-black hair and smooth skin made him look very young. His attitude was one of respect mixed with worry.

His older brother was less respectful. "We're not even making two knots right now, Cristobál, and you know it! If we continue one more day like this, we'll have mutiny on our hands!" Martín Pinzón made no effort to keep his voice down, and Pedro, tucked away in the corner, was sure that every word could be heard by those immediately outside. And they would soon be passed on to the rest.

12

AN ULTIMATUM

Glaring at Martín Pinzón, Don Cristobál furiously motioned for him to keep his voice down. But the captain of the *Pinta* was too angry. "I can't even be certain of my officers, anymore! They, too, suspect you're shortening the daily estimates, and they're convincing the others."

"I'm afraid he's right, sir." Vicente crossed his arms over his officer's jacket, his tangled hair falling over his ears as he talked. "The same is true on the *Niña*."

Don Cristobál looked from one captain to the other. Pedro could see that he was angry at his authority being challenged. But he could also see that the Pinzóns still regarded him as the expedition's over-all commander. Yet, if he did not bend now . . . if he refused to listen . . .

"I recruited most of these men," the elder Pinzón reminded him. "They're good sailors, some of the best in Spain. You cannot sacrifice them to save your dream. We must come about. *Now*."

The gloom in the cabin grew with each passing second. Pedro tried to fight off what he was feeling. The Pinzóns were asking Don Cristobál to give up *everything*. All his dreams. All the years of waiting for a sovereign to believe in him enough to sponsor such a dangerous trip. This voyage was the Captain's mission in life, his life's calling. He would not get another chance. If they turned back now, before finding Asia, Don Cristobál Colón would become the laughingstock of Europe.

And yet, what the Pinzóns were requesting was the only thing that made any sense. Their water was barely drinkable and would soon be gone.

Pedro propped a foot on the slanted wall behind him and gazed at the Captain's bronze face. It was a blur of misery. His thin lips quivered, when he finally spoke. "I've been sailing since I was a boy. I've studied the great cartographers, gone over their most recent maps. I believe in the Scriptures and have prayed for insight. I am convinced we are heading in the direction God has given me."

He slumped down into his straight-back chair, still in the same position he had left it when they arrived. With his elbows on the chair's arms, he tapped his forefingers together. "But I also know the men cannot take much more. Many have already made up their minds against me, whispering and giving me looks. Their fear will soon eat us up, as surely as any sea monster."

Pedro realized he had been holding his own breath. He swallowed the lump in his throat and tried to breathe.

Don Cristóbal stared out the porthole at the setting sun, for what seemed like an eternity. As far as Pedro was concerned, the next few moments were the longest in his life. The creaking of the ship's timbers became more like a groan. The seawater lapping at the hull kept up a slow melodic rhythm. Time seemed to stand still.

Yet something supernatural occurred in the little cabin that evening. For the rest of his life Pedro would never be able to quite put his finger on what it was; all he knew was that it had happened during the Captain's pause. And this something altered the course of his life, and the lives of the other sailors, forever.

"I need one more thing," the Captain murmured, so softly that Pedro almost missed it.

But Martín Pinzón heard him and shifted his weight from one leg to the other, not at all sure he was going to like what he was about to hear. Vicente remained guarded.

"The birds." The Captain's voice seemed to gain strength, and his words now had a renewed air of confidence. "We spotted birds."

The Pinzón brothers shrugged, as if on cue. Pedro, too, had seen the fowl earlier that day—three white royal terns with their slender orange bills, plunge-diving for fish in the sea.

"And birds mean land!" the Captain declared. "Give me three more days! One for each tern! If we have not sighted land by the twelfth of October, we will come about and head home."

"Cristóbal, I don't think the men have three days left in them!" Martín Pinzón retorted, anger furrowing his brow. "I don't think I have three days left in *me*!"

"Me, either!" exclaimed Vicente, apparently siding with his brother now, against the Captain. But then his black eyes shifted from the overhead beams to the chart table, and he finally added in a subdued tone, "Very well, then. I agree to three more days. But I want us to steer a southwest course to go where those birds seemed to be coming from."

"Agreed!" said the Captain quickly. "Tell your men, seventy-two more hours. If we don't find land by then, we come about." He turned to the grommet and smiled. "Pedro, we'll have our wine now."

That night, Pedro braced himself against the bulkhead right outside the Captain's door. The cabin boy hugged his knees to his chest and rested his weary head in his arms. His body was bone tired and ready to sleep, but his brain wouldn't settle down. Scrunching his eyes and humming a peaceful tune didn't help. His eyes seemed to have a mind of their own, flipping open at every sound to gape at the full moon's dark blue lengthy shadows dancing and shimmering on the water, like tiny ghosts in the night.

All of a sudden, a vague drone could be heard in the northeastern sky. Pedro craned his neck like an egret, but his squinting eyes couldn't detect anything, even in the light of the moon. Slowly, the distant sound grew louder. It was a fluttering and a gabbling, almost like the wind itself was talking. Only this wasn't the wind. It was the flapping of wings and a high-pitched screeching.

Birds!

Sure enough, within a few seconds, Pedro caught their silhouettes in the full moon. A small flock of seabirds, the color of the night sky, glided in a V over the ships' decks. They were headed southwest.

And so were three tiny Spanish vessels in the middle of the vast black sea.

13

THREE DAYS

The early morning mist that had settled on Pedro's hooded jacket during the night felt especially damp this morning. The October wind from the northeast sent a chill through his bones, still stiff from sleeping on his makeshift cot on the quarterdeck, a hard plank outside the Captain's window. The boy hopped to his feet, brushed off the arms of his jacket as well as his damp britches, and twisted his rope belt tighter.

"Pedro!"

"Aye, sir, I'm coming!" He stepped carefully around the end of the lateen sail's boom, trying not to wake up any of the other men still sprawled around the deck, snoring as sailors do.

As the rising sun cast its light upwards onto the bottom of the clouds creating spectacular colors, the memory of last night's meeting with the Pinzóns was still fresh in Pedro's mind. Without thinking, his body naturally compensated for the increased pitching and rolling of the ship.

Glancing forward, he could barely make out the bowsprit that seemed to be plunging down and up more than it had at any time in the past two weeks. Before he could open the cabin door, a cool salty spray splashed his unsuspecting face.

"Yes, sir?" He stepped inside with a salute, water dripping off his chin. The doorframe offered welcome support, as the ship abruptly pitched forward more than usual.

"Wind's picking up. She's running at least seven knots now, lad. Stand fast."

"Aye, aye, sir!"

The Captain stood with his hands clasped behind him, gazing out at the boiling wake now rising behind. His bedclothes, which Pedro had left neatly arranged, had not been used in two days. His journal lay open on his desk. In the middle of the right page, big enough to see from the doorway, the Latin words

CHRISTO–FERENS

had been penned in beautiful calligraphy. Pedro knew their meaning: "Christ-bearer." He also knew their significance to the Captain and to this voyage. On the dock at Palos, shortly before their departure, Pedro had heard Father Peréz take the captain aside and explain that the Sovereigns were going to write to the Holy Father in Rome and tell him that Don Cristobál was sailing at their bidding and with their blessing.

Pedro also knew that the Captain's given name, Cristobál (or in English, Christopher) came from those two words, and that for many years the Captain had felt that even his name was a sign of God's plan for his life.

Father Peréz felt that regardless of the fabled riches of the Orient, "bearing the light of Christ" to the west was the primary purpose of the Captain's mission. It was why God would favor it, and why the abbot felt good about allowing young Pedro to go. And he told Pedro he would pray every day for the safe return of La Rábida's youngest missionary.

Something gleamed on the table. Peering more intently, Pedro saw that in the journal's centerfold, between the day's log entry and the calligraphy, was the breathtakingly beautiful Crimson Cross. The Captain must have removed it from its red leather pouch sometime during the night.

Pedro inhaled. That cross was the heart of the Captain's dream—to take its truth to those who had not yet heard about Jesus. And now he could see that Don Cristobál had begun to draw a picture of the cross below the carefully lettered words. That parchment displayed his vision, pure and simple, a vision that must come to pass soon. Very soon.

"Sir?" asked Pedro, reluctant to break in on the Captain's thoughts, "may I get you . . ."

A loud hollering from outside the cabin cut off Pedro's question.

As he and the Captain rushed through the door, they saw Chachu, standing on the forecastle, his right hand gouging the air with his wood crutch. "Turn back! Turn back!" Both his words and his pock-mocked face screamed rebellion.

Within moments, the chant was picked up by other sailors, swarming the flagship's decks like cockroaches from the flour kegs. Louder and louder came the chant, as more and more men joined in.

"Turn back! Turn back!" The chant crossed the waters.

As the *Niña* and the *Pinta* clipped through the ocean's waves on either side of the flagship, the other crews stared in their direction and then joined in.

"Turn back! Turn back!"

Don Cristóbal, his face set like flint, stared straight forward, as if he did not hear them. Peralonso and his other officers, seeing the depth of his resolve, firmed up their own. The shouted chant grew even louder.

And then, as suddenly as it sprang up, it died away.

But the anger had not subsided. Every Spanish eye glared at the Genoese captain, this foreigner who was taking them to their death. The tension on board the flagship was as thick as the carpet of seaweed that had held them in its grip a few weeks back. This was the crisis, and Pedro knew it. The apprentice bit his top lip and held still, as if in a trance.

"The sea's makin' up too fast!" an older sailor cried from the main deck, his foot planted on one of the protruding beams for the crosses they had hoped to raise.

"We'll never see our families again!" added a younger mariner from a ratline.

"Turn back, Captain! Or we'll turn her back for ye!" This, from De la Cosa, whose expression matched the look of the serpent tattooed to his arm. And Chachu, arms folded over his chest, was standing right behind him.

It was then that the Captain spoke—so loud and clear that his voice boomed like a cannon, carrying to all three ships. *"Now, by Saint Ferdinand, you will cease this immediately!"*

In all their weeks at sea, Pedro had never heard Don Cristóbal swear. He would, in fact, stop any sailor who did. But today was different than any other day. Today could end in mutiny—Pedro, the Captain and anyone else that was loyal to him, thrown over the side.

"We were commissioned by the Sovereigns, Ferdinand and Isabella, to find the Indies! We have not found them, but we will! It was God who set us on this course, and it is God who will see us through!"

The Captain now turned his gaze to De la Cosa, obviously the ringleader aboard the *Santa Maria*, and held his eyes. "The other captains and I have agreed. We sail west for three more days. If we don't sight land by dawn on the morning of the twelfth," he stiffened, "you may do to me as Jonah's shipmates did to him."

Pedro blinked and shook his head. Had he heard correctly? Was Don Cristóbal *inviting* them to cast him overboard? Three days—against his *life*! Had the Captain just told the entire crew that he was willing to *die* for this cause?

But . . . somehow, the Captain's words dispelled the mutinous moment.

For the remainder of the day, the mood aboard ship was as solemn as if they were attending a funeral. And the winds seemed to be gathering, driving them ever faster, farther and farther from Spain.

"Ahoy, starboard! Lay hold of the clew!"

"Heave on the buntline!"

"Lend a hand at the brace!"

On and on, the orders flew, without any rest. The men felt as if they were driven to the point of collapse.

"Five inches and holding, sir," called Pedro to Señor Lonso from the hold. He nearly tripped over a mound of fish netting and was too tired to care. At least, the putrid bilge water was not rising, though its stench was worse than ever. Not only was the food rotten and full of worms, the small amount of "fresh" water sloshing around the bottom of the barrels was so bad it turned Pedro's stomach sour. Not a soul on board believed they had more than one more day's supply in them, including Pedro.

"Lonso?" The noise from the gusts against the canvas and the frenzy of activity among the sailors whipped Pedro's words out of his mouth.

Gripping the rail, the weary pilot stepped carefully onto a pile of planks covered with ropes. The dark circles under his eyes seemed to be deepening. He had just checked the sea running by to estimate their speed. They were flying.

"Will her timbers stand it, sir?" Pedro knotted the yarn to tighten the hood of his billowing jacket around his face. His black bangs flapped wildly in the unceasing wind.

"The Captain knows what she can take, lad." Lonso scratched markings on the black slate. Then he hollered up to Don Cristobál on the quarterdeck. "I make it *nine*, Cap'n!"

Pedro's eyes widened. Nine knots! Faster than they'd ever gone before!

The Captain's gaze never wavered from the blazing orange ball now dipping below the western horizon. The ruffles of his linen shirt waved violently, but he had yet to send Pedro inside to fetch his coat. He just stood there like a Roman statute, his seaman's hands clasped behind his back. Waiting. Watching. Knowing.

And this was still Day One.

14

A SURPRISE AT SEA

By sundown of the first day, they were in the grip of a full-blown gale. It was practically hurling them west. And with each passing hour, every soul on board knew that they were being driven that much further from their homes.

The cook had just set out the night's meal of dry hardtack, olive oil, and slimy sardines in two heavy iron skillets near the fogon. No cooked meal tonight. They were traveling too fast to risk a fire. Slowly, bedraggled sailors ventured by to pick up their food.

"I've never met anyone like the Captain, Lonso; someone who's willing to die for his faith. He's either crazy or the most amazing man I've ever met!" The water mixed with wine in Pedro's mug sloshed about, until it spilled over. Wrinkling his nose against the obnoxious odor, he closed his eyes and downed a thick swig.

The old pilot vigorously rubbed the outside arms of his hooded smock to warm himself. "The conflict here, lad, is one between imagination and doubt." A weevil tried to burrow back into his biscuit, but he quickly flicked it out and chomped down, sucking in the moistened hardtack in through his missing front tooth. "The Captain has chosen to hold onto the imagination his belief has fired in him." He smiled thoughtfully. "It's called the walk of faith."

"I don't have that kind of faith, Lonso," Pedro murmured, shaking his head. He wiped his mouth with the back of his hand.

"Faith isn't always feelings, Pedro. Sometimes it's just standing firm, like the Captain is right now up on the quarterdeck. It's believing, when everything—and everyone—around you says, 'Don't believe.'"

Slowly Pedro nodded. Peralonso Niño surely had that right. Here they were, racing into—what? Nothingness. Maybe even off the face of the earth. There were a lot of reasons not to believe.

Yet on this evening Don Cristóbal was not just standing firm; he was praying. And he was doing it out loud, under this canopy of stars, without seeming to care about who might hear him.

Later that night, with most of the crew asleep, the moonlight cast the long shadow of his tall kneeling frame, now clothed in his fur-collared burgundy cloak, over the rail and down onto main deck.

Listening intently, Pedro could make out his words. "Lord, I know You called for this voyage. I know You've led us this far. And I know we cannot do this without You. But I *don't* know, if You will see us through. I believe You will, but I don't *know* You will."

Pedro shivered. If the Captain, in his heart of hearts, was that uncertain, then this grommet felt more afraid than he had ever felt in his fifteen years. And more alone, too. Others had always taken care of him: his grandfather, the friars, even the Captain. Now? He didn't have a soul. What was happening to him—what was happening to all of them—was totally out of their hands.

Their fate was in God's hands, and God's alone.

Pedro decided it was time he tried it, too, this praying, this talking to God. Not using someone else's words but using his own. If God would listen to the Captain, maybe He would listen to Pedro, too.

"Lord," Pedro stammered silently in his heart, where only he could hear. "I don't know You very well, but I guess now is as good a time as any. I'm scared, God. Really scared. Please, help us."

Back at the monastery, Pedro had heard the padres talk about miracles in the Bible, like the parting of the Red Sea and God's provision of manna in the desert. But they had been things of the past—or so he'd thought, until the second day, Thursday, October 11th.

"Ahoy, below! Look to port!" The words barged into what was far from a normal sailing day, because the ships were still making record speed.

Way up in the crow's nest of the *Santa Maria*, the lookout yelled down to his shipmates three decks below. "Yo, mates! Over there!"

Shielding his eyes from the sun, Pedro looked where he was pointing. There was a branch on the next wave! It was covered with tiny blossoms and leaves; they were still green! There was no questioning its significance. Land! And it had to be nearby.

That afternoon the *Pinta* drew close enough for the crew's shouts to be heard by the flagship.

"What is it?" called Emilio through cupped hands.

In the middle of a half-circle of men, a bearded sailor, his face one huge smile, held up a crude cane in one hand and a piece of wood, still dark from its ocean soaking, in the other. The crowd around him was whooping and hollering.

"Captain! Captain!" Pedro flung the Captain's door open, forgetting to knock. "You must see!" he panted without even saluting. "You must see!"

Outside in the sun, the Captain's face relaxed back into its normal dignified countenance. He combed his fingers through his long, windblown hair. His thin lips curved into a smile, and his blue eyes, the color of the sky, shone. Something was happening, and it was good.

One of the men aboard the *Pinta* yelled, "It's carved! There are man-made markings on it!" The rest of his explanation was whipped away by the gale-force winds.

But it was enough. On all three ships the mood shifted from somber to exuberant. In spite of a clear western horizon, the signs of their nearness to land were now unmistakable and exciting, as real as the solid oak planks under Pedro's bare feet.

Throughout the day, whenever he finished a chore or errand for the Captain, the young sailor could be found with the other off-duty mariners scanning the horizon for any sign of land.

"D'ye think it's soon?" Pedro asked Emilio, who was sitting on one of the beams for the landing crosses.

"Don't know," replied the grommet, not taking his eyes off the horizon. "But I do know this: I plan to win that ten thousand *maravedi* prize the Sovereigns promised to give the first one to sight it. I got things to do with that money."

"Not before I do," Pedro said, with a laugh. "I got me a ship to buy." He tucked the frayed end of a long hemp rope, now wrapped around his left elbow and hand, between two tight strands of the tough fiber and then flung the coil over the top of a nearby square post for safekeeping.

"Well, ye best stand fast then, boy," Emilio retorted, his black eyes flashing. "No sleep for ye this night!"

By eight that evening, as the *ampoletta* announced the changing of the watch, the sun was well down, and another brisk trade wind caught the ship and increased its speed back up to nine knots, more than eleven miles per hour. As the wind shifted around to the flagship's starboard side, her able seamen trimmed her sails accordingly. The *Santa Maria* was like an

Andalusian racehorse. Pedro grinned at that thought. He felt like a jockey with the wind in his face, letting his mount fly and hanging on for dear life.

"Nine and a half knots, Don Cristobál!" called Señor Lonso jubilantly.

"Shift course to due west," called the Captain, permitting himself a smile.

"Are you sure, sir?" Lonso cleared his throat, scratchy from yelling through the wind for the last two days. "Should we not heave to, for the night? If we're truly close to land, we could encounter reefs or rocks, sir. Wouldn't see them in the dark."

"This is not the time for prudence, Señor Niño," the Captain reminded him. "This wind is like gold, and I intend to spend every bit of it! We must make all possible use of this wind. We shall change direction, sir. No more southwest for us. *Oeste!* Due west, I say! Use the smoke signal to alert our sister ships. Cipangu is due west."

Later that night, with the horizon no longer visible, the drifting October moon made the three tiny ships' sails glisten like ghostly silver.

To Pedro, the night seemed magical.

Suddenly Chachu blew his whistle. There was a loud shuffling of bare feet as the crew quickly appeared from every nook and cranny of the ship and assembled on the main deck and the half deck. The Captain was going to speak. Pedro stood next to some other grommets near the forecastle, wondering what he was going to say.

"The Lord is blessing us with signs," Cristobál assured them. His right forefinger pointed straight up in the wind. "This westerly is directly from Him. An answer to our prayer. Keep a sharp lookout in the moon's light," he beamed. "And a silk doublet in addition to the ten thousand *maravedis* to the first man to sight land!"

As the sailors dispersed to their duties Pedro could hear them chattering noisily to each other. The pitch of excitement on the cruising flagship this night would keep every man wide awake, and all eyes scanning the horizon.

Then something up by the bow caught his eye. "*Look!*" he called to Emilio, pointing at the foaming bow wave. It seemed illuminated from within by a faint green light.

His friend nodded. "The sea does that, sometimes. Usually in tropic latitudes."

"And usually close to land?"

When Emilio had no reply, Pedro smiled. Was it another sign from God? Maybe He was listening, after all.

15

DAY THREE

Keep 'er far away from any reefs, Señor Arias, or I'll have to come down and take the stick m'self. I'll not lose 'er after comin' this far." De la Cosa's grunting could be heard fore and aft. Clearly miffed that the captain was taking this kind of chance with his ship, the master paced the quarter-deck like a hunting dog that needed exercise.

"Take it up with the captain," Arias answered back sharply up the ladder to the master, as the giant tiller vibrated both hands. "That's yer job."

"I can't do everything," De la Cosa barked. "Listen for the breakers, Señor Arias, and keep yer blasted ears open." The irritated master bit a dirty fingernail on his left hand.

Pedro actually felt sorry for him. The worst thing that could happen to a ship's owner was to have his ship wrecked. They were sailing mighty fast tonight, with only a lopsided moon now hiding behind a thin stretch of clouds to guide them. No wonder De la Cosa was nervous.

The cabin boy maneuvered over the beams for the crosses and around the coils of rope along one side of the steerage. It was his job to flip the *ampoletta* this watch until midnight. The helmsman's small lantern flickered next to the binnacle, creating an even ruddier appearance than normal in the steerage.

"We ain't goin' to sight land for two more days," Emilio declared quietly, squatting near the capstan.

"How do you know?" Pedro inquired. Emilio had this way of thinking he knew it all, a fact that annoyed Pedro no end. After all, the other cabin boy was just seventeen, and he'd only been out to sea two more times than Pedro. He wasn't *that* smart.

"Had a dream."

"So what? Everyone has dreams."

"Yea, but mine tell the future," Emilio piped up, hugging his knees. "It'll be two days, and I'll lay ye a wager on it: one hundred *maravedis*."

Pedro ignored the bet, remembering Father Antonio's caution about sailors. He eyed the upper chamber of the fragile glass container. Slowly but surely, the last few grains dribbled into the bottom. Carefully, the cabin boy flipped it over, returned it to its peg, and sang, "Blessed be the hour our Lord was born . . ."

It was ten o'clock, two hours before Day Three and still no land.

Suddenly he heard a cry from the Captain, who had been pacing the quarterdeck. "A light! I see a light!"

"Aye, sir, I see it too!" a sailor on the main deck chimed in.

And then it was gone.

"It must have been land," Cristobál groaned to no one in particular. "It looked like a candle being raised and lowered."

By two o'clock in the morning, the Captain's cabin boy was finding it more and more difficult to keep his eyes open. If he could just stay awake long enough, maybe he could spot land first. Thoughts of the reward tumbled through his mind again. And a doublet, too! He'd never owned a nice jacket. And the money—oh, what he could do with that money!

The quarter moon was now high over Orion on the port side and clear of any clouds.

"Jupiter is rising." Pedro directed his comment toward Lonso, who had just stepped toward the starboard rail, polished earlier in the day.

"Aye, lad, and Saturn's already set."

Lonso tugged the wet sleeves of his jacket down below his wrists.

"The *Pinta*'s sailing ahead, sir," Don Cristobál's long-time friend announced to him, as the Captain positioned himself near the bowsprit on the forecastle.

"I see 'er, Señor Niño. The *Pinta*'s a faster rig, to be sure. I'm thinking Martín Pinzón wants that prize."

The Captain had not slept in two days, but no one could tell it from the way he gave orders, or the way he watched from the bow. It was as if each nautical mile furnished his body with more energy.

"Wouldn't mind that purse myself, Cap'n." The pilot wiped the sea spray from the plunging bow off his whiskered cheeks. Only a few curly gray locks showed under his sailor's cap, tugged securely halfway down his weathered brow.

"I don't think any of us would, my friend," replied the Captain with a chuckle. "I'm still convinced that strange light I saw earlier tonight came from land. There is no other explanation. Certainly it could not have come from a ship. Our vessels are the only three on this side of the world."

Pedro glanced up toward the heavens to find the two brightest stars marking the edge of the dipper farthest from the North Star. "There are the two guards of Polaris, sir." The boy was trying to make conversation. One, because he didn't want to fall victim to his own exhaustion, and two, because he knew they were only four hours away from dawn of the third and final day.

"Aye, lad. And there's Pegasus." The Captain pointed to the constellation.

At that moment, a loud cry electrified the night.

"*Tierra! Tierra!* Land!" From the *Pinta*'s forecastle, the lookout's words reached them, despite the wind behind them. "White cliffs, ahead!"

In the pale light of the moon, on the horizon ahead of them, the jagged outline of chalky white cliffs appeared. The blast of the *Pinta*'s cannon shattered the normal sounds of the Ocean Sea, and every sleepy eye flew open to see.

Land! It was really land!

"Señor Pinzón, you've found land!" Don Cristobál shouted over to the caravel, where it was barely heard above the cheering of the men, now slapping one another and dancing on the deck.

"Aye, sir!" The *Pinta*'s captain placed his soft brimmed cap over his heart.

"I'll give you half the prize as a present!" Pedro realized that the captain was claiming half the prize for himself, for the light he thought he had seen earlier.

Turning to the officer of the watch, he gave a new course. "South, Señor De la Cosa! Bring her about now, sir! And lower all sails except the main, and let her have plenty of way."

Before Chachu's pipe could sound its instructions, a boisterous chorus of Spanish song graced the night sky. The men were singing, and their music was as full of adoration and worship as any cathedral choir. Within seconds, all three ships' crews of ninety sailors, tired but ecstatic, were giving thanks for the miracle each man knew this to be.

The fleet maintained its southerly course for the rest of the night, to stay well offshore of any barrier reefs lurking just beneath the surface. No one slept. No one could. Every man who wasn't working, was watching and wondering, hoping and dreaming.

For Pedro, every moment was memorable. He savored the experience, as if he were eating Father Antonio's favorite baked rosemary and oregano bread. The boy danced little jigs with the rest of the men. He laughed. He wiped hints of moisture from the corners of both eyes. He stared in amazement at the dimly lit shoreline, considering Chinese pagodas and gold and the stories he would now have to tell his children.

Inside the Captain's cabin a short while later, Pedro asked a question. "Sir, do you think we'll land on the mainland?" The Captain's inkhorn was almost full. Pedro carefully poured the last few drops until the ink shimmered at the top.

"We'll find out soon enough, lad." Wax from the large white beeswax candle on the edge of the Captain's desk had been dripping down its side and was spilling onto the pewter stand. Under the candle's light, the Captain carefully pricked their location on the map and penned in the date: Friday, October 12, 1492.

"Fetch me a rolled parchment from my trunk over there, Pedro." The dark color of the ink mellowed with each breath the Captain blew on it.

"Sir, is Japan very big?" For a brief moment, the familiar scent of fresh parchment from the waxed leather trunk transported Pedro back to the library at La Rábida. He carefully rummaged through the parchments, rolled and neatly stacked on top of each other.

"As I understand it, Cipagnu is actually a group of four large islands and many smaller islands, Pedro, off the mainland of Cathay. Its name means 'country where the sun rises.'"

"Marco Polo called it a land of gold and riches," Pedro added, remembering his readings with pride.

"That he did, lad."

The parchment map had the slick feel of goat's skin, much like some of the ones in Father Antonio's stockpile at home. He handed it to the Captain.

"Here is where we are." With one finger, Cristobál outlined the coast of Japan. "We're sailing along the 28th parallel. We've hit it exactly."

The young apprentice's ponytail tickled the back of his long neck as he shook his head. This navigational miracle was hard to believe. This Captain had gone where no other European had ever gone before, across a sea few people believed could be crossed. And Pedro had come with him. All the boy's doubts melted into respect and admiration. The voyage had truly become a voyage of destiny, no longer a nightmare but a miracle, a dream come true for his Captain. And now, for him as well.

"God still sits on his throne, Pedro, and His Spirit knows all things. Now put this back for me, while I start my letter to the sovereigns."

The cabin boy returned the map in its place in the pine bench under the window and waited quietly beside the desk, as the Captain wrote:

Oh, most Blessed Sovereigns,
I shall soon erect a cross on the
beach of this new land
as a token of Jesus Christ Our Lord.
And I shall conduct a ceremony
taking possession of this land on behalf of Spain,
naming it San Salvador, or Holy Savior.

"Sir? If I might . . ." He usually didn't make suggestions to the Captain, but his concern tonight outweighed his hesitation. "Sir, should you not get a bit of sleep before we land?"

Cristóbal settled his quill pen in its holder and breathed a loud sigh, the kind of breath that silently embraces one's thoughts. "You're probably right, lad. But I fear sleep will elude me now. The world, as we know it, is changing today. I've waited too many years to sleep through any second of this experience."

As the boy turned to go, the Captain added, "One more thing, Pedro: Tell Lonso to have the men ready the ship's boat and retrieve two beams for the first landing cross. We shall plant the cross this day."

Pedro's salute was lost on the Captain, who had already bowed his head for a word of prayer.

As the lad stepped over the well-weathered threshold to the outside, his eyes were drawn once again to the long, low silhouette awaiting them. And he wondered in his heart. What would it be like, this strange new land? Would they find people there, and would they be friendly? What unseen dangers might lurk in these Asiatic waters?

16

TO GOD BE THE GLORY

A fiery orange orb decorated the eastern horizon, as if the universe, feeling hospitable this morning, was offering up its favorite morning dish. Before the dawn *ampoletta* chant echoed through the ship, the once-familiar shrieking of water fowl snapped Pedro up and out of his slumber.

But these weren't gulls. There were three of them, and they were much bigger; their wingspan must be nearly ten feet! He stared at them in awe, as they soared upward in tight circles on a rising October air current, searching for some unsuspecting prey. All of a sudden, one of them folded its wings and plunged like an arrow into the sea, emerging a moment later with a big fish flopping in the pouch beneath its long bill.

Pelicans! Only these were brown and bigger than the ones at home.

The early morning air was already rich with humidity. Pedro yawned and stretched his aching calves. He could feel the exhaustion. His back and neck warmed and loosened as he forced himself to run in place, his bare feet smacking the hard deck planks. This promised to be a big day, and he had to get his blood moving.

Blessed be the light of day
And the Holy Cross, we say . . .
Blessed be the light of day
And He who sends the night away.

The familiar morning ditty was truer today than any other day of the voyage. God had sent the night away and ushered in a breathtaking morning.

Like children in a candy store, every sailor eyed the scene around him. The sea around them was emerald blue-green, and so clear that one could see the bottom several fathoms down. Ashore, mountains of gray limestone overlooked long coral reefs creating barriers between the shore and the open sea, like huge sea gardens, growing parallel to the shore. Joining the herring gulls flying about them was an exotic tropical bird with a long white tail. What a wonderful and strange new world!

During the last two hours of the night, the fleet had drifted south to the southeastern tip of the land.

"She's lookin' more and more like an island, Cap'n," Señor Lonso panted, his biceps bulging, as he helped another sailor haul in a rope through a pulley block.

"Indeed, Lonso," Don Cristobál responded, scanning the barrier reef for an opening that would let them into the shallow bay, where he might anchor safely and send boats ashore. "Cipangu has many islands."

Suddenly the Captain ordered, "Now! Brace 'er sharp, Señor De la Cosa!" He had sighted a break in the barrier ledge.

Within minutes, the ship was where he wanted her. "Drop anchor!" he commanded, and immediately sailors began pushing the long wooden handles protruding from the round capstan. Slowly the heavy anchor rope unspooled, and the iron anchor plunged deeper, till it found a purchase on the inlet's sandy bottom. Once one of its two hooks had caught, the men reversed their efforts at the capstan, till the anchor rope was taut.

"Pedro, in my cabin!" ordered the Captain from the quarterdeck.

The darkness of the cabin made it feel musty and dank. Pedro blinked his eyes and tried to focus. "My doublet, boy. There in the closet. Quick!"

The close fitting wool jacket hung on one side of the tiny cedar closet. The Captain had only worn it once before, during his meeting with the Pinzóns. The white cotton blouse right next to it tumbled to the closet floor when Pedro lifted the jacket off its wooden hanger.

"Worry about that later. Where's my good shirt and my boots?"

Pedro had never seen Don Cristobál this ruffled. He could issue commands with more authority than any officer or captain. And his faith in this God-given mission had never faltered. Yet now he was uncharacteristically frantic and ill-tempered.

The cabin boy's hands felt as heavy as sounding leads. He fought off what he was feeling. Here they were, about to set foot on new soil, and he was shaking because he had to brush white lint off the Captain's deep red coat. His exhaustion was getting the best of him. Swallowing hard, he rushed about feeling as if a sea dragon was breathing fire at his backside.

"My helmet, lad."

"Helmet, sir?"

"Yes, yes, on the top shelf of the hutch there!"

The weight of the steel helmet surprised Pedro. Embossed with a geometrical design of squares and circles, the helmet fit snugly over the Captain's wide head.

"Now, my sword!"

The sword, hanging on an iron hook in the other small closet, was a patterned blade of Damascus steel that Don Cristóbal had purchased at a bazaar in North Africa. Even the shadowy cabin did not diminish its gleam. Elegant in its scabbard, it fit securely to the Captain's leather belt.

"How do I look, boy?"

"Like an admiral, sir." Pedro smiled with a formal salute that covered his nervousness.

"Indeed," responded the Captain, half to himself. Then he smiled. "Indeed!"

Opening the door of his cabin, he turned momentarily back. "So, lad, are you coming?"

The world seemed to have a special luster today, thought Pedro, as four of the crew rowed the *Santa Maria*'s small boat towards the beach. Also in the boat were the Captain, De la Cosa, and Lonzo. And the two pieces of the wooden cross that they would assemble and plant.

Behind the gleaming white sand was thick dark-green underbrush with exotic bright-red blooms, and tall palm trees. Pedro marveled at this strange tree's fanlike fronds, waving hello in the morning's gentle breeze. He shook his head and smiled. This looked like paradise.

As the bow of the tender ground ashore, he leaped over the side, taking care to miss the oars jutting out into the water. Heaving the bow farther up on the sand, he steadied it for those about to disembark. How good the wet sand felt beneath his toes, after more than four weeks at sea!

Now the sailors shipped their oars and joined him, pulling the boat farther up on the sand, so the Captain's boots would not get wet. To the left and right, the boats from the *Niña* and the *Pinta*, also arrived.

Hardly any words were spoken. Everyone seemed to regard this as a solemn occasion. Somehow words would dispel the enchantment of the occasion, moments that seemed to be filled with a sense of the miraculous.

Silently Pedro helped Lonso assemble the eight-foot-tall oak cross. When it was ready, the Captain called all present to gather at the foot of it. On one side, Martín Pinzón held the flag of the Sovereigns, Ferdinand of Aragon and Isabella of Castile. On the other side, his younger brother held the white banner with the red Crusaders' cross emblazoned on it.

The Captain raised his eyes to the top of the cross and to heaven above. "Almighty and Everlasting God," he proclaimed, his bright scarlet doublet and glistening helmet giving him a regal appearance. As the rest of the company knelt on one knee and bowed their heads, Don Cristóbal spoke with the authority of one who had long believed in his mission and was now, at last, seeing it come to pass. "Forgive us for our doubts, Lord."

That pierced Pedro to his very soul. Through the last part of the voyage, Pedro had been a doubting Thomas. Father Peréz used to say doubt was like a disease, and right now, it was making him feel sick with shame.

"Thou hast created the heaven and the earth and the sea," the Captain continued. "Blessed be Thy name."

Señor Lonso had been right: Here was a man who had faced life's battle against doubt and had won. When the odds were against him, he had chosen to believe. Don Cristóbal Colón—Christopher Columbus—had believed when everything and everyone had said not to. He truly deserved his new title: Admiral of the Ocean Sea.

With his back to the sparkling sleepy cove, Pedro forced himself to keep his eyes open, squinting against the glare. Open eyes, he reasoned, would chase away these gnawing feelings of shame.

"You have used us, Your humble servants, to proclaim Your Holy Name in this second part of the earth." The Admiral's helmet shone, as he lifted his face toward heaven again, turning his gloved palms upward and opening his arms wide. "We dedicate this land to You, O God. We christen it *San Salvador,* in honor of our Holy Savior."

Just then, an insect landed on Pedro's right eyebrow, which was wet with the sweat that now trickled down his forehead. Pedro swatted at the pesky creature, but the giant fly buzzed him a second time, enticed by the salty taste. With gritted teeth, the boy whacked at the pest again. The sting of salt pricked his eyes, now opened wide, as he determined to get rid of the annoying insect.

Out of the corner of his eye, he caught a movement in the underbrush. Was it just the breeze moving the palms? Or was it something else?

17

STRANGERS

As Pedro watched, transfixed, a form emerged from the dense under-brush. It was a man, dark-skinned, clad in only a loincloth. And now, here came another, and another. And after them, a woman, wearing only some kind of skirt. And several more men. They appeared to be as amazed by the new visitors, as the small group gathered at the base of the cross was by their approach.

The boldest, a young lad about Pedro's age, with a large shell earring on his right ear and a spiny oyster-shell necklace around his neck, came right up to him and sniffed him! And declared something to his companions, who smiled.

"Stay calm, men," murmured the Admiral, suppressing a chuckle.

A woman, her face painted white, now touched the Admiral's jacket and snatched back her finger, as if the cloth was hot. When she did it again, the Admiral laughed and declared, "I think the natives have found us. And they certainly seem friendly enough."

"What do we call them, Admiral?" asked Vicente Pinzón, as an older native stared intently at the gold buttons on his blue topcoat.

The Admiral turned to him, as more dark hands reached to touch his metal helmet. "Well, since we seem to have arrived at the Indies, it is only appropriate that we call them Indians."

Indians it was. And a small crowd of them now greeted the wide-eyed explorers. Some of the sailors had seen natives before on voyages down the coast of Africa. But those had been black, not brown like these. And none of the men had ever experienced a welcome like this. Like bees to honey, a swarm of Indians arrived to investigate the strange white-skinned creatures that had arrived in giant canoes pulled by white clouds.

The islanders were actually quite handsome. They were well built with lean frames and wide angular faces. Painted colors of black, red, and white covered parts of their bodies, including their slightly oblique black eyes and broad noses. Shell ornaments of various shapes and colors adorned their necks, as did jewelry made of different animal bones.

The Indians were chattering like mallard ducks in a tongue no one knew.

"Let's try sign language," Pedro suggested, remembering how Marco Polo's father had used hand gestures during his early visits to Cathay, before he learned to speak Chinese.

Just then, the young Indian who was Pedro's age, tiptoed up to him, his toes dusty with white sand. The boy angled his head to one side, squinted his dark eyes, and scrunched his coppery face together almost into a frown.

Pedro saw this as his chance. Thumping his own chest, he uttered the word, "Spaniard," slowly and distinctly. The Indian's bushy eyebrows lowered even more, while his lips, now open and revealing large square teeth, imitated the movements of Pedro's lips, trying to get the sounds from his own ears to his mouth.

Pedro repeated the word.

The boy gently touched Pedro's lips, following their formations with the tips of his long fingers. Three shiny metallic bracelets dangling on the Indian's right arm jangled toward his elbow. Pedro mouthed the word slowly once again.

"San . . . erd," the boy finally replied, almost in a whisper.

Pedro's enthusiastic nodding prompted the Indian to try the word a second time, and then a third, each time a bit louder and quicker. "San . . . erd," he repeated. "Sanerd."

In spite of the heat, tiny goose bumps produced a tingling sensation on Pedro's arm. Gradually, the commotion on the beach that surrounded the young Spanish sailor from the Old World and the young native Indian from the New World faded into the background, as if there were no other sounds on the earth but theirs.

All at once, the native thrust out his muscular chest and squared his jaw. "Ar . . . a . . . wak," he proclaimed, waving both hands in wide circles to the jingle of his bracelets.

Pedro had to think a moment. Was the boy telling him his name? Or doing what he himself had done, giving him the name of his tribe? The circling arms offered Pedro the clue. "Arawak," Pedro affirmed the tribal name, gesturing to the other Indians.

The islander then poked at his own bare chest, thumping it over and over. "Macu. Macu," the boy said in a tone that carried a sense of pride.

Pedro smiled and pointed at him. "You, Macu!"

Grinning the Indian pointed at Pedro, his eyebrows raised.

"Me? Pedro," the young Spaniard replied. "Pedro."

"Pay . . . dro" the Indian slowly repeated.

What should he do next, Pedro wondered. He turned and threw a questioning glance to Lonso.

"Why don't you offer him your red cap? It'll be a sign of friendship."

So Pedro did. Other sailors did the same, and soon a number of Arawak, both men and women, were strutting about the beach in red sailors' caps, like peacocks with new plumes.

Blue waves lapped the shore, as their children danced in the foamy current to the jingling of Spanish hawks' bells tied around their wrists. The little circular metal bells, worth little in Spain, were used to keep track of hawks being trained to catch other birds. The Admiral had brought them with him, along with glass beads, for just such occasions as this, and the Indians seemed to prize the fascinating tiny bells and the beads which shone in the sun as much as their new knitted caps.

As the sun heated the sand beneath their bare feet, the Admiral removed his helmet and thick coat, laid aside his sword, and pushed up his ruffled sleeves. The sailors and the natives were now exchanging trinkets and food and began learning quite a bit through sign language and specific words. Macu's tribe, the Arawak, inhabited not only this island, which they called Guanahaí, but other islands nearby. They were a gentle people, whose only weapons were darts tipped with jagged fish teeth. The Caribs, on the other hand, were a warlike tribe to the north, much feared by the Arawak.

All day long the exchanges continued. The ships' boats brought all the men ashore in relays. The only work assigned to them that day was to scour out the water casks and refill them with fresh water from a sparkling stream that emptied into the inlet.

Pedro would never forget his first sip of that stream—the best water he had ever tasted!

In the afternoon Pedro joined other sailors, downstream from where they were refilling the water casks, as they set about to clean themselves. Removing their clothes, till they were as naked as the Arawak, they waded in, taking care not to go further in than waist deep, as only Pedro and one or two others knew how to swim. Using rocks and brush, they scrubbed the dirt off of themselves, and then off of their clothing. And for the first time since they had left the Canaries, Pedro felt really clean.

Finally, as the three pelicans hovered over the inlet hunting for supper, the Admiral announced that their new friends would soon be giving them supper. Then he returned to the conversation he and the Pinzón brothers were having with the Arawak chief, who was called a cacique.

"Pedro, have ye tried this?" Emilio called to him, as he used his hand-forged sailor's knife to slice the green rind off a wedge of yellow fruit. "Juicy," he slurped, letting the sticky juice course down his chin and offering a piece to his friend. "They've got baskets of them over there, and no one seems to mind how much you eat."

Sure enough, near the palmetto bushes and ferns bordering the forest, five baskets woven with dried palm fronds had been crammed with all kinds of exotic foods. Eager sailors hovered around them, greedily consuming whatever they could get their hands on.

As he bit into the succulent fruit, Pedro's stomach growled like a ravenous dog. He hadn't realized how hungry he was. Food! Real food! No more weevils and worms. No more hardtack or thick wine or dirty water. No more cockroaches!

Pedro's knees almost gave way as he reached into one of the baskets for a roasted crab. Savoring the chunks of sweet fresh crabmeat, he observed Macu squatting at the shore, his silhouette framed by the pinks and grays of the setting sun. The young Arawak was caressing each individual glass bead on the necklace Pedro had given him, as if it was the most precious thing he had ever owned.

All too soon, the boatswain's high-pitched whistle instructed the sailors to return to their ships for the night. Pedro burrowed his toes along the squiggly lines of the tide's ebbing current in front of the tender, searching for tiny live cochina crabs and waiting for the Admiral, who was now striding toward the shore.

As he reached the boat, De la Cosa came up to him, pulling along an elderly Arawak by his ear. "Admiral, I have somethin' here that might interest ye."

The Admiral turned slowly. Both Pinzóns hesitated before stepping into their respective ships' boats.

"It's gold, sir," De la Cosa announced, pointing at the old man's nose ring and forcing him down in the sand.

"Señor De la Cosa, we will not treat these people harshly, do you understand? And that's an order." Cristóbal's voice was stern with warning.

De la Cosa's eyes narrowed, but he released his grip on the man.

The freed native now kissed the Admiral's hand, as if Cristóbal were a king. Then he twisted his round nose ring until it came out of his hole and handed it to the Admiral.

Don Cristóbal turned it this way and that, holding it up to the setting sun. "Are you sure it's gold?" he asked De la Cosa.

"Well, it ain't fool's gold, I can tell ye that. Their word for gold is *caona*, and apparently all the islands have it."

Holding the valuable ornament high in the evening's glow, the Admiral boomed, "May God be praised! All gold belongs to the Sovereigns!"

"Riches to Spain!" Martín Pinzón bellowed. "The treasures of Asia will soon be ours!"

18

A NEW FRIEND

Saturday's trip to shore couldn't come fast enough for Pedro. He finished his chores before the noon ditty and hopped into the ship's boat. With his hair freshly combed, the young seaman adjusted the leather straps holding his goatskin satchel across his bare back. He had to find Macu today, so the two of them could explore together. Pedro wanted to see it all—the village, the lakes, the birds and animals, and anything else that came up.

Especially food. His mouth watered from the memory of the morning's fresh fruit left by the natives who'd climbed aboard the flagship yesterday. The boy had peeled a soft yellow skin off a new fruit and swallowed its mellow insides, one bite at a time. Three bananas later, he learned that the fruit grew in huge bunches on island trees with leaves up to ten feet long.

Another basket contained a thick, hard yellow-green skin and sword-shaped leaves that had to be cut before he could get to the fruit. The prickly pineapple skin sliced Pedro's fingers twice, but his persistence paid off. The fruit was delicious, something he wanted the fathers to try back home, especially Father Antonio whose appetite for new flavors was as big as his expanding girth.

Pedro had not eaten many new foods in his lifetime, but this trip was changing all that. He was willing to sample almost anything now, as long as it didn't have bugs and mildew. As the boat took them towards shore, the apprentice seaman knew the sea was calling his name more than ever. If every trip turned out to be this good, life was sure to become one great big adventure with thousands of stories to tell.

The smell of the sand and the ocean filled the lagoon, making it a place of pure peace. Under its surface lay an azure world of exotic flora and fauna. Underwater, the coral reef looked like deer antlers, only colored in greens, purples, yellows, oranges, and tans. A huge turtle, camouflaged by its brown shell with dark and light streaks, with a hawk-like beak nibbled on a red and purple sponge. Tiny copper-colored hermit crabs flitted in and out of the small caverns in the reef, scavenging for food in its crevices. A bright orange starfish crawled along the rock as two of its five arms floated with the water's current.

Out beyond the line of breaking surf, a huge gray creature with a whiskered snout and wrinkled face chomped on some brown sea grass, lazily propelling itself with its two flippers, as if it didn't have a care in the world. The Arawak's dugout canoes, long boats fashioned from the island's mahogany trees, glided back and forth between the three ships and the shore, linking the known with the unknown.

"Pedro! Pedro!"

The heavy accent was definitely not Castilian.

Pedro swiveled to find his new Arawak friend in a nearby *piragua'*, or dugout, frantically waving one hand and pointing the other hand toward the shore.

"Hola. ¿Cómo estás?" cried Pedro in Spanish. "How are you?"

The question mark on Macu's face quickly converted into a smile and an Arawak reply. *"Guarico!"* The accompanying gesture, however, was so exaggerated that his entire canoe capsized, sending all three men aboard into the water. They soon re-emerged and joined in the laughter of the men aboard the boat, as their righted their canoe and quickly climbed back into it.

When all were ashore, Macu took Pedro to his village. It was a picture of serenity, set under a canopy of giant palms near a great lake that extended far into the background. As the sun's noon rays shown through the branches and spiny green pines, Pedro entered another world, an ancient world that had existed for thousands of years.

Round wood-framed dwellings with palm thatched roofs surrounded a huge square with a rectangular hut right in the middle—the cacique's. The quiet setting was disturbed only by the clatter of three native women weaving colored cotton yarn back and forth on a spindle loom, making a blanket.

Taking Pedro's hand, Macu guided him toward a small hut on the south side of the village. Two pieces of pottery with grotesque heads guarded the entrance, reminding Pedro of the gargoyle water spouts he had once seen on a trip with Father Antonio to the nearest cathedral, in Cadiz. Well swept and clean, the shelter seemed to invite Pedro to enter and made him feel welcomed.

The first thing that caught his attention were odd-shaped gourds hanging down from the rafters and a clay bowl with fresh greens in it on the hut's table. The second thing was an aroma of something good cooking.

He turned to Macu, who beamed and introduced him to his wife, "Liani."

Kneeling before a low fire, the young woman was extracting a white-skinned vegetable from a stationery metal spit. Her black hair, long and thick, brushed the earthen floor like a feather duster. Smiling shyly, she juggled the potato between both hands and breathed on it. In a few moments, Pedro's smacking noises, as he bit into the hot potato, pleased his new friends very much.

The two young men now set off to survey the island. Pedro quickly learned that except for its sand dunes, the north-south island was fairly flat. The Arawak had worn a path to the lake through a labyrinth of green shrubs and water vines.

Ah! To dig his bare toes into the dark rich soil again felt so good that all Pedro wanted to do was walk and walk and never stop. His feet, still tough, felt like they'd come home at last. So much of this island was like home. The rocky shore and the sand. The palmetto bushes and the familiar smell of the pines.

His ears picked up the buzzing of bees while his nose sniffed fragrant trumpet-shaped white honeysuckle. Vibrant red hibiscus flowers, much like those lining the adobe walls of the monastery, made him feel closer to home, too. At one point, he thought he had stepped into a magic garden, as a cloud of bright yellow butterflies flittered about his head.

Finally the two boys worked their way around some bristly water plants near the murky water's edge. The salty lake shimmered like a mirror in front of them. An ivory-billed woodpecker busily chiseled wood high above their heads, while long-legged white egrets leisurely stalked crayfish along the muddy shore.

"Shh—"

Pedro nearly crashed into Macu, who had abruptly stopped near the lake's shore. The Indian pointed his thumb at a large green stone beside the water. Perfectly camouflaged against a rock covered with lichen, was the biggest lizard Pedro had ever laid eyes on. It was almost six feet long and must have weighed at least forty pounds! The reptile was basking in the direct sunlight, its eyes like slits and its nostrils slowly opening and closing. A crest of spiky scales ran down its back to a razor-sharp tail. Pedro swallowed hard at the sight of its long sharp claws.

This time the Arawak's "shh—" was a silent finger in front of his pursed lips. The native slipped the three metal bracelets off his right arm and put them on the ground. With the grace of a dancer, he crept toward the creature. Pedro tried to ignore the gnats now dive bombing his sweaty eyes, as he watched the scene unfold before him.

With a quick thrust of his right hand, the Indian dug into a sandy hole at the base of the rock. Startled, the female *iguana* dove off the rock and into the water, creating splashing ringlets. A smiling Macu held up two eggs from a burrow that must have contained fifty unhatched eggs, enough food for Macu's family and the flagship as well.

For the rest of the afternoon, Pedro lounged on the lake's mud banks watching the dragon lizard that was as big as a dog and enjoying his time with his new friend. Before long, the first distant boatswain's whistle summoned the Spaniard and the Arawak back to the village.

As the setting sun colored the western sky over Macu's hut, Pedro rummaged through his knapsack until he touched the trinkets he had brought with him.

"For Liani." Pedro presented the Arawak with two colorful beaded bracelets and a necklace, a gesture of continuing friendship.

"Pedro," the Indian replied, slipping one of the wide bracelets back off his own arm and handing it to his friend. *"Datiao,"* he grinned, with a generosity that touched Pedro deeply.

"Datiao," Pedro replied with a smile. The Arawak word for "friend" held new meaning for him today. Here across the Ocean Sea, this native Arawak had bestowed on him a valuable treasure unlike any he had ever owned, with no hint of stinginess or greed or payback. The piece of gold jewelry had been freely given.

And it now belonged to Pedro.

19

SHIFTING SANDS

Somehow the light filtering through the branches and leaves above him seemed brighter this evening. Somehow the gnats hovering around his face didn't bother him as much. Somehow the bottoms of his feet couldn't feel the dried needles and fallen twigs along the path.

Pedro twirled the gold bracelet around his left wrist. He felt rich, richer than he had ever felt in his life. What a trip this was! Now he would be like the sailors he had met at the Palos dock, full of wild adventures and incredible stories. Now he could be proud of his life and his accomplishments. Proud of who he felt he was becoming—a Spanish explorer.

By the time of the boatswain's second whistle, Pedro was nearly back to the thick forest around the inlet. Every forest hum invited him to linger—the male ground crickets rubbing their forewings together to attract females with their special chirping. The brown forest thrush, whose haunting refrains mesmerized him as he ambled along. The distant rhythmic sound of the surf growing closer with every step. Each one beckoned him to stay—just a little bit longer.

All of a sudden, the sound of two husky voices drew his attention toward a clearing on the other side of some dense underbrush. Pedro squared the pack on his back and inched toward a cabbage palm. The palm fronds pricked at his hand as he slid two branches to one side.

Standing in a small open area were Juan De la Cosa and Chachu!

"This gold is ours fer the takin', you idiot." The green and black serpent tattoo on De la Cosa's right arm looked like it was slithering forward, as he thrust his right fist in the air. "These heathen ain't people like us."

"I ain't arguing with ye, mate, but I don't think we has to hurt them." Chachu's feet were planted in a bed of brown pine needles. "We only needs this to get what we want." The sharp curved blade of the steel knife in Chachu's right hand flashed. "Look at 'em," the boatswain scoffed. "Nothin' more than whimpering fools."

Pedro's eyes widened. Sprawled on the dirt at the sailors' feet were three Arawak braves, their eyes as white as cotton wool.

"Grab that one's nose ring and let's get outta here, afore we're missed," De la Cosa barked.

Before Pedro could blink, Chachu flicked the knife into his other hand. Leaning over one of the men, he dug the blade's point into the flesh of the man's nose and jerked the gold ring out. The Arawak, now crumpled into a ball, moaned with blood dripping from his nose.

Just then, a gnat whirred its way into Pedro's gaping mouth all the way to the back of his tongue. "Aagh," the boy gagged and let out a loud cough.

De la Cosa and Chachu both whirled around.

"What are ye lookin' at, ye little piece of trash?" De la Cosa sneered, his eyes sharper than Chachu's blade. "Ye don't belong here!"

Still holding his throat, Pedro stumbled up and through the palm bush. He wasn't about to let these two baboons scare him. "You don't have to hurt them," he managed to gasp through his coughs.

"Why not?" De la Cosa hissed. "I'm jest doin' what the Admiral ordered."

With that, De la Cosa snatched the gold nose ring from Chachu's hand and plunked it in the leather pouch attached to his rope belt. "Let's get outta here," he hissed.

As soon as the sailors were out of sight, Pedro helped the wounded Indian to his feet. The other two brushed off their stomachs and knees. Pedro stared at them, as they disappeared through the foliage.

The smell of the sea grew stronger as Pedro emerged from the lushness of the island's tropical forest onto the beach. A few hours before, he had been overwhelmed with the beauty of this place, but now he felt only despair over what he'd just witnessed. How could this be happening? These people were so gentle and generous. They would have gladly given the sailors their jewelry. All De la Cosa and Chachu would have had to do was ask.

A commotion at the shoreline startled him out of his thoughts. Huddled in a tight circle around the cacique was a group of Arawak braves, clamoring for the tribal leader's attention. Waving their arms, they jumped up and down chattering like herring gulls over a school of fish.

Pedro spotted Emilio heaving a bolt-rope into the bottom of the ship's tender.

"What's going on?"

"The Admiral wants to take 'em with us." Emilio slung a second rope into the boat and wiped his brow. "Thinks they can lead us to the gold."

"Where?" A wave lapped over Pedro's feet.

"On other islands."

Just then the cacique emerged from the throng. The blue and red feathers in his graying hair waved in the wind and the scallop shells wrapped around his knees clipped as he walked toward the boat. Six men, their faces painted black and yellow, followed him.

The boat shifted in the sand, as the men climbed in. The cacique's eyes folded into the wrinkles surrounding them. Although he was thin, his skin was weathered from age. With the palms of both hands facing out, he drew two huge arcs in the salty air toward the western and southern horizons as a sign of blessing for the men. Then he turned and walked away.

"Guess we got us some guides." Emilio tugged at the rope attached to the ship's bow while Pedro lifted the wooden anchor into the boat. Both boys crawled in. "Looks like we're goin' gold digging,' after all."

All of a sudden, something made the hairs on Pedro's arms stand up. Part of him shook it off as a cool breeze, but the other part wondered if it was an uneasy feeling about what was going to happen.

Martín Pinzón's visits to the flagship had been more frequent since their landing. Tonight, the captain of the *Pinta* was dining with the Admiral in the cabin. Pedro stepped through the doorway, carefully balancing two large wooden bowls of food in each hand. The fishy smell of the raw oysters on open shells made his nose wrinkle. Oysters weren't his favorite dish, but the Admiral really liked them. In fact, this was the third dish of mollusks the Admiral had ordered in the last two days. Pedro carefully placed both dishes on the Admiral's table already set with two clean but wrinkled linen napkins and a fresh beeswax candle from the cupboard.

"Admiral," said Pinzón, "I don't see how this can be Japan." He examined an oyster from the bowl Pedro had just set before him. "There aren't any royal palaces or streets of gold. We haven't found one pagoda or anybody with slanted eyes. And how do we know these natives going with us even know we're talking about gold?"

"This is just one of the islands, Martín. Japan isn't the only one along the coast." The Admiral's chair scraped the floor as he shoved it back and stood up. "Look here." His finger circled a group of islands on the map now hanging on one wall. "If we sail southwest, we should find Cipangu itself. If we miss it, we're certain to land on the Chinese mainland."

"I'm still not convinced, Don Cristobál. I think we should head north, not south."

"Will that be all, sir?" The cabin boy stepped to one side and straightened his muslin shirt, badly in need of a wash.

"Actually, you'd best bring more, Pedro. I seem to have a real hunger tonight."

The Admiral drew his chair back up to the table. "Let's not quibble, Martín. When you return to your ship, let your men know we'll explore this island's coast tomorrow and then, on to Japan!"

Just after sunset, the smell of smoking whale oil in the steerage seeped up through the cracks in the overhead beams. The light from the papyrus wick in the compass binnacle lamp wobbled, casting eerie shadows above and below. Since the wick was no longer getting enough oxygen, it needed to be trimmed. Tonight the trimming was Pedro's job.

The lid to the cask containing the oil was slippery as usual. Pedro tried to wipe it with the bottom of his shirt, but the lid wasn't cooperating, and Pedro's patience was wearing thin.

Lonso came to help him. "Ye best ask the Admiral about that bracelet," he said, wiping a stained cloth around one side of the oily rim.

"I did. He told me I could keep it. Just so long as I don't make a big deal about it."

The ancient mariner eyed the boy's face. "What's wrong, lad?"

Pedro gritted his teeth. "The day wasn't so good, after all," he replied, dipping the ladle into the oil.

"Did ye see Macu?"

Pedro nodded. "Aye and more of the island, too." The boy was careful not to let the oil spill over the top of the burner. "But now, I don't know what to do," he murmured, tracing the burner's rim with one finger.

The old pilot waited.

"They were hurting a native, Lonso."

"Who?"

"De la Cosa and Chachu. They made his nose bleed, too."

Lonso shook his head slowly, as he began to understand. "For gold?"

Pedro nodded. "Chachu cut his nose ring out with his knife."

As the wick soaked in the whale oil, Pedro told Lonso the whole story.

"God could not be pleased with that, Pedro," the ancient mariner finally replied, his voice nearly lost in the hull's rhythmic groaning and creaking. "Mark my words: If we treat the natives this way, we're inviting trouble."

20

GOLD SEEKERS

"At least this water doesn't stink as bad." Emilio jerked up the plunger to suck out the bilge water in the hold. It sloshed onto the curved deck at their feet and ran off toward the sides.

Pedro smacked his lips on a raw sweet potato. "I'm going to make sure some of these get home with us." He chomped on another bite.

"Them Indians seem to be likin' that molasses," Emilio quipped, the muscles in his arm swelling with the work of the bilge pump. "I ain't ever seen anyone get so excited."

Standing near the port rail, the natives were sampling their first taste of the syrup on some cassava bread, a golden brown flat-bread that was bitter to the taste but a starchy staple of the Arawak diet. One Indian pointed toward the barrel, his cheeks stuffed with the sweetened bread. Another licked his fingers while a third cackled, as the thick syrup slipped through his fingers and onto the deck. The bread was too bitter for Pedro's taste, although watching them made him wonder about trying it smothered with the sweetener.

The morning sun promised a clear day today, and the hum of the rigging suggested a strong Atlantic wind to carry them to their next island stop. The high, fair-weather cirrus clouds reflecting pinks and blues looked like wisps of white hair. The canvas sails flapped in the sea breeze, as the three vessels began the next leg of their voyage.

The fleet was heading southwest, threading its way through numerous smaller islands and rocky shoals toward the biggest island of all Cipangu, the land of ivory cities, curved stone bridges, and gold.

Suddenly, a scream jolted the normal sounds of the ship.

"Caribs! Caribs!"

One of the Arawak natives was yelling and flailing his right arm towards the starboard rail, his forgotten biscuit crumbling on the deck. As he gripped the weathered rail, his bronze knuckles turned almost white. Two long canoes, filled with dark-skinned men with long black hair and spears, were rounding a bend on the northern point of the crooked island. Instantly, the Arawak hunkered down with his two companions in a tight knot, and all three began to rock back and forth on their heels.

"They sure don't like them Caribs!" Emilio observed, yanking the plunger one last time.

"Macu had a big scar on his stomach," Pedro added. "I wondered if he got it fighting the Caribs." He swallowed his last bite of sweet potato and downed a swig of water.

Emilio wiped his grimy hands on his britches. "Who knows, maybe them Caribs are, you know, man-eaters; cannibals that delight in the taste of boiled meaty flesh." He gobbled imaginary food, smacking his lips so loudly the nearby sailors eyed him suspiciously. "Hmm . . . a sliver of skin . . . a morsel of fingers . . ."

"Your imagination's gettin' to you," responded Pedro with a chuckle. Then, not wanting to entertain any bad omens for the trip, he added, "You need somethin' else to do."

Though they paddled hard, the Carib war party was no match for the speed of the three ships with a following wind. They were soon left far behind.

Toward the late afternoon, a pod of bottleneck dolphins was escorting them to their next port of call—an island that seemed quite large. As their gray tail flukes broke the surface, the mammals twisted and turned in perfect harmony with one another. A mother whistled to her baby, following close behind, to nose it away from the flagship. Somehow the dolphins made Pedro feel safe, as if they were guarding the fleet to keep it out of harm's way.

"Our latitude, Pedro!" The door to the Admiral's cabin, peeling even more from the blistering noon sun, remained ajar in spite of the ship's rolling and pitching.

The wooden quadrant dangled on a nail on the bulkhead. Pedro grabbed it. From the quarterdeck, the seaman apprentice lined up the edge of the quarter-circle with the sun and, holding the plane as perpendicular as he could with the rolling ship, waited for the silk cord to stop swinging.

"It looks like we're around 23° north, sir."

"That we are, lad."

Pedro was still learning, and the Admiral was still teaching him. From using the quadrant to the art of dead reckoning to making point, the novice sailor honed his navigational skills, using the latest techniques every captain must know. On this day, a captain had to know how to tack to the west along the treacherous shoals of this very long island and find a way into shore.

"Señor Torreros, what is your recommendation?" Don Cristóbal asked his student, as they eyed the rocky highlands of the island's eastern shore off the forecastle.

His heart might be pounding inside of him, but the young apprentice was not about to show it. The Admiral had been clear from the start: No grommet was ever allowed to pilot the ship or man the tiller. Yet, here he was, giving Pedro the chance to prove himself. No good captain would show any hint of fear, and Pedro certainly aimed to be a good captain. He stood firm, hoping his knees wouldn't cave in under him.

"Señor Lonso? Our sounding, sir." Pedro spoke with only a hint of nervousness, trying to copy the Admiral's voice, always so full of authority.

"Ten fathoms, Señor Torreros," Lonso replied, his voice clipped by the wind and that same grandfatherly twinkle in his dark eyes. "Steady at ten fathoms."

Pedro's face felt scratchy as he rubbed his chin. He had to think. He'd been at sea two months; he could figure this out. Long rocky horizontal platforms of gray limestone and visible sea caverns backed by steep cliffs sculpted the island's lee shore. If they couldn't come up with anchorage by nightfall, they would have to lay-to. It was almost the first dogwatch, or seven o'clock. Night would soon be upon them.

"Admiral, I think we should stand off for the night, anchor here, and tomorrow send in the ship's boat for more supplies."

The Admiral cocked his head and tipped an imaginary hat at the boy. This boy was learning and learning fast. "I quite agree, lad. Señor Peralonso, have the boatswain whistle us up. Alert our sister ships, and we'll furl sails. Tomorrow we'll plant another cross and search for gold."

By low tide the next morning, the cross was planted on a beach sandwiched between a cave and rocky ledge. The Admiral named this island *Fernandina* in honor of King Ferdinand.

"Let's go!" Emilio exclaimed, as he dashed toward a sandy path through the dunes near the shore. "Come on!" he yelled. "I mean to find some gold."

The trail was lined with slender white weeds waving in the wind. What Pedro didn't realize was that glistening weed harbored a deadly enemy for anyone who dared to walk barefoot along the seashore. Sandspurs! Before the boy knew what was happening, a cluster of the hidden prickly weeds had stabbed the bottom of his left foot.

"Ow!" he screamed, so loud he surprised even himself. Grabbing his punctured foot with his left hand only made things worse, as two of the burs jabbed the soft palm of his hand, sticking into his flesh. Even though Pedro's feet stopped moving, his heart was beating faster than a hound chasing a deer. The boy hobbled to a nearby rock outside the entrance to a cave, plopped his body down, and began to pluck the spurs out of his hand, one at a time.

Emilio was nowhere to be seen, leaving Pedro feeling rather sorry for himself. Just as he was extracting one of the sharp splinters from his foot, however, a strange-looking dog straggled down the path from the direction of the beach. His tangled wet black fur was full of cockleburs, and his ears drooped to match his eyes.

"Hey, boy." Pedro kept his voice friendly. "Do ye live near here?"

The dog's black eyes narrowed into slits, and he slunk back a few steps, but he didn't growl. In fact, the only sound was the nearby crashing of waves along the rocky coast.

Using a mellow voice, Pedro tried again, as he rubbed his wounded foot. "It's all right, boy. I'm not going to hurt ya."

The dog's grimy teeth were sharp through his silent snarl. It was as if the animal wanted to talk but couldn't. Then, just as abruptly as he had shown up, the canine trotted off in the direction of the cave.

"It don't bark," a human voice growled behind Pedro. Marco's wooden cane clacked hard against the rock twice, as if he wanted to wake the boy up. The helmsman limped past Pedro. "The Admiral is lookin' fer gold, boy, not dogs."

21

A NEW DISCOVERY

After Pedro had crept a distance into the damp and musty cave, he wondered if this was such a good idea. He was following the strange dog that didn't bark, but even though it was low tide, each wave splashed up to his waist. Still, the warm, gentle waves made him forget his encounter with the sandspurs a few minutes before.

The cavern felt as hollow as a tomb. Illuminated by a shaft of sunlight from somewhere above, water droplets from the roof dripped into a large pool in the center, creating liquid flower petals wherever they hit. Enormous gray sloping boulders towered above him, giving him the feeling of being as tiny as the iridescent fish swimming in the pool. The angular ledge above his head gave him something to hold on to, as he inched his way toward a sandy shore further inside, visible with the low tide.

"Come on, boy," he called to the dog that was sitting on the sand, watching him. "I'm not going to hurt you." His words reverberated across the damp walls.

With his head cocked to one side, the dog eyed him warily.

Something snagged Pedro's hand. Not again, he thought. Wincing, he glanced up. A red and white gooseneck barnacle hung from the stony ceiling right beside some colorful marine algae. He made a mental note to be sure to avoid that spot on his way out.

A few minutes later, his feet touched the soft sand. The dog's ears still drooped, and his tail still wasn't wagging, but at least he wasn't baring his teeth.

"I'm just going to sit here a spell, boy," he calmly assured the animal while hunkering down on his heels, to give his eyes time to adjust to the dark interior of the room.

The cave was a single chamber about three hundred feet long with a labyrinth of underwater sea reefs. In the dimness of the cave's light, he could make out white squiggly lines around the walls high above his head, indicating the water level at high tide.

The place gave Pedro the creeps—and he couldn't figure out why.

Then he spotted them. All over the wall, right behind him.

Still conscious of the dog's stare, he put his hands on his knees, which cracked as he slowly got to his feet. The dog didn't move. When Pedro turned around, his jaw dropped open.

Chiseled shapes of human faces and skulls haunted the walls from bottom to top—ghostly forms etched into the stone. Skeletons with wide sunken eye-sockets grinned at Pedro. A host of disturbing figures in all shapes and sizes stared at him. What must have been fire came out of one grotesque fiend's mouth, while another portrayed a tormented sun with scissors of light carved around its head.

The indentations, rough to the touch, felt strange. He jerked back his hand. Talk about bad omens! He shuddered, more from the demonic feel of the cave art than from the chill on his damp britches and bare chest.

Pedro took a deep breath in the damp cave—and at that moment, grasped an important truth: The Indians had a religion. They obviously believed in some form of power higher than themselves.

Pedro peered at the frightening pictures. Perhaps they represented lots of different gods. Or the natives may have etched them to ward off evil spirits. Maybe they held special feasts or ceremonies here, when the tide was low, to honor certain gods. Pedro could only imagine the stories and rituals these figures were portraying. But one thing was certain: He had to tell the Admiral, as soon as possible.

Late that night, he got his chance.

"I hear you made an acquaintance with a dog that doesn't bark, Pedro." The Admiral removed the last smudge of sardine oil from the corners of his mouth with his napkin. Only a few kernels of the Indian food called *maize* remained on the pewter plate.

"Aye, Admiral. A strange one, he is. He seemed mean at first, but he didn't bother me when I went exploring in the cave."

"Cave, you say?" The Admiral's eye thick gray eyebrows lifted with the question.

"Yes, sir. A sea cave, just back from the beach. I found something in it I wanted to tell you about." The Admiral's empty mug clanked, as Pedro placed it on top of the pewter plate and cleared off his desk.

"Where's my pick?" The Admiral's desk drawer squeaked, as he pulled it out. "These kernels seem to have found hidden crevices in my teeth." Retrieving the willow toothpick, he put it to good use, beginning with the slight gap between his two front teeth. "Now, tell me, boy. What have you found?"

As the Admiral listened, Pedro related the whole story, from the strange dog to the eerie cave art. "These Indians do believe in something, sir," he concluded.

The Admiral gazed out the porthole at the night sky. "It appears they do, lad. I would like to see these for myself tomorrow." He paused thoughtfully. "All men need to believe, Pedro. It's part of our nature. But not all men know what to believe." He returned the pick to his drawer and smiled. "That's where we come in. The Lord left us with a Great Commission: To tell the world about Him. That is why God called this voyage into being."

Pedro nodded. If they returned to San Salvador, he would try to tell Macu about God. Meanwhile, noting how short-lived the Admiral's smile was, he added, "I'm sorry we didn't find gold on this island, sir."

"It's all right, lad. I can smell other islands. We'll find some."

"Smell, sir?"

"When a man has been at sea for any length of time, boy, he can smell land before he sees it. Ye'll see soon enough."

Pedro smiled to himself. Don Cristobál Colón himself was like the sea. Strong. Steady. Certain. The admiration the cabin boy felt for him rose inside him like a high tide. Pedro wanted to be just like him. A good captain. No, a great captain. One who loved the sea and his men. He would be one, too.

One day.

Under sunny skies as blue as robins' eggs and night skies as black as ink, the fleet continued its search, propelled forward by the force of the natives' constant indications of an island to the south and east.

One day toward the end of October, however, the weather changed.

It was only one or two droplets at first. Pedro didn't think much about them. Since morning, the sky had been rich with cotton-ball clouds. No one was expecting a sea change.

Until it happened.

The shrill whistle of the boatswain commanded all hands on deck.

"Haul in the topsails!" it shrilled with one refrain. "Lend a hand on the yards!" ordered another.

Within minutes, the rain was pouring down, drumming like Father Antonio's fingers on his mahogany desk, only much louder. And it was cold! It seemed to slice into Pedro's skin, chilling him to the bone. He could barely see two feet in front of him, his hair a soggy tangled mask over his dark eyes.

"Give the spritsail a little sheet!" Señor Lonso ordered through the blinding rain.

"Hold her, man! This gale's blowin' so hard, we can't come about!" yelled De la Cosa, as he hollered down through the hatch to the helmsman below. "Hold her steady down there!"

It was nearly November. The rainy season had struck the Indies, and there was no land in sight.

22

EXPLORING

The seasonal rains continued over the next few weeks, sometimes hindering the fleet from anchoring; other times driving them to shelter on the lee side of a nearby shore. When the rains stopped, though, they brought out the best in nature. On the clean air came the happy chirping of the tropical birds, both land and sea. And every vista of rugged coastline or butter-colored beaches appeared brighter and more colorful. Fresh winds ushered island fragrances across the water, delighting the sailors' sense of smell.

"I wish I'd thought to bring a naturalist," the Admiral murmured, gazing at the Crimson Cross, before returning it to its red leather pouch. Having finished his evening prayers, he'd sent Pedro to bring two mugs of hot sassafras tea, as he'd invited his old friend, Lonso, to join him in his cabin.

"I quite agree," the pilot replied, collapsing into the slatted chair and obviously enjoying the chance to rest a bit. "I can recognize a few plants like the palmetto bush and the pine from home, but many of these new ones are lost on me. Someone who knows plants would be a big help right now."

The Admiral placed his silver bookmark between the open pages of his Latin Bible and folded its soft leather cover shut. "I must admit, Lonso, I'm battling some disappointment. No Japan yet. And no gold. If we don't find the mainland soon, I'm going to be truly baffled." He returned his two most precious possessions, the Bible and the cross, to his desk drawer.

His old friend sought to lift his spirits. "Ah, the Khan's palace will be a magnificent sight to behold, Don Cristóbal. Ivory columns and silk tapestries. To think that we should live to see such things!"

The Admiral smiled and turned to Pedro. "Which reminds me; lad, how are your sketches coming?"

Retrieving a few truant white goose feathers that had escaped the Admiral's linen pillowcase, Pedro fluffed it for the night. "Well sir, . . . I think."

He was never really sure whether his drawings were any good. Whether it was a new long-tailed tropical bird or a dragon lizard or a spiny pineapple, he did his best to capture the important details, as Father Antonio had taught him. So that when they returned home, the drawings might be useful to some learned naturalist.

But he also sketched scenes from their adventures. The lookout up in the crow's nest, pointing to land. The planting of the first cross. The first natives timidly emerging from the forest. The Arawak village. Macu fingering his beaded necklace at the beach. The drawings in the cave that the barkless dog had led him to. The Admiral with ink-stained hands, carefully journaling long paragraphs by candlelight to the Sovereigns. The first sighting of the last island they'd left behind them, which the Admiral named *Isabela*. Pedro had even done a sketch of his old friend, Lonso, contentedly chewing on a spindly straw.

"Me thinks yer pictures will be quite the draw when we return, lad." The aging mariner chuckled at his own joke. "I quite liked that one of m'self during the last storm. Do I really look that old?" His smile etched even deeper wrinkles in his leathery skin. "The sailing of ocean seas is creepin' up on this ole soul, Cristóbal."

This was one of the few times Pedro heard the pilot refer to the Admiral in a familiar way. It didn't happen often, and it only happened when the two relaxed alone after a long day. The two mariners had sailed together for many years. *Many* years.

Pedro never got tired of hearing how they met, even when Lonso retold it, as he did now. "First set eyes on 'im, on that Portuguese frigate. A tiny ship she was, not more than twenty ton. But she was seaworthy. The Admiral and me, we was shipmates back then, sailin' to Elmina and the Gold Coast of Africa. Long about '73, if my old mind serves me right."

The sailor's eyes glazed over with the memory. "He asked me to go with 'im to the spice bazaar one day. Baskets chocked full of nutmeg and cloves. More cinnamon than *mi madre* could use in a lifetime. And the gold? Neither one of us could believe it. Stories were, it lay in nuggets along the river."

The old pilot sighed. "Been sailin' with 'im ever since."

"Yer getting to be quite the wizened old salt, Lonso," the Admiral piped up quickly, pulling Pedro's thoughts back to the cabin. "That ripe old age of forty-five is creeping up fast, is it not?" Lonso's friend couldn't pass up the lighthearted jab.

"True, sir. But as I recollect, ye ain't far behind." The seaman was never one to be outdone.

The back two legs of the wooden chair creaked as the pilot shifted his weight to tilt it against the cabin's wall. "How many years young are ye now? Forty what?" Lonso squinted his black eyes, like an old man needing a magnifying glass to think.

While the men were bantering, Pedro peered through one of the open windows aft. The fleet was safely anchored in the mouth of a river that was so wide that maneuvering in had been easy. Beyond the stained-glass panels, he could see that the river's sandy shoreline was lined with bright green royal palms. The lush vegetation was heavy with the inviting fragrance of night-blooming jasmine. The Admiral had named this land *Juana* after the infant Don Juan, heir to the Spanish throne. The natives called it *Cuba*.

In the distance, Pedro could barely make out the stilt-like legs and webbed feet of a coral red flamingo, sloshing the water into ripples while it hunted for crayfish.

The young explorer's curiosity was at a fever pitch. "Sir, may I go with the delegation tomorrow? I'd like to meet the Chinese Emperor." The thought excited the boy. Imagine meeting the Grand Khan, absolute ruler of the vastest country in the known world. And it would have been largely unknown to Europeans, were it not for the intrepid Marco Polo. The descriptions of his travels to China a century earlier had been read by all boys who could read. And now the Admiral was about to lead an expedition to find the Khan's palace and the streets of gold. This was too good an opportunity to miss.

There was one other thing, a little thing to be sure, but one he would not care to admit. Pedro was secretly hoping to escape the grueling, two-day chore of scraping the barnacles off the flagship's hull, on the ship's log for tomorrow, October 29th. Finding the Khan sounded like much more fun.

The Admiral's tan brow furrowed. The thumbs on his clasped hands played somersaults around one another while he thought. Cristóbal glanced at the pilot, whose straw scrap now hung limply out of the side of his mouth.

"I'm not sure about your going, lad," he said thoughtfully. "Our native guides have spoken about Caribs being in these parts." Pedro shifted his weight from his left foot to his right and back again. "Father Peréz would not be pleased, if I came home with the report that you had been eaten."

Pedro shook his head vigorously, not wanting to hear that he was too young to go. He was fifteen and a half! Almost an adult. Some boys his age had been at sea for years. By Saint Simon the Apostle, he was old enough to take care of himself!

And yet, he had too much respect for the Admiral's wisdom to challenge him here.

Was this what the Admiral was really saying? That he was too young to go? Or was it something else?

Maybe the Admiral felt like Father Antonio, and even Pedro's grandfather, who probably would have expressed uneasiness. They wouldn't have let him go without some thought. The Caribs *were* cannibals; that was no sea tale.

Pedro had never known his own father, but this must be what it felt like to have one. Perhaps Don Cristobál was showing that he really cared and didn't want anything to happen to him. "Thank you, sir. I appreciate it," Pedro replied honestly, though he still hoped that somehow . . .

"I don't see no harm in his coming, Cristobál," said the old pilot smiling. "And if he brings his charcoal and paper, he might be useful."

The Admiral pursed his lips, considering the pros and cons.

"We'll only be gone six days," Lonso added.

The Admiral looked at his old friend. "You'll watch out for him?"

"Like he was my son. Count on it."

"Very well," the Admiral said with a smile. He turned to Pedro. "Take care that you do *exactly* what Señor Peralonso asks of you."

"Aye, sir."

"Do not make me regret this decision."

"Aye, aye, sir!"

Thrilled, it was all Pedro could do, to keep from hugging him.

23

SEARCHING FOR
THE GRAND KHAN

Led by Don Cristóbal Colón, Admiral of the Ocean Sea, the Spanish expedition, equipped with swords and helmets, first scouted the valley near the river, then turned inland in search of the Grand Khan. Purple flowering orchids and colorful red hibiscus speckled the lush tropical green foliage with color. Open fields of wild white cotton bolls slept lazily in the bright sun.

But after two days of trekking, the only thing they'd found to spur them on were samples of native pepper and what they thought might be cinnamon—their first taste of the fabulous spices of the Indies.

At last, early on the afternoon of the third day, they came upon a cultivated field of tall Indian corn and flowering sweet-potato vines. Excitedly they convinced themselves that they were approaching Chinese farms. Farms meant people, people meant villages, and villages meant—the Grand Khan.

Sure enough, a few minutes later, they stumbled upon a village. An empty village.

"Where *is* everyone?" One of the sailors muttered, giving voice to what everyone was thinking. "Ain't no one here!"

Seven dilapidated palm-thatched huts encircled an open fire pit, with charcoaled sticks that had clearly been cold for a long time. Two stray dogs, their ribs visible through mangy yellow fur, sniffed at the men, hoping perhaps that they might give them something to eat.

The Admiral looked at Peralonso. "Are you thinking what I'm thinking?"

The old pilot nodded. "Caribs. They must have chased them off."

Cristóbal thought for a moment. "We will not spend much time here. The other captains and I will check the huts on this side of the clearing;

Señor De la Cosa, you and Señor Peralonso and the two grommets check the others. When you hear me call, we will push on."

Inside the first hut De la Cosa's group investigated was nothing but a dirt floor with dried palm branches and flat stones. Grotesque figures carved in wood had been dumped into a pile, now a home for hundreds of busy fire ants. And no evidence of human inhabitants, alive or dead.

"Wonder who lives here?" mused Lonso, removing his helmet, his curly hair scribbled into ringlets from sweat. Dust covered his burlap knapsack when he dropped it to the ground.

"You mean, who *used* to live here," De la Cosa interjected, surveying the scene. "Not much goin' on now, that's fer sure."

"Let's look for skulls!" Emilio whispered to Pedro, who just shook his head in disgust. Emilio flipped back the frayed cloth of the next hut's doorway and stepped inside. Right behind him, Pedro saw that the hut was totally empty, except for a shabby woven sling five to six feet long that had been hung between two peeling wooden stakes pounded into the ground.

"What's it for, do you think?" Emilio asked.

Pedro's entire hand fit through the loosely woven netting. "Don't know," he replied. "Looks like some sort of bed."

"The natives call them *hamacas*." De la Cosa's brittle voice grew louder, as he crossed the threshold. "It's for sleeping. Why don't ye try it?"

"Why not?" Pedro was always up for a challenge—or at least always wanted to *appear* up for a challenge.

First he clutched one side of the wobbly netting with his left hand. Then he elevated his left leg at the knee, followed by his foot. Once he had stretched out his leg, he positioned it carefully in the center of the netting. With curled toes he hoped could grab the net should he fall, he eased his backside on, both elbows arched out for support. Maybe this wasn't going to be so bad.

Before he could blink, Pedro spun over and hit the dirt. "Ouch!" he howled, rubbing his rear.

"Havin' a mite of trouble, are we?" De la Cosa didn't usually smile, but this one uncovered all of his stained bottom front teeth, as crooked as wrought-iron railing.

The flagship's owner was making Pedro mad now. "I can do this," he shot back.

With that, Pedro tried again, only this time he gripped both sides and jumped into the webbing, all at once. It worked! The boy nestled his black head into the palms of both hands.

"Not bad for a beginner," he declared, puffing up like a blowfish. "Nothing to it."

"Right," Emilio smirked. "Nothin' to it."

De la Cosa scratched his thick neck, covered with caked dirt. "I hear the Admiral said ye can keep that there bracelet on yer wrist," he remarked, his tone low and without emotion. "You know, one of them would buy a good stallion."

Pedro stared at him. While he liked the bracelet, its gold might be able to buy him something else he really wanted. "How many would it take to buy a ship?" he asked, sitting up and flinging his bare feet back on the dirt floor to balance as quickly as possible.

"Oh, eighteen or twenty, I'd say." De la Cosa's response wasn't lost on the cabin boy, as they all stepped back out into the direct sunlight.

In the third hut, under some dried palm fronds De la Cosa found a large face mask, two thin anklets, and a big nose plug—all made out of pure gold.

"Waitin' fer the takin'," he murmured under his breath, as he examined the mask.

Pedro held the nose ring up close. "Look, Señor Lonso," he said. "There's something etched on it. Could it be Chinese?"

"Stow that stuff in my knapsack, lad," Lonso ordered, taking the mask from De la Cosa, before the latter could object. "We'll give it to the Admiral, soon as we get going."

As if on cue, the Admiral called the expedition to re-assemble. When they'd gathered, from the talk it appeared that the only items they'd found of real interest were those in Lonso's pack.

The expedition resumed its march. Before long, they came to a forest of short scrubby trees, gnarled and anchored in thick mud. Long spreading roots created thickets that crept into a brown murky current of saltwater around the base of the trees. Stagnant water, the breeding ground for mosquitoes, swallowed the roots.

The explorers had entered the mystical world of a mangrove swamp.

A huge brown pelican swooped over their heads to land in a patch of mossy grass. Five white gulls in a triangular formation veered along with the flow of one of the sluggish stinking rivers.

Pedro looked down at the muck he was standing in. It was getting softer with each step—dangerously soft.

"What *is* that smell?" Emilio grimaced, as if he were about to vomit.

"Swamp land," Lonso muttered. "I've seen such swamps before. They sometimes have bogs of quicksand. Nasty stuff."

"Can we get through?" asked the Admiral.

The old pilot hesitated before replying. He knew how much Don Cristobál wanted to find the Great Khan.

"It's your decision, sir. But I would advise turning back."

The Admiral gazed at the swamp that stretched in both directions, as far as the eye could see. At length, with a deep sigh, he gave the order. "Return to the ships."

Pedro felt a lump in his throat. He knew that Don Cristobál had already penned a letter to the Sovereigns, telling them all he hoped to find. Now he would have to tear it up.

"We best keep our eyes pealed for serpents. They love swamps!" Emilio said softly to Pedro, as he took up the rear of the column.

"Serpents?" Pedro's curiosity was getting the better of him. Maybe he could sketch one. He had heard Lonso tell a story once about a great Nile River scaled serpent that could take down a cow.

"Watch for the horseflies on the water," Emilio cautioned. "Might really be the reptile's eyes or maybe his snout."

"Forget about reptiles," barked Lonso, overhearing them. "Think about where you are putting your feet. Quicksand is the real danger in here."

24

THE SMOKING WEED

The trek back to the ships went without incident, until the afternoon of the second day. Bedraggled and sweaty, the Spanish explorers were hiking along a dirt path through a thicket of pointy palmetto bushes and towering pines. Shafts of light formed lines and patches on the men's bronze skin.

Pedro's muslin shirt, drenched with sweat, bunched up when he scratched at his chest. His stringy bangs tickled his brow and were getting more annoying with each step. The pebble indentations in the bottom of his feet were becoming permanent.

"The sounds are changin'," Emilio commented, as he stepped on a brittle fallen limb, snapping it in two.

"What do you mean?"

"There aren't any."

Pedro listened. Emilio was right.

"The crickets and birds must be taking a siesta," Pedro quipped, looking for anything to help pass the time. "I wish we were. I could use a nap."

"Not me," responded Emilio. "Every hour we keep walking means we're an hour closer to the *Santa Maria*. She's gonna' be a sight for sore eyes."

Pedro could certainly agree with that. Thoughts of the cool blue water off the flagship's bow renewed his determination to keep going. One single jump . . . the wind in his hair, as he flew down . . . the freedom of bare skin, then the splash of the water . . . Surely, the ships couldn't be much farther.

At the head of the column, the Admiral raised his hand, signaling a halt.

They could hear the clacking sound of shell ornaments coming towards them.

"Shh—" Lonso held up his hand. "People."

Instantly the men feared the worst. *Caribs!*

"Into the bushes!" Lonso whispered. "Quick!"

The men dived into the thick vegetation as the clacking grew louder, accompanied by the sound of laughter.

"They don't sound too evil to me." Small needles stabbed Pedro's knees as he crawled around the bristling palm bush to take a look.

"Me either." Emilio had squatted down right beside him.

"What's that smell?" Emilio wrinkled his nose.

"Ain't never smelled it 'afore." De la Cosa's comment was loud enough for Pedro to hear.

The odor grew stronger as the Indians approached. As a group of Indian men came into view, Pedro saw a strange gray vapor surrounding them, like a cloud of mist on a stormy day.

Strangely enough, the natives seemed to know the Spaniards were there. As soon as they reached the place where the explorers were hiding, the Indians gestured toward them in a most friendly manner, smiling. When the sailors came out of the bushes, the natives poked and fingered their new acquaintances, and touched their hair. Pedro doubted he'd ever get used this native practice, but he decided that he would put up with it, as long as they weren't Caribs!

"They're smoking rolled leaves up their noses." Emilio grimaced as the commotion of their encounter died down.

One young native who had been prodding Pedro's cheek pointed to a flexible brown leaf wrapper stuffed with shredded leaves he had just retrieved from his quiver. *"Tobacos,"* he said. The man's broad smile revealed large square teeth, stained the same color as the tobacco.

The cigar's tip lit quickly from a smoking torch one of them was carrying. As soon as the Indian had inhaled its smoke, he offered it to Pedro.

"It ain't bad, lads!" De la Cosa announced to anyone listening, as he passed a cigar back and forth with his new Indian acquaintance. "Ain't bad at all. Give it a try."

Pedro wasn't so sure. Within seconds, a number of his colleagues were coughing and gagging and clutching their throats. The sour look on Lonso's face wasn't encouraging.

The Indian tapped Pedro's shoulder, sniffed the cigar again, and offered it to the boy. Pedro's reluctance was overcome by his desire to try it, at least in the name of friendship.

No sooner had he inhaled twice than his gag reflex kicked in. He coughed. He choked. With both hands smothering his mouth and nose, he tried not to spit up. The scene blurred around him, and Pedro quickly sat down on some crunchy leaves to try and stop his head from spinning.

After a short while though, a few of the seamen had decided the tobacco wasn't so bad. They laughed and traded glass beads and brass tambourine jingles for cigars.

"I'll be smokin' these on the trip home," Emilio boasted, tying the string on his duffel bag into a square knot. Two cigars prodded their way out of the hole in the top. "I got me a bag full of 'em." The grommet patted the overloaded bag. "These should last awhile."

Food for fools, Pedro thought. "I doubt that," he replied as he hopped back to his feet and dusted the cracked leaves off the seat of his britches. "You know the Admiral. He won't allow fire on the ship. Too dangerous."

"Nothin's gonna' happen to the ship." Emilio had a way of dismissing things he didn't want to hear.

Pedro couldn't shake the uneasy feeling creeping into him like a black cat. Realizing it might be some sort of premonition, he shoved it back down. No, he wasn't going to think about it. Emilio was right. Nothing bad was going to happen to them *or* to the ship. *Nothing*, he whispered to himself.

Nothing.

By the time the exploring party returned, the hulls of all three ships had been scraped and repaired, their sails mended, and all water casks filled with fresh water. To Pedro, they seemed to be straining at their anchors, like coursing hounds ready for the chase. Get aboard, they seemed to be saying. Let us up anchor and get underway!

Pedro grinned. He liked this life of adventure. He could keep this up for a while. A long while.

While they waited for the ships' boats to come to shore to pick them up, Pedro showed the Admiral the drawings he had made on the expedition. "Here's my drawing of the swamp, sir," he said, handing the Admiral his depiction of the tangled and twisted roots growing into the water.

"That's good work, lad," exclaimed Don Cristobál, impressed.

"And here's one of the ghost village." He paused. "I'm only sorry there's not one of the Great Khan and his palace."

"And no gold," the Admiral mused, "beyond the mask and a few pieces of jewelry."

Standing nearby, Lonso observed, "We may not have found gold, Admiral. But we were in the Almighty's hands. We didn't meet a single Carib. And not one man was injured, or even sick. In fact, Doctor Sanchez has had precious little business this entire trip." He looked at his old friend. "You and I both know what a miracle that is!"

When the Admiral failed to respond, he pressed further. "God has been with us all the way. He has held us in the hollow of His hand. He quelled the mutiny and squeezed five days into three, to get us to our first landfall."

"I know, I know, Lonso," the Admiral finally replied. "But it's already November. We'll make Christian converts among the natives, once we can converse with them, but how can I fund a crusade for the Sovereigns, much less lead one, without gold? *Fields* of gold."

Lead a crusade? Fields of gold? Pedro stared at him, open-mouthed. Was this what he had been writing and dreaming about, night after night? What had happened to their mission of bearing the light of Christ west to heathen in undiscovered lands? He looked down at the gold bracelet on his arm. Everything began to change after they saw the gold ornaments of the Arawak. Macu had given him this bracelet as a sign of their friendship. It was meant to bring happiness, but Pedro had a feeling that gold was going to bring far more misery than happiness.

25

SAILING AWAY

That afternoon, in an attempt to make the Admiral feel better about the lack of gold, Pedro spread the woven sling on the deck before him, explaining that they'd found it hanging in one of the huts.

Don Cristóbal frowned. "An odd-looking contraption." He stuck a big fist through one of the holes. "What do you call this thing?"

"The native word is *hamaca*."

"What do they use it for?"

"With these two strings at either end, they hang it from something and sleep on it—or rather, *in* it." Pedro chuckled. "I climbed in without falling—at least, without falling more than once."

"How was it?"

The cabin boy laughed. "Surprisingly comfortable!"

Cristóbal rubbed his chin thoughtfully. "Perhaps we could tie one or two of these *hamacas* up in the hold for the men to try."

Pedro grimaced. Sleeping down in the foul-smelling, roach-infested belly of the ship? No, thank you very much. He preferred good old freshly swabbed, no-rats-in-the-water, hard planks.

At that moment, the Admiral's attention was turned to one of the sailors on the main deck smoking a cigar. "Lonso, pass the word: No more cigars. They can smoke them on land, but not on board. Ever. And that's an order."

At sunrise the next morning with a fair wind on their port quarter, the little Spanish fleet set sail to explore the inlets along the coast. By noon the Admiral realized that *Juana* was actually a huge island and not mainland China. Disappointed, he altered their course to east-southeast, based on what he thought the Indian guides were telling them.

"I hope them Indians know where we're headed," Emilio complained one afternoon, while he and Pedro observed a sailor repair another wooden barrel lid that was too loose. The eight Arawak Indians spent most of their time near the steerage on the main deck. Chachu was in charge of them. "So far, the only places they've showed us are deserted villages and swamps."

"The Admiral's beginning to learn their language, but it's still hard," Pedro commented, resting his elbows on his knees. He'd been thinking about something recently and had decided to voice it. "Emilio, are the Arawak acting a little . . . odd?"

Emilio shrugged. "No more 'n usual. The whip probably scares 'em a bit. Don't suppose they've ever been whipped before. And Chachu can really crack it, when he has a mind to." He shuddered. "I sure wouldn't want to be on the receiving end."

Pedro shook his head. "No, what I mean is, they stay to themselves all the time. They barely talk to one another, let alone anyone else. And they're not eating, at least not much."

"Maybe they don't like Cook's food," Emilio laughed. Pedro had to admit this might be true. This morning's hardtack wasn't exactly his favorite meal, either.

"But they didn't eat supper last night or breakfast this morning." The more Pedro talked, the more he realized how much this was bothering him.

"They're probably just missing their families." Emilio flipped a deck of thirty-two cards out of his back pocket. "How about some Picket?" He began to shuffle. "Can't say as I blame 'em. Who knows when we'll get 'em back, if ever." Emilio picked up an ace that slipped out and shuffled again.

"I think something's wrong," Pedro persisted.

"They're ignorant heathen, boy. Leave 'em alone. C'mon, I'll deal."

A short while later, Pedro was scrubbing the quarterdeck when he heard the sound of whistling wind, followed by a sharp crack, and cries of pain.

"I said, fetch that bucket over there!" Chachu ordered at the top of his lungs.

Pedro ran over to the rail overlooking the main deck. One of the natives was sprawled on the deck. On the back of his leg was a stripe of dark red, oozing blood.

The Admiral, who had heard it, too, now viewed the scene from the top of the ladder.

Pedro waited for him to speak. He was shocked when Don Cristobál, without speaking turned and went back into his cabin, shutting the door.

The wounded Indian crawled slowly toward the bucket and picked it up. The other seven huddled together around the main mast, visibly trembling.

Pedro went immediately to Lonso. "How can he—how can *we* do this?"

"Every country has its own rules for right and wrong, Pedro. Every ship does, too. It's the way it is," he answered quietly.

The way it is? Pedro couldn't understand. Chachu had whipped a human being for failing to fetch a bucket. And the Admiral hadn't said a word! The scene sickened him inside. The water beads collecting on the deck didn't help Pedro scrub down the growing fear inside him. This trip was not turning out like he had imagined.

The flagship's timbers creaked with each roll, as the mounting sea winds backed the fleet in its new heading. The points on the Admiral's chart grew in number. Sighting island after island, the ships cruised along, sometimes anchoring in a bay or inlet and other times sailing so close to the shore that Pedro grew alarmed about the shoals and rocky reefs.

"These natives are gettin' on my nerves." Pedro heard Chachu talking to someone a few days later as he climbed up the freshly swabbed ladder from the hold. He slowed down to eavesdrop on the conversation.

"We're a bit too close to these islands fer my taste, too." De la Cosa stuffed the frayed end of a rope between two twisted strands and dropped the heavy coil on the deck. "We're gonna run onto a reef if we're not careful. But I don't see us runnin' into any more gold."

"How much have we got?"

"Not enough," the master retorted, as the lid to the trunk of gold jewelry and masks thudded back down. "Not nearly enough."

After the knife scene back on San Salvador and the whipping on the ship, Pedro wasn't about to trust these two any farther than he could throw a cannon ball. They were up to something, and he determined to keep an eye on them.

At that moment, the sound of shrieking catapulted across the decks. Using the banister, Pedro heaved himself up and over the last three wooden steps. Four of the natives were wailing at the starboard rail. Within seconds the boy realized what had happened. Two of the Arawak had jumped ship and were furiously swimming toward the nearby island.

"What are they doing?" Pedro asked Lonso at the rail.

"Escaping. They're afraid and homesick."

"Why don't we just let them all go?"

The pilot's face was expressionless. "I don't think the Admiral's gonna let them go, boy. He means to take them back to Spain."

"Against their will?" The realization flooded Pedro's soul like a tidal wave.

"What the Admiral is doing is no different than any other captain of any other country does these days, boy, although I'm not sure God is pleased about it." The pilot's battered eyebrows lowered as he talked. "If Don Cristobál continues, if he ever comes back for more gold and more captives, our beloved Spain may become known all over the world as the nation that enslaves innocent people."

From books he had read, Pedro had learned that slave traders were selling people taken captive against their will in North Africa to wealthy plantation owners in Europe, who were using the slaves as cheap forced labor. It was the way things were.

But he hated the thought of it, imagining how he would feel if he were a slave. That night, he felt exhausted, and after his watch immediately curled up on the quarterdeck just outside the Admiral's cabin, and dropped off into a deep sleep.

Just before dawn, the lookout's piercing cry jolted everyone awake on the flagship. "The *Pinta!* The *Pinta!*" He shouted from the crow's nest, bellowing like a town crier publicizing the news at the top of his lungs.

Pedro was amazed the Admiral's cabin door didn't fly off its rusty hinges, when he burst out on deck. They both watched. Martín Pinzón's caravel had altered course and was sailing off toward the dawn's eastern light.

"Where's she going, sir?" Pedro hoped the *Santa Maria* wouldn't heel to the side, as nearly every sailor jammed against the port railing in disbelief.

"I fear Martín Pinzón thinks he can find gold somewhere else and beat us back to Spain." The Admiral's eyes looked sad and weary. Pedro knew what he was thinking: How could he do this to me? Why, Captain Martín's energy and faith in the Admiral's vision had helped Don Cristobál convince the local mariners to join them on this treacherous voyage.

Would Martín's brother, Vicente, do the same thing? Surely not such fine sons from the most famous seafaring family in Palos! They were so well respected and such a vital part of the community. Pedro found the words the Admiral had just spoken hard to believe. Yet there was the *Pinta*, growing smaller and smaller by the minute.

These were not good signs. First the taking of the Arawaks, then the *Pinta* leaving. The troubles were mounting. It was then that he remembered Lonso's words. "Ships have a tendency to bring out the worst in people."

It didn't look to Pedro like God was pleased.

26

ALMOST THERE

To the Admiral's intense relief, Vicente Pinzón decided to remain with the Admiral and not sail off after his brother. Fair winds blew them from one island to the next during the next three weeks. At times heavy rain and unfavorable winds detained the ships, but by early December, the Spanish explorers had discovered the finest natural harbor in the Indies. Deep and surrounded by land on three sides, it offered the ships a mooring so close to the shore that they could actually lay their gangplanks on the grass.

At the relieving of the dawn watch about eight o'clock, the flagship's heavy plank dropped over the starboard side like a sturdy bridge over a wide castle moat. The last time Pedro had felt the plank's slight wobbling under his feet was when he left Palos nearly four months ago. Once again, the boatswain's slow and solemn shrill piped them over the side, for today the Admiral was disembarking, too.

As his first act ashore, he planted another large cross, which would stand sentinel over the bay. As Pedro and the others with him removed their caps and bowed their heads, the Admiral prayed.

"Once again, we give thanks, O God, for this great land. We dedicate it to You, and we christen it *La Isla Española*."

He'd picked the right name, Pedro thought. Of all the islands they had visited so far, this one was most like home. In the distance, mountains touched the sky and brought bittersweet memories of Andalusia and his grandfather. The wide path in the fertile valley at the head of the harbor looked so much like the monastery trail along the Rio Tinto that Pedro could scarcely believe it. Mockingbirds chirped in the trees, reminding him of the nightingales that serenaded his tiny cell window every night at La Rábida. Even the skins of the islanders that stood around them on the shore were as white as a Spaniard's. The Admiral was right. *The Spanish Island* was the perfect name for this place.

At just that moment, the sun abruptly disappeared, and an increasingly loud cawing invited everyone to look up. Some tropical birds called parrots were flying by. Not just a few, but a flock so enormous that it blocked the sun!

The sailors all pointed up and exclaimed about the sheer number of birds and their brilliance. Dazzling feathers of greens and reds and yellows coated the azure blue sky like oils on an artist's palette. Flattened head crests, graceful flapping wings and long tails added to the splendor. While each bird was dramatic by itself, the sight of the whole flock was so magnificent that only God Himself could have woven such a stunning heavenly tapestry. It was as if the parrots had joined the crews at the perfect moment to give praise to the Almighty for this beautiful land.

"Lonso, come look at this!" The Admiral's expression was like a small child watching a troubadour. In the palm of his hand was a mottled yellow nut, slit open with his pen-knife. Inside was a reddish egg-shaped seed.

"Nutmeg."

"Indeed, sir?" The pilot hobbled through the sand, followed by Pedro who had been standing at his side.

"*Sí!* And here!" A few large oval leaves floated to the ground, as the Admiral tugged off a pale green flower bud. "It isn't red yet, but these should be cloves when they ripen."

Lonso sniffed the bud and handed it to Pedro, whose nose recognized the vague scent of a clove.

"Just imagine the future of this place, Lonso!" The Admiral's right arm swept the salt air in a broad arc. "Dozens of Spanish merchant ships entering the harbor. A spice bazaar as big as the one in Elmira. Christian natives welcoming traders. And all of it happening right here!"

Pedro's imagination soared with the Admiral's. They'd done it! They'd reached the *Moluccas*, the famed Spice Islands of the Indies, where only Japanese or Chinese merchants had once been able to sail. The dream of every European trader had come true. Europe would no longer be dependent on the Muslim-ruled bazaars in Africa, because Spain had discovered a sea route to the Indies. Not only would this fulfill the Admiral's dream, it would help the Spanish build wealth to finance another crusade to the Holy Land. King Ferdinand and Queen Isabella would most certainly be pleased with this!

Just then, a young cacique not much older than Pedro approached them, accompanied by two of the Arawak interpreters. A headdress of bright parrot-like feathers concealed most of his black coarse hair, while the brown and red paint on his face almost disguised his nose and mouth. Three wide gold necklaces circled his long neck extending down to his breastbone, completely covered in yellow and brown. A green and red parrot, perched on his left arm, pruned its feathers and squawked in the cacique's ear. In his right hand, the tribal leader carried a gold ornament that looked like a leaf and was as big as his hand.

"These people call themselves Taino, sir," Lonso began, "and this here young one is called a cacique. He's some kind of prince or something. They want us to go with 'em."

The well-beaten path from the harbor led into a valley and a village—a huge one. There were too many palm-hatched huts to count, more than a thousand, Pedro guessed. Children played with barkless dogs. Women dug sweet potatoes from nearby fields, and harvested yucca from plants around the perimeters of the fields. Inquisitive and friendly, the women and children crowded around the strange white gods, as if they were herring gulls hovering over bread crumbs.

Pedro was amazed at the amount of gold they wore—scores of shimmering masks and necklaces, bracelets and anklets.

Once again, the gentleness and hospitality of these natives was almost overwhelming. Large beautifully woven palm baskets overflowing with such fish as freshwater tilapia and inshore mullet were placed in the common area for the sailors to enjoy. Chunks of cucumbers and tomatoes satisfied their hunger for fresh vegetables. Corn by the bowl and cassava bread by the plateful were eagerly devoured.

The generosity of the Taino extended to their personal belongings as well. The natives willing traded their gold necklaces and masks and anklets for the novel sounds of the tinkling hawks' bells and tambourine jingles. The children danced around Pedro and the other grommets, who handed out colored baubles to each pleading hand.

As they did now, with each group of natives they met, the Spaniards made clear their interest in finding more gold. The young cacique nodded and smiled, and invited the sailors into the center of the village. It was there that Don Cristóbal met the old man.

He rested quietly on one of the benches and smiled at their approach, as if he had been waiting for the Admiral and for this moment, for a very long time. The point of the cane arrow he held in his left hand was very sharp. His aged skin was covered with hundreds of wrinkles, and the skeleton-like fingers of his raised right hand pointed toward the west. He patted the bench beside him and pointed to the Admiral, who sat down next to him.

As he began to talk, Peralonso, with the help of their Arawak interpreters, began to explain, as best he could.

"There's a great island out there." The man's Taino words were hoarse, and the whites of his eyes yellow with age. "A great island of gold."

"He's talking about Cathay," the Admiral murmured. "I can feel it in my bones." He rubbed his hands together. "It isn't far now."

The elderly Taino went on. "Caribs." The old man jabbed the pointed end of his handmade spear into the dark sand. "Caribs!" he proclaimed a second time.

All of a sudden, the Admiral shot off the bench. With the knuckles of his hands planted on each side of his leather belt, he declared, "Of course! Why didn't I think of it before? The Caribs are subjects of the Great Khan! Now it all makes sense! They are either Chinese pirates or sea raiders making slave raids on the Taino. That's why these people are so afraid!"

"Sir, I do believe you're right." Lonso expressed the amazement every Spaniard within listening distance was feeling, including Pedro.

It made perfect sense! No wonder the Indians were so frightened. The Khan was a powerful ruler of a rich and powerful nation, who could easily enslave these gentle people. Yes, the Admiral was most certainly right. The explorers were close to their goal now, so close it made Pedro nervous.

What if this great and mighty Khan saw them as enemies, too?

27

GOLD FEVER

Little feelers probed every inch of dirt in front of them. Tiny yucca crumbs, pieces of green palmetto leaves, even a few dead flies jostled along atop tiny antennae as the tiny legs scurried along the trails, as magnificent and intricate as the roads to Seville. It was unlike anything Pedro had ever seen back home—a splendid display of an insect colony working together to survive.

A young Taino lad had almost dragged Pedro to see the anthill, a gigantic pile of sand, pine needles and soil. The hill was just far enough from the cacique's sleeping quarters not to be dangerous. The native boy didn't seem afraid of the small black ants, but Pedro was not so sure. Once he'd mistakenly stumbled on a red anthill in his bare feet. The ants were fiery mad and let him know it in an instant. Father Antonio's solution of oil of lavender mixed with olive oil had only soothed the bites somewhat. Pedro rubbed his right calf, still scarred from the big painful itching red welts.

The two boys had scaled the ridged trunk of a mahogany tree to sit themselves on the lowest branches and watch. Pedro focused on some ants depositing food at one of the nest's entrances when he heard voices. Spanish voices.

"He told us to get all we could fer the Sovereigns. I'm jest doin' my part." The mocking words were faint but audible.

"But the cacique's gold leaf? Ye stole it." This second voice was closer now.

"He won't miss it," the first one jeered. "This here gold doesn't mean that much to him."

Pedro could hear the soft sounds of footsteps on pine needles and small twigs. He edged forward on the sturdy branch.

"The Admiral ain't gonna' like this."

"Who's gonna' tell 'im?" the first sailor answered crossly. "Just think what this thing will be worth back home! We can stop workin'. Go fishin'. Maybe hire a servant or two. I tell ya, this be our chance, mate."

The sailors were so close now, Pedro could almost smell their sweat.

"You gonna' put it in the trunk?"

"How dumb do you think I am, Chachu? My pouch stays right here on my belt. It'll keep this here leaf real safe fer the time bein'.'"

Pedro held his breath till the men were out of sight. De la Cosa and Chachu! Again! Part of him recoiled at the thought of stealing gold from the natives, let alone a cacique. And then stealing it again by not adding it to the Admiral's treasure chest.

Yet, on one point, he was inclined to agree with De la Cosa. The gold meant nothing to these people. They wouldn't miss it. Was it really stealing, if the people themselves didn't really care?

As a seaman apprentice, Pedro was making only 666 *maravedis* a month. No one could live on that. As an able seaman, he wouldn't fare much better. They made only 1,000 a month, barely enough to survive. Later, he might become a first mate or a pilot, and as such he would bring in 2,000. That might support a small dwelling, but it wasn't nearly enough to buy a ship for himself. He had to find another way to raise the money.

The idea percolated up from the deep recesses of his mind like bubbles in a cauldron. A quick shift of his eyes convinced Pedro that no one else was around. Maybe this was *his* chance now. This native boy wouldn't miss a thing. After all, he could get more gold any time he wanted some. And a piece of jewelry like that thick gold bracelet on the boy's right arm would make a big difference to someone like Pedro, someone who needed the funds to buy his own ship one day.

The sinister thought actually felt pretty good. This was beginning to make sense. After all, Father Antonio had told him to make the most of his opportunity, hadn't he? He would be doing just that, wouldn't he? Seizing the chance while he had it. Who knew what the Spanish explorers would find after this? Maybe there would be more gold, but maybe there wouldn't. Should he let this chance go by? No, of course not! *That* would be foolish.

Any twinges of conscience slipped down the slope of his thoughts and were gone in an instant. Not only was this a *good* idea, it was the *right* idea! And it would help Pedro get what he wanted.

Pedro motioned to the young native boy, still perched on a nearby tree limb. Both boys scrambled down.

The hawks' bells tinkled as Pedro pulled them out of his pocket and opened his palm. The Indian's eyes were bright with interest when Pedro offered the bells to him. Maybe this wouldn't be so hard after all, Pedro thought. The boy examined them, sniffing and jingling them close to his right ear.

Pedro pointed toward the thick bracelet. The Indian hesitated and wrinkled his thick brows. He didn't look very interested in the swap. Pedro flipped his hands back and forth in a gesture of exchange. The Taino boy stepped back.

This wasn't going to be as easy as Pedro had hoped. It didn't matter; this kid wasn't strong, like Pedro. He didn't stand a chance. Pedro inched forward. The Indian moved back again, this time clutching the bracelet with his left hand. For some unknown reason, this kid did not want to part with it.

Pedro pounced on the boy like a ravenous hawk on an unsuspecting rabbit. When the boy toppled to the ground, Pedro grabbed the gold band and snatched it off the boy's arm. With no resistance, the boy didn't even murmur. Pedro then quickly removed the other two bracelets from the boy's left arm and dashed off into the woods, leaving the surprised Indian sprawled on the ground.

After a minute, Pedro slowed down. His heart thumped in his chest as he tucked the three pieces of valuable jewelry into his right pants pocket. No one would see them. They would be safe there for now. Quite safe. Patting his bulging pocket with a feeling of satisfaction, he headed back toward the shore.

Within a few days, the two Spanish vessels weighed anchor and departed from the paradise of Española in search of more gold.

"Do ye see anything?" Señor Lonso's voice traveled up to the yardarm of the foremast, where Pedro was now positioned.

"Nothin' from up here, sir." Pedro balanced himself and yelled his reply down through cupped hands. Beneath him, the canvas sail billowed out with the wind.

"Emilio?"

The second grommet was stretched out on the bowsprit. Like a spider monkey, he gripped the slender spar with hands and feet. "No shoals here, sir. We're clear right now."

"Keep a sharp eye, lads!" the pilot barked.

Stationed at high places on the masts and the crows nest, the grommets helped the flagship feel her way through the outlying reefs into another bay. The *Niña*, slightly ahead, was already there.

Pedro could hear the orders.

"Are we lined up, Señor De la Cosa? It's that wooded island right there!" From the forecastle, the Admiral pointed toward an island not far from the shore. The wind pulled at his white hair and open shirt.

"Aye, sir. She's dead ahead."

"Steer straight then, but keep her on this side of the channel. How's the line, Lonso?"

"So far, so good, Admiral," the pilot replied. "Ten fathoms."

Pedro could hear the grunts of the men in the steerage hauling in the fathom line. He knew how important it was that they get the measurement right, because the ship's life depended on it. A shoal could rip out a ship's hull in minutes. Yet, Cristobál never flinched. As he was fond of saying, "Each man to his job, and we'll get the job done." Under the calm and confident command of the Admiral of the Ocean Sea, the flagship continued to sail steadily around the dangerous island reefs unharmed.

"This is going to be a different kind of Christmas," Emilio remarked from his perch. The date was December 22nd, and the men were feeling a bit homesick.

Pedro remained up high, where he could smell the fresh salty air and have a good view of what was going on. Lately, he'd been thinking about all the preparations for Christ's birth at the monastery and the huge feast of roast lamb to celebrate it. Father Peréz would be preparing his sermon and dispatching his special letter of thanks to the Sovereigns, as he did every year. There was always an air of expectancy, as the Advent season drew to a close. It was his favorite time of year, because there was always so much happening.

But even more was happening here. The sense of majesty and beauty that surrounded the two ships almost took Pedro's breath away. It was a gift from heaven just in time for Christmas. The clear turquoise water, beautiful as ever, tickled a stunning white beach. In the background, tall rugged mountains of green jutted into the blue heavens. Clouds like white cotton balls dotted the sky as far as they could see.

Today, the harbor itself was jammed with dugouts and swimmers of all ages splashing toward the two ships, anchored about a league from shore. As the canoes drew closer, the sounds of squawking parrots and laughing children intensified. Pedro even understood some of the Taino words, such as *guarico* for "come" and *Y'ay'a* for "Great Spirit."

Fresh water splashed over the rims of earthenware vessels tied to the bottoms of the canoes. Baskets brimming with yellow and green and red fruits and freshly baked breads made of yams made Pedro salivate. Talk about Christmas! Things were looking better all the time.

Not only had the islanders brought food because it was a time of celebration, they also wore gold. Lots of it. In their hair. Around their necks. On their wrists and ankles. In their ears. In their noses and in their navels. The gold glistened in the tropical sun.

"Me thinks he's tellin' us another cacique lives up the coast, sir." De la Cosa was interpreting one of the native's words and gestures aloud. "Guacanagari."

Cristobál nodded his head.

"It appears this Guacanagari man is very powerful, some kind of grand cacique, and he wants us to visit."

"Aye, sir," Lonso agreed, his hairy arms folded across his bare chest. "There's that word again, sir. *Cybao.* I'm thinkin' like you, Cap'n. He means *Cipangu.*"

"This Guacanagari lives close to Japan, Lonso!" The Admiral was so excited that he nearly tripped over a coiled rope behind him. "I'll send the ship's boat ahead with a few men to accept the invitation. We'll set sail day after tomorrow. Lonso," he exclaimed jubilantly, "we're almost there!"

28

CHRISTMAS EVE

The sailing on Christmas Eve was hard. With the coastline off the starboard bow, the *Santa Maria* and the *Niña* crawled east toward the Guacanagari's village. It was slow going. Trade winds from the east kept beating the ships back, causing the Admiral to tack in and out along the island's shore. The current rushed west against them. The workload was tremendous, and every sailor, sweaty and tired, had felt the frustration, including Pedro.

That evening, however, the easterlies died down altogether. There was no wind at all, and the sails hung limp like canvas shrouds from the flagship's yardarms. A soft crescent moon gave off just enough light for a sleepy Pedro to make out the shadow of the *Niña* ahead of them. Both ships were now floating along Guacanagari's island, just outside the island's barrier reef that divided the nearby bay from the ocean. The sea was calm and the night so quiet that from the quarterdeck Pedro could actually hear the surf swishing on a coral reef.

He was on watch duty but couldn't see much in the dark, as he propped his arms on the oak rail and gazed forward over the main deck.

Life at sea—the seaman apprentice couldn't help but ponder the wonder of it all. The ocean held its own magic. It was a place where time stood still. Were it not for the regular hymns and prayers that marked every half-hour, Pedro could almost have lost his sense of time. Somehow, past and future merged into present here. Life jelled into one string of moments. At this one, Pedro was once again marveling at how alive he really felt on the ocean. While tired tonight, he felt more *alive* on the sea than in any other place he had ever known.

His gold—the three bracelets he had taken from the young native boy on Española, in addition to the one Macu had given him—was safely stashed in his satchel. Thoughts of it offered him a certain comfort, as the night wore on. In fact, tonight a blanket of comfort seemed to envelop the entire voyage. Their expedition was turning into a success. They were on their way to meet the Grand Khan. The Admiral felt confident about the course, and his confidence filtered all the way down to the grommets. The seaman apprentice was truly on his way to owning his own ship one day.

The decks on the flagship were quiet. No one played card games or threw dice tonight. There were no songs from the plumwood recorder or wood flute. Even the six Arawak natives had long since closed their eyes. The sailors on watch yawned under the twinkling black canopy overhead, lost in the depths of their half-awake thoughts.

"I reckon maybe we've covered a quarter mile in the last hour, sir." De la Cosa's words to the Admiral carried across the deck. "She's hardly movin'."

"The sea's mighty calm," Don Cristóbal mused. "As if it's gone to sleep."

"Not even a crosscurrent, as best I can tell," the ship's master observed. "We're floatin' in place without even setting an anchor. Don't happen often."

"No, it doesn't," the Admiral yawned. "I think I'll turn in then."

No wax candle would flicker from the Admiral's cabin tonight. No summons would come for his cabin boy to help him check the log or relay a course correction to the pilot tonight. Before long, the Admiral's pronounced snoring would join the loud chorus of raspy breathing from all the sailors who had been waiting for the Admiral's cue. Even the lookout had curled up in the crow's nest and dozed in the ship's gentle sway.

Eleven o'clock, and all was well.

Like everyone else tonight, Pedro was too tired to care. Two excruciatingly long days. Natives everywhere. Constant trading. Trying to understand the language again. Exploring another island. Again.

And that wasn't all: the expedition had not really rested since they'd arrived in the Indies. Not one idle day in the last ten weeks. A new world. New people. New food. Scraping barnacled hulls and tramping through swampy forests. They had hoisted halyards and overhauled the ship's boat, now being towed astern. They had weighed anchor and dropped it again and again. The list was almost too long to think about.

Exhaustion consumed every ounce of Pedro's body and mind. His right cheek stung from his own slaps, but his attempts to keep himself alert didn't perk him up. How in the world would he ever stay awake through the remainder of this watch?

"Steer by a star, Señor Arias." De la Cosa, the officer of the watch, called off-handedly down the open hatch to the helmsman. "The Admiral's in, and I'm gonna' get some shut-eye."

No one answered from below.

"Call me if the wind picks up."

The coarse rope ladder to the main deck was wet from the night dew, as Pedro hopped down to the main deck from the quarterdeck. Just before he had to sing the next ditty at half past the hour, he entered the steerage.

In the dim light of the oil lamp, Marco's shadowed head leaned toward his right shoulder. Sensing Pedro's presence, the helmsman jerked his head back up.

"Sir," Pedro told him, "I'm here to turn the *ampoletta* and sing the ditty. I'll be through in a moment."

The helmsman let out a "humph," as his head slid back toward his shoulder.

Pedro turned the *ampoletta* and had just sung the ditty when something jabbed sharply into his back.

"Listen, boy, I've already dozed off twice." Marco's whispered words, spoken through toothless gums, were sharp. He retrieved his wooden crutch. "You take 'er fer awhile."

Pedro cleared the sleep from his throat, aware of the blood pulsing through his body now. "Meaning no disrespect, sir, but that's against the rule."

"She's ain't goin' nowhere, boy. Sea's dead calm tonight." The helmsman was obviously irritated by Pedro's reply. "There's nothin' to it. Jest hold 'er steady." Marco shifted his left stump over to the other side of the wide wooden bar attached to the tiller.

"But, sir, I'm just a grommet," Pedro was pleading now. "The Admiral forbids it."

"Never mind that!" The mariner's tone was cold as ice. "I'm tellin' ye to take this here tiller. And that's an order!" With that, the old man slid his body off the bar, dragged himself a few feet across the deck and lay down.

Pedro knew the rules, and he was breaking them. On more times than he could count, he had watched Señor Arias push and pull the long smooth handle, to turn the stern-mounted rudder through the tiller port. On a few occasions during a storm, he had actually helped to steady the tiller and had felt the rudder's strong tug against the waves. But never once had he manned her. Not solo, on his own. Never.

The groaning of ship's timbers, the singing and rattling of her rigging, and the creaking of the great rudder were all absent on this still night. The silence in the low dark steerage seemed to enfold him in its arms. A full *ampoletta* of sand would have to run out before it was 11:30. Then thirty more minutes after that he was off watch.

His freshly washed muslin shirt clung to his damp shoulders. The long tiller, its square edges rounded smooth from years of wear felt cumbersome in his hands, though there was no pressure on it from any direction. He could do this, he told himself. He'd have to; he had been ordered to.

Maybe, however, this was actually an opportunity. After all, a seaman apprentice needed to know how to man a tiller. He should have been learning to do this anyway, if he was to be a real sea captain one day. It couldn't be that hard. If Marco could do it, he could do it. Pedro made up his mind to seize the moment, but not without the fleeting thought that somehow the moment had actually seized him.

His chest swelled with one long deep breath, first in and then out, and his pulse slowed back down to normal. The cabin boy brushed the straggly strands of his ponytail off his neck and leaned against the tiller. Maybe this wasn't going to be so bad after all.

There was a hint of movement now, a soft gentle rocking that may have indicated a current. But it was so soft and so gentle that the *Santa Maria* had become like a huge cradle, lulling Pedro to sleep. Standing up.

It happened without warning.

With a slight jar, the rocking stopped.

Yawning, Pedro opened his eyes. He shifted his weight and noticed the tiller felt hard, whereas before it had been so pliable he could move it with the lightest touch.

The boy now tugged it hard with both hands. It refused to give an inch.

Pedro slammed on it with all his might.

Nothing.

The terror of it sent panic through his bones. The tiller was jammed!

The cabin boy's wonderful dreamy night had just become his worst nightmare.

29

DISASTER!

"The helm don't answer, sir!" Marco, now thoroughly awake and badly shaken, called up topside to De la Cosa, the officer of the watch.

But it was the Admiral who replied and had taken command of the situation.

"Señor Niño!" he bellowed, loud enough to wake anyone who was sleeping. "What's her condition?"

"She's takin' water aft, sir!" The pilot's voice was strained as he dashed up the steps from the hold.

"All hands on deck, men!" The Admiral's voice exploded across the night sky. "We have only a few minutes to save her!"

Straightaway the boatswain piped "all hands on deck," but no one needed it; with the pounding of feet, all the sailors rushed to their assigned emergency positions.

Except Pedro, who was frozen with the enormity of what he'd done.

The flagship had struck a coral reef, and the rudder was held by it. And it was his fault.

"Sir . . ." he managed to say to Marco, "I . . ."

"Clear away, you cur! Look what you've done!" He sniffed at Pedro as if the boy's mere presence created a stink.

This can't be happening, Pedro thought, as tears sprang to his eyes. The storm of commotion around him wasn't real, he told himself, wishing that he would wake up from this nightmare.

"Get out of the way, boy!" roared a sailor at him, as he and two others heaved the anchor rope from the capstan through the steerage toward the portal. "Move aside!"

"Move!" screamed another. "You heard the man!"

Pedro stepped backward out of the way, but his mind remained trapped in a quicksand of disbelief. None of this was real; it couldn't be. It was a dream. Of course, it had to be a dream.

A very bad dream.

The worst he'd ever had.

"De la Cosa!" cried the Admiral, topside. "Get in the ship's boat, take the anchor in her with four men, row it out as far as you can and drop it! We'll kedge her off!"

Gradually Pedro realized what had happened. There may have been no wind. The *Santa Maria* may have been simply floating. But she must have drifted into a current, which would explain the soft, lulling rocking he vaguely remembered.

Slowly, imperceptibly, the current had gently taken her over the coral reef. Then the ebbing tide had lowered her onto the reef, and the jagged, razor sharp coral now held her fast—at least, by her stern. And the Admiral, master mariner that he was, knew that their one chance was to row the anchor into deep water, drop it, hook it, and with the strongest mates at the capstan, attempt to pull her free.

But with each passing moment, she was getting caught more and more firmly. And now, as the receding tide no longer supported her, her own weight was starting to open her seams, which explained Lonso's damage report of water coming in at the stern.

"Up here, Pedro!" he heard Emilio yelling.

He ran topside.

Emilio was up on the mainsail's yardarm. "We need help up here!"

The seamen's expertise was being tested tonight. They weren't straining to hoist in one or two sails; they were dragging all five heavy limp shrouds in at one time, from foresail to lateen. And they were doing it as fast as they could.

But Pedro was paralyzed. Everything seemed unreal, as if he was watching it all, from far above. Shoulder to shoulder, his mates worked on the sails, racing against time itself. Not one ounce of energy was wasted. If this was a test of endurance, they weren't going to fail it. If this was a battle of might, they weren't going to lose it. They knew this ship, every square inch of her. The *Santa Maria* had been their home, their connection to the motherland. She had been their protector and their guide. They weren't going to fail her now.

All of a sudden, Emilio's voice cut through the din. "Look out there!" he yelled. "They're not comin' about!"

All eyes turned towards the ship's boat. It was not coming to the bow, to load the anchor; it was making for the *Niña*, as fast as her oarsmen could row.

"What are they doing?" Pedro asked Lonso, who was shouting orders to the men aloft.

"De la Cosa!" the old pilot spat out the name in disgust. "He thinks we're sinking, so he's saving his skin!"

He shook his head. "There goes our last chance. We jest lost our lady, boy," and his voice broke, as he uttered the words.

Lonso nodded towards the quarterdeck. "Ye best get up there, lad. He'll be needin' you now."

The Admiral! Pedro had completely forgotten about the Admiral. With two leaps, he bounded up onto the quarterdeck. He could not see Cristóbal's expression, but the slump in his shoulders said it all. He was losing a loved one, and there was not a thing he could do to save her.

At that moment, the cabin boy felt more sorrow than he had ever known. While Don Cristóbal Colón had discovered a sea route to the Indies and now bore the well-deserved title of Admiral of the Ocean Sea, he would always be remembered as the captain who lost the *Santa Maria*. This accident would stain his reputation for generations to come.

The ship moaned now, with each surge, as if she were in agony and weeping. Her timbers were opening. The sea was rushing in. She knew she was dying. With a great prolonged groan, she said goodbye.

And I've killed her, Pedro thought with a sob.

The Admiral gave one more command to his pilot. "Cut her masts, Señor Niño. We must lighten her." But the command did not have the edge of authority and determination that the previous orders had. Pedro sensed that the Admiral did not have much hope that this last measure would be successful.

Two men worked with the great saw hard, but without hope or joy. They, too, sensed it was a futile effort. Sailors took smaller saws aloft, to strip away her yardarms. In a matter of minutes, the tangled mass was over the side.

But it did no good. And now all her seams were open, and she was starting to come apart.

The Admiral took his speaking horn and hailed the *Niña*. "Captain Pinzón, we must abandon ship. Send your boat, and the *Santa Maria*'s, over here to begin ferrying the crew over there, with as much supplies and provisions as we can salvage."

By the time the two cutters had come alongside, the *Santa Maria* was listing far to starboard. The huge rock off the coast of La Isla Española would forever be her tombstone and the Ocean Sea her grave.

To the forlorn call of the boatswain's pipe, the sailors from the *Santa Maria* silently disembarked and crossed the water to the safety of the *Niña*.

No one on board the caravel said anything for a long time.

But one conversation carried to them all, as the Admiral confronted the flagship's owner. Staring out at the wreckage of the *Santa Maria*, he declared, "This was your fault, De la Cosa. You were the officer of the watch. What have you to say for yourself?"

De la Cosa shrugged.

"Why did you take the cutter and go to the *Niña*?

"I figured you got her on, so you could get her off." The master's words oozed out like slime in a bog.

"How dare you show insubordination to me!" the Admiral countered, his square jaw set like stone. "It was your watch and your responsibility!"

The *Niña*'s main deck was far too small for this many men. Squeezed between Emilio and Marco, Pedro could barely breathe. Suddenly, Marco's cane clapped Pedro on his left thigh, as De la Cosa grabbed the helmsman by his right arm.

"Arias here, was on the tiller," the master exclaimed, trying to shift the blame. "He's yer man."

The Admiral shook his head. "No! Let history record that you lost your own ship, De la Cosa!"

He turned to Marco, but before he could say a word, the helmsman stammered, "I wasn't on the tiller. T'weren't me at all." The helmsman clawed at his ragged shirt. "'Twas Pedro here. He had the helm!"

"Pedro?"

Every eye of every man on deck turned toward the boy. And in the twinkling of an eye, Pedro knew his life would never be the same.

"Pedro! How could you?" The Admiral's anger rose like an erupting volcano. "Grommets don't sail ships! You *know* that!"

The shock of the Admiral yelling at him was forever etched into the boy's memory. In that moment, the boy's entire world collapsed around him. The Admiral blamed him!

He was the one who had broken the rule.

He was the one—the only one—who had wrecked the *Santa Maria!*

30

DISGRACE

By dawn, the entire broken hull of the *Santa Maria*, caught and doomed on the coral reef, was mostly exposed. She was a sad sight, with stumps for masts, her once proud rigging stripped away. The two small boats continued to make trips back and forth from the ship to the shore, taking off everything of value that could be salvaged.

"Admiral, we should retrieve her timbers, too, sir, if we can. They may be useful."

Cristobál looked up at Lonso with moist eyes. Pedro watched as their gazes met and realized that the old pilot was making his friend consider what might be the next step. What *must* be the next step.

"Cristobál," said Lonso gently, "the time for exploring is over. It is time to go home. We cannot all fit aboard the *Niña*. Some will have to remain here in *La Navidad, until we can return.*"

La Navidad? Pedro had not heard the name before. The Admiral must have decided to name this place the Nativity, since they'd arrived here on the anniversary of the Savior's birth. Under other circumstances, Pedro would have delighted in the name. But the shadow of what he had done had fallen over this place; in his memory it would be forever cursed.

The Admiral gave a great sigh. "You're right, old friend. Her timbers and beams will be useful in erecting shelter. But we won't be able to get them all, before the tide returns."

"Why don't we send Vicente Pinzón in his boat, to ask Guacanagari for help? I'll take our boat back with some men, and we'll start dismantling her."

The Admiral nodded, too sick at heart to speak further.

By mid-morning, the cacique had arrived with canoes and people to help. Pedro was part of the salvage crew, working with sailors, as they chopped through the deck to get to the cargo below. Some of the Indians actually guarded the ship so that nothing was stolen. By sundown, the enormous undertaking was almost finished, and the shoreline was strewn with wooden planks and beams and ribs, coils of rope, and even the Admiral's desk.

For Pedro the hours aboard the *Niña* were like a foul stench in the air. He could hear the men talking about him, and what he had done. Shame assaulted him with each shifting eye. Rejection washed over him with the turn of each head. And there was no escaping the condemnation; it clung to him like moss on a tree.

Then there was the Admiral. A grown man, crying. Out in public, where everyone could see him. All day long, he just sat there, grieving for the loss of the love of his life.

Pedro heard every moan—until finally he could stand it no longer. He had to get away.

He looked to the forested mountains in the distance. The forest was thick enough to hide him, big enough to lose him for good. There would be plenty of food and water there. He could build a shelter out of palm fronds, and he could fish in the sea. He could live by himself. Alone. Forever.

He chewed on his bottom lip. One thing was certain: he could never return to Spain. From birth, Pedro had been taught to be proud of his heritage, and proud he was. His family had descended from the powerful Visigoths, great warrior-rulers of Spain until the 700s. He'd grown up on the stories of their exploits, as they ventured forth from their turreted stone castles. He could almost hear his grandfather's gravelly voice as he related their legends, while he and Pedro dug in the red soil for fishing worms or dropped their poles in a mountain stream, hoping to hook a trout for supper. They were stories rich with history and meaning. Tonight Pedro missed those stories.

He had never known his own father. A captain in the queen's army, he had been killed during a battle with the Muslims a few months before his birth. The purple ribbon, a badge of courage, had shimmied in the afternoon sun on the adobe wall above Grandfather's straw mattress. Pedro wondered if it was still there.

Even now, on the other side of the world, Pedro could close his eyes and rekindle the story of his father in full army regalia sitting astride a black stallion, marching off to war. In his mind, he could hear the cries of admiration from the throngs of people waving him goodbye from their village. Grandfather's tales brought everything to life.

Yet none of that mattered anymore. Not here, half way around the world, where he had brought disgrace to the family name.

Right now Pedro missed his grandfather more than he ever thought possible. It was a longing that flowed from some unexplainable place deep within his soul, the most intense pain he had ever known. Where was he now? Why wasn't he here?

At one time Pedro had understood why his grandfather couldn't care for him anymore. At eighty, Grandfather was simply too old. His grandmother had been gone for over three years. Somehow, Pedro had been able to accept the life of the monastery and its friars, who had always shown such loving care. Not today, though. Last night he had brought eternal shame to La Rábida, where in the future the mere mention of his name would cause the monks to turn away in pain. What had Father Antonio said to him, just before he left? "Make us proud of you, Pedro de Torreros." Well, he'd certainly done a good job of that, hadn't he!

He had brought shame to his family, to La Rábida, and to the man whom he'd come to regard as his second father.

Pedro looked over at him, his head sunk in his hands. Tears coming again, he went over to the Admiral and put a hand on his shoulder. "Sir? I'm . . . so sorry!"

Red-eyed, the Admiral raised his head, and seeing who it was, angrily brushed Pedro's hand off his shoulder. "Get away from me!"

In numb shock Pedro staggered back, and then he turned and ran down the beach, farther and farther, until he turned inland and started running for the mountains.

Within minutes, he encountered a mangrove swamp. The masses of tangled stilt-like roots were hard to navigate, and he slipped more than once, plunging into the muddy water down to his thighs. His drenched rolled-up britches quickly turned from tan to dark brown, as did his feet and legs.

The sounds of the swamp were everywhere. Crickets. Frogs. Brown pelicans overhead. Egrets along the banks. And then—a strange small splash. Pedro froze. To his right a large-eyed, striped mud snake slithered up out of the swamp and onto the muddy bank, not ten feet away.

With eyes as wide as ship's dishes, Pedro held his breath, clutching the burlap bag at his waist, to keep the three gold bracelets from jangling. Dingy water had settled around his ankles. He dared not move, not an inch. He had no idea whether this snake was poisonous, and he was not about to find out.

No sounds from the men on the beach reached him here, and without human voices, the music of the marshy wetland now exploded around him. A giant bullfrog croaked on the nearby bank, some four feet away from the snake, now posed as a large tree branch on the mud. A flock of green herons issued their hoarse trumpeting calls in concert with the short chirping whistles of some black winged ospreys. Over the next few minutes, the chatter of the swamp's natural world turned into a cacophony of boisterous noises.

In the midst of it all, Pedro realized he was truly alone.

At last.

The boy squinted and shifted his black eyes toward the snake. All at once, the reptile lunged into a green shrub. Ever so slowly, it curled back out, a huge lump protruding just behind its head. No need to listen for the frog anymore. It was inside the snake's stomach for dinner.

Strands of Pedro's black hair clung to his neck and his brow. Cuts and scratches on his arms showed through the torn sleeves of his shirt, mud-splattered and almost threadbare. His lips were parched from lack of water. His feet in the swamp water were shriveled and waterlogged.

Pedro was tired. And he hadn't even been gone an hour.

He'd find a way out of this swamp, he assured himself, and away from that nightmare back on the beach. Somehow, he'd get there—wherever "there" was.

31

ALONE

With each step, his mud-caked feet sank in less far, until by the time the setting sun was greeting the horizon, Pedro had reached a high stone ridge overlooking the bay. A great boulder of solid granite allowed him to survey the scene.

To his left, a rugged mountainous island jutted out of the Atlantic waters, shimmering with the colors of sunset. Deep red mahogany trees towered on the evergreen hills around him. A distant meadow of colorful wildflowers waved with the wind near a broad canopy of the now-familiar mango trees.

Pedro's chest expanded, as his lungs welcomed the island's fresh sea air. Had he not known better, he might have thought the tiny wrecked hull down there on the barrier reef, and the little caravel anchored in the lagoon, had been plundered by pirates and left to die. There seemed to be no one on this island but him.

Time to get going, he told himself. He marched into the deep underbrush. Slapping back palm fronds and hopping over thick fern beds, he soon reached a small stream threading its way down a jungle ravine. He decided to join it. Meandering his way down the steep slope, Pedro heard the sound of surging water ahead.

Before long, he found the source. Like a terraced stairway, fresh rushing water twisted and dropped over glistening boulders to form two distinct waterfalls that spilled into one great pool. Framed by green ferns, brush and tropical trees, the falls provided a lush rainforest haven for both reptiles and birds. The ends of some leaves dangled out of a rock iguana's mouth, where he lunged on a ledge still warm from the late afternoon sun. In the pond, two green-backed herons tucked their heads between their shoulders, to fool their supper into swimming closer.

The back pocket of Pedro's cotton britches snagged on a low limb from one of the tall trees, as he scurried down the closest ledge. He didn't stop.

He didn't even care, when a branch sliced his arm and drew blood. He couldn't get down fast enough.

With a splash that reverberated through the clearing, the water cooled the boy's parched body. He couldn't remember when swimming had ever felt so good!

Clothes and all, Pedro dove to the bottom and popped back up through the lily pads, to surface for air. Moored to their thick roots, the broad green leaves bobbed up and down on the water with each wave. Pedro lapped up the liquid and spit it out again, as if he were a human fountain. Like a frolicking dolphin, he flipped over, rolled onto his back, and kicked his feet. Finally, he tugged off his sopping shirt, britches, and pouch and tossed them onto a nearby sprawling shrub, hoping they might dry a bit while he swam.

At length, refreshed and a little less tired, he crawled out and flopped down, and lay on the grass for a short while. As water beads trickled down his temples, Pedro gathered his hair into a ponytail and wrung it out. Above him he could see the lavender darkening sky through the canopy of overhead trees.

Night was coming soon. This was probably as good a place to stay, as any. No one would find him here—at least, not anytime soon.

Pedro took stock of his situation. He was alone on a strange island somewhere near mainland China, hundreds of leagues from home. He'd wrecked the flagship, and that was the end of it. He'd let everyone down, and worse, he'd let himself down. Yes, he'd been ordered, but he could have refused the order. He knew the rule: grommets do not steer ships. Long ago Father Antonio had taught him that consequences always follow choices. Well, he had made the wrong choice, and now he must live with the consequences, which would affect the rest of his life.

The mud felt soft, as the boy dug his heels into it and sat up. At the loud clamor of a common crane, he sighed and forced himself to get his mind off the immediate past and focus on the immediate future. He was living with new choices now, which he must handle. By Saint Elmo, the patron saint of Castilian sailors, he *had* to handle this!

But his mind, like an unruly child in church, would not obey. It kept returning to the past, to pick open the scab that was trying to form over the wound.

The seaman apprentice had almost made it to the Promised Land. He had been eager. He had believed in his dream and in his ability to accomplish it. He had been part of one of the most exciting explorations in history. It had all been there, within his grasp.

And now, everything was changed. Now he would never become a sea captain. He wouldn't even make it to pilot or master. He was a ship-wrecker. The cabin boy who'd wrecked the *Santa Maria*. He had become a bad omen that no captain would want on his ship.

Gradually he realized that this sick feeling in his gut came from more than wrecking the flagship. Pedro's feet squirmed in the sand, as another truth stared him in the face. His pouch, lying on his clothes, still bulged with the bracelets. Four gold bracelets. Three of which he had stolen.

Now guilt gnawed at his heart. Unlike Macu, who'd gladly given Pedro a bracelet, the young Taino boy had not wanted to give him his bracelets. So Pedro had thrown him down, hurting him, and wrenched the bracelets off his arms.

And he hadn't put them in the Admiral's treasure chest, along with the other gold jewelry that had been traded for. The Admiral's rule was that all gold collected belonged to the Sovereigns. The gold Pedro had hidden away in his pouch didn't belong to him. He knew it—and had known it, all along.

Somehow he had to find a way to live with all of this. But for now, all he could do was wipe away the tears. He hated to cry—and he was crying like a little boy again, for the second time in the space of a day. It had been four years since he'd cried. And as he remembered the reason for those long-ago tears—Father Antonio whipping him for having taken another boy's cap—more tears came.

Pedro de Torreros was nothing but a thief, a no-good, common thief.

Sometime later Pedro's empty stomach began to growl. He tried to ignore it but the more he pushed thoughts of food away, the stronger they came back. But what would he eat?

His clothes were as dry as they were going to get. Time to put them back on. When he tugged them off the bush, however, a clump of purple fruit, barely visible in the gathering twilight, emerged between the leaves.

Food! They looked like the wine grapes harvested by the Franciscan fathers back home. Pedro popped one into his mouth. Not nearly as sweet but very juicy. He gobbled down a handful, then another, all he could find.

But now they had whetted his appetite. Hastily, he donned his clothes and refastened the pouch to his rope belt to search for more food.

Within a few minutes he had discovered another edible treasure, oval yellow-skinned fruit growing on a large evergreen shrub with small, white, fragrant flowers. Drops of its tangy juice dribbled down Pedro's scruffy chin.

His stomach full, Pedro became aware of the immense fatigue he was feeling. He had not slept in two days. And now he was about to spend the night in a tropical forest. Alone.

But the calm night sounds of the amphibians soothed his tired nerves. As darkness settled into the clearing, a small green sea turtle floated by, its shell showing just above the water's surface and its flippers silently propelling it under the surface. A white egret stood still, its straight yellow bill closed, no longer hunting for food. Even the thick gray limb, drifting near Pedro's submerged wiggling toes, seemed to have no particular place to go. It was a perfect night for sleeping. As he started to doze off, his last waking thought was that if he had to spend the rest of his life alone, this idyllic spot was not a bad place to spend it.

"*Oww!*" The pain in Pedro's right foot was excruciating. He howled so loudly a hidden flock of parrots took flight from the branches above him.

As he grabbed his bloody foot, the floating log lunged at him, its broad olive-colored tail thrashing the water behind it. The 'log's' massive upper jaw overlapped its lower jaw and with a loud hiss, the giant lizard opened its mouth and snapped at the boy again.

Instantly Pedro scuttled away from the water's edge like a crab. But the reptile clambered up the bank right after him, its short, stocky legs giving it amazing speed! The bony ridge connecting its two beady eyes looked almost like evil spectacles sticking out of its skull.

Pedro whipped around and darted toward the nearest tree, whose lower limbs offered him sanctuary.

Below, the serpent glared up at him, grunting and snapping and swishing its huge tail. Sooner or later, that light-skinned animal up there with the tasty toes, would have to come down. The serpent settled in to wait.

Up in the tree, Pedro rubbed his throbbing foot, which was already swelling to twice its normal size. He shifted to another broader limb that would support him better.

The serpent moved around the tree with him, to be ready in case he should fall.

Pedro sighed. It was going to be a long night.

32

CAPTURED!

In the gloom of the jungle night, Pedro couldn't see the ground below him. But every so often a low grunt from the monster assured him that his captor was keeping its vigil.

He reached down and rubbed his bitten foot, which was quite stiff now. But what he had thought was a puncture wound, was actually a long tear in the skin. He was relieved; there was less chance of infection.

He rubbed his backside, numb from his rough bark perch. His back ached from being in one position for so long, and he ruefully smiled; as sore as it was, it was infinitely preferable to being chewed on by the monster lizard. He leaned back against the trunk of the tree and listened to the night sounds of the jungle.

Two distant owls were carrying on a leisurely dialogue. The familiar slow musical trill of a water thrush provided a bit of comfort but not much. And there were the crickets and the *rivets* from the bullfrogs.

He yawned. Did this night have no end? It wasn't enough to have a foot throbbing with pain. His mind was being bombarded with fearful thoughts. And he knew that thanks to that grunting monster down there, he had to come to grips with those fears. With a wince he remembered that in times past, he'd believed that he could handle anything! But, the truth was that he'd always had someone close by to help—his grandfather; Father Antonio and the other friars at the monastery; aboard ship, Peralonso and even the Admiral.

Now? There was no one. He had no idea how he was going to cope with that spiny invention of the devil that had already had a taste of him and clearly wanted more.

Moreover, he could not shake the deep-seated feeling that he was only getting what he deserved. Was this his punishment?

What he needed was courage—a lot of it. The real kind, that faced fear head on and said, "I'm going to get through this! I'll fight this thing to the death!" Then from deep inside him came the thought, "With God's help, I'll find a way!"

But would God help someone who stole from defenseless boys? Who disobeyed rules and wrecked ships? Who ran away and got himself treed by some toe-munching creature?

"Just what kind of God are You, anyway?" he heard his own voice ask out loud. "Can you hear me? I'm down here in this tree! I can't get down, because there's a monster down there who wants to eat me!"

But heaven was silent.

When God didn't answer, he tried a different tack. "Look, God, I'm hurt, and I'm tired, and I want to go home. I mean, what kind of God allows such terrible things to happen to boys? I'm only fifteen!"

Now his back really hurt, and he got angry. "And what about the Admiral? He *believes* in You! He started this whole adventure, because he thought You wanted him to. Look at all he went through for You on this voyage. All *we* endured, because we believed in his faith."

Below there was a reptilian grunt. Monster was irked that his breakfast was making so much racket up in the tree.

But Pedro wasn't finished; in fact, he was just starting. "After all of that, You first allowed him to be abandoned by Martín Pinzón, and then You allowed him to lose his flagship, so he has no choice but to return. Without reaching Cathay. Without even reaching Cipangu. He deserved to come home a hero, but now he'll be returning as a goat."

Those were pretty strong charges. He paused to give God a chance to answer them. When there was only silence, he continued, even angrier. "If that's how You treat someone who has that much faith in You, I'm not sure I really want to have faith!"

He was about to say more, but the words stuck in his throat. He had the strangest feeling that somehow Father Antonio and Father Peréz knew what he was saying, and that it greatly saddened them. And his grandfather, too, who had been a praying man.

Pedro himself was surprised at the depth of his feelings. But there was something else: Underneath the anger and the shame was a truth he had never faced before. He did want faith; he wanted it badly. He just didn't know how to get it.

When it came down to it, Pedro knew he had a choice. He could believe that God was alive and listening. And that He loved him and would help him, in spite of all that he had said and done.

Or, he could choose not to believe. And remain miserable for the rest of his life. Which might be over as soon as he came down from the tree.

Pedro chose to believe.

So, now what do I do?

That's not hard; I pray.

Prayer seemed to work while they were at sea.

Well then, what do I have to lose now?

"Father," he whispered out loud, "I have sinned. I am a thief and a liar. A bully and a coward, afraid to stand up for what I knew was right."

He paused and wondered what to say next. "All I know to do is to ask You to forgive me, Lord."

He sniffed as the wind rustled the tops of the trees. "Please, help me to get out of this. I promise I'll tell the Admiral that I took the bracelets, and I will give them back. And if we ever get back to Española, I'll find that boy and give him my bracelet, since I doubt I'll be able to give him back his own." He finished with "amen" and made the sign of the cross.

The moment his fingers crossed from his left shoulder to his right, a strange relief seeped up from deep within him. Somehow—in his heart, not his head—he knew what it meant. Fifteen-year-old Pedro de Torreros had placed himself in God's hands.

Soon Pedro's nose detected a faint aroma. A light tapping on the leaves around him was followed by soft tiny droplets tickling the hair on his extended legs, then his arms and finally his cheeks. It was too dark to see them, but gentle, steady raindrops began to soak the jungle air and the already muddy ground.

As the boy shuffled slightly to his right, the leaves dumped water on him. He shivered from the drenching and rubbed both forearms for warmth. Yet the coolness of the rain actually felt good on his swollen foot, as the water bathed the wound.

Perhaps it would clean the wound enough so that he really wouldn't get an infection. At the thought, his imagination ran wild. He had seen one-legged sailors leaning on sticks. Whether it was from shot or accident, it usually began with an infection. And when the limb was dying and had maggots crawling in it, off it came, to save the life of the sailor.

"No!" he cried aloud. He was not going to allow his mind to dwell on that. He had chosen to believe God was in control of his destiny, and he would stick with that plan. He would somehow get out of this.

Within moments, however, his slender faith was under assault again, by the overwhelming fear he would fall asleep and tumble to his death, as Monster was waiting for him to do. How would those great powerful jaws feel, when they clamped down on his head?

"God help me!" he shouted in the night. And the terrifying thoughts did seem to recede—a bit.

Finally the night dampness turned into the gray mist of early light. And Pedro made a wondrous discovery. Monster was gone! The only thing that remained of it at the base of the tree was the imprint of his body and long tail! Annoyed by the rain, it must have slithered off and returned to the depths of the pond.

Weary but relieved, he made his way down the tree and slumped on the ground.

What next? He certainly wasn't going to hang around this pool very long. No telling where Monster had gone, or whether it had any friends.

He examined his foot. A black crust edged the still painful wound. He winced every time he moved it.

Before he could decide where to go, or how he was going to protect his foot, his exhausted body wilted on the tree's protruding roots, and he fell into a deep sleep.

Out of the distant morning mist, a raucous noise startled him awake. As he inched back against the trunk, he discovered his swollen foot wouldn't support any pressure. Which meant he could not stand up at all.

The clatter in the forest grew louder. Voices. Voices speaking words that had a familiar sound to them. They were speaking Arawak!

Pedro's tired spirits soared! God had answered his prayers!

"Help me!" he cried aloud. *"Ayudamé!"*

He laughed for joy. Those were real human voices, coming closer. They were almost here.

He squinted. Long straight bamboo tubes with colorful feathers and dangling animal-skin pouches emerged from the forest followed by natives whose red skin had been dyed in browns, yellows, and whites. The men were jabbering very loudly now. Pedro's ears felt like they had been stuffed with cotton. He couldn't hear very well, and he certainly wasn't seeing very well.

These Arawak had painted their skin, too. As the men encircled him, however, they were not exactly friendly. They poked at his chest and legs with the blunt ends of their blowguns.

As they prodded his injured foot, despite his pleas for them to be careful, Pedro recoiled in the sharp pain. This didn't make any sense! They were *hurting* him!

A merciful gray fog came over his eyes, as he lost consciousness.

33

SEASONED FOR SACRIFICE

The round wood-framed dwelling kept the sun out but retained its heat. Pedro moaned as he shifted onto his sore back, the ground hard underneath him. Where was he? His brain wouldn't register anything, except the distant memory of jagged coral reefs and a giant lizard.

Opening his eyes, he made out in the shadows some round objects dangling from the rafters. They looked like the heads of dolls, only they were misshapen and bore hideous expressions. Against the wall was a long, spear-like weapon. Whiffs of bitter smoke wafted into the tent.

With a groan, he rolled on his side, bringing his knees to his chest and curling up. It seemed like every bone in his body hurt, especially his swollen foot. One moment his body was hot, and the next it was cold. Morning now merged into afternoon and afternoon into night. He was losing all track of time.

A stab in his right hip with the point of a bamboo spear brought him back to the present. He switched positions on the ground, wanting the annoyance to go away. A second jab in his thigh forced him fully into consciousness. Pedro woke up.

The stubble on his face felt grubby, his hair tangled with pebbles and dirt. His cracked lips burned when he pressed them together, and grit covered his tongue. Slowly, he breathed in the heavy air and opened his caked eyes.

The shadow towering over him was dark and menacing. The warrior's black eyes held a certain cruelty, and the deep crease bridging his hairy brows gave him a wicked look. While Pedro couldn't understand the man's words, there was no mistaking their deathly tone. Black and yellow stripes decorated the man's chest, but it was the fire-hardened javelin in his left hand that brought Pedro into reality.

The neck of Pedro's striped shirt nearly choked him, when the painted warrior jerked him up off the ground. Half dazed, the wounded boy stumbled through the tent's flap toward the light and sprawled onto the hard ground, to the vibrant whoops and hollers of more warriors.

As they picked Pedro up and tied his arms to a tree behind him, he shook his head, to clear away the fog. Those heads back in the hut . . . they weren't dolls' heads . . . they were the heads of captured enemies, somehow shrunken . . .

He had been captured by Caribs!

To his left, smoke curled around jagged lava rocks set in a circle, while a scorching fire licked burning wood. Dancing bodies in straw skirts chanted to the sound of bamboo pipes and pulsating drum rhythms. Pedro shuddered and felt his scalp tighten. He did not want to think about what they might be celebrating, or what that fire might have been prepared for.

The bark of the coconut palm dug into Pedro's wrists, now tied securely behind the tree. He must be dreaming, he told himself. But even in his worst nightmares, he did not feel pain. And he was feeling it now. This was no dream.

He shifted slightly to one side. *Uno . . . dos . . . tres . . .* He counted seven men. Only seven. In his foggy dream-like haze, he began to consider the possibility of escape.

But not for long. Two white-faced warriors lunged at him and screeched, their faces an inch away from his. Suddenly, his wrists were freed, and he was being dragged back into the darkening tent. Before he knew what was happening, yellow and black paint was being slapped all over his bare chest, mostly in circles.

Within minutes, he was so covered with paint, he could barely see his own skin. One of the warriors ripped the rope belt off his waist, while another dug into the pouch. The warrior slipped the three bracelets over Pedro's left hand and up to his elbow, until they dug into his skin. Chattering loudly with his partner, the man pointed toward the tent's flapping doorway. The two of them dragged Pedro, now ceremonially painted, back into the murky shadows of dusk.

The smell of smoldering wood and tobacco assailed his nostrils. The throbbing in his head wasn't just his headache. Horrified, he watched as two Carib drummers pounded long sticks on taut animal-skin drumheads. The dancers squealed while they leaped and swirled around the fire. The crashing rhythm dominated the scene, with each series of hits. Gradually, the resonant sounds of the drumming outweighed the chanting, until only the pulsing of the drums was left.

And then, in an instant, everything ceased. There was total silence. Time stood still.

Pedro's ears buzzed in the quiet. Could this worst of all dreams be coming to an end? The pulsing inside his head kept him from thinking about anything other than the moment. Petrified with fright, he had to keep remembering to breathe.

Through the smoke he recognized the huge fluted lip of a gray conch shell when a Carib raised it to his lips. As the man blew on it, one long deep note flowed out of the shell. Its eerie sound ricocheted through the cavernous forest around them. The trumpeter then lifted the shell up toward the sky, now dark with night. His shell anklets tinkled when he twisted in the four directions. North. East. South. West. In each direction, he stopped and blew again, sending the note to the far reaches of the night. Then he raised the shell to the heavens, as if making an offering.

It came to Pedro that he was observing a tribal worship ceremony. Memories of a story he had once read about African rituals associated with worship swirled up in his head. All he could remember was that the ceremonies usually related to the natural world, with natural objects, like conch shells, having supernatural meanings. Somehow the arid smoke and the shell's deep tone imparted a supernatural significance to these people. He had a dreadful premonition that tonight they were celebrating his imminent death, probably spitted and roasted over that slow fire.

Just then the odor of burning grass and sage punctuated the air. In moments, a Carib was pouring burned herbs into a large oval abalone shell. With great ceremony, two of the men danced up toward Pedro and started to fan the smoke toward his face.

Over the din of drumming, piping, and singing, Pedro couldn't hear the rustling of the nearby palmetto bushes.

Until they exploded right in front of his face.

Through the brush, short wooden bows with horsehair strings suddenly released a flight of arrows into the midst of the dancers.

Then from all sides came deep-throated battle cries. Spanish battle cries. Into the fire circle came helmeted Spaniards, swords drawn and reflecting in the firelight.

Screeching with terror, the Caribs dropped their pipes and drums and ran off into the woods, their cries becoming fainter and fainter, the farther they ran.

"We've got to get you out of here, " said a voice whose Genoan accent Pedro recognized. "Quick, boy. Come!"

"Admiral . . ."

"Never ye mind, lad. We've got you."

The familiar voice was growing very distant . . .

34

WAKING UP

He knew it was time to get up. He had the morning watch, and his chores were waiting for him. Why hadn't he heard the morning ditty? Where was Emilio? His eyelids seemed to be matted shut, though he could feel shafts of sunlight on them.

He must really be late. He tried to force his lids open, but they seemed as heavy as the cross beams stowed on the *Santa Maria*'s deck.

The *Santa Maria*!

The memories flooded back in, as sure as the tide that was washing over the hulk that had once been the flagship of the Admiral of the Ocean Sea. Pedro's eyes flew open—and closed again, against the blinding sunlight.

Oh, why hadn't they just let him die? How would he ever live down the shame of the wreck and the guilt of what he'd done? The thought of being back with the crew bore no comfort. Who would want to work or sit or stand alongside a ship-killer? He wanted to crawl away in a hole and die.

"Ah, I see ye're coming back from the dead," said a gentle voice. It was Lonso. "We've been missin' ye, lad."

The lump returned to Pedro's throat, and the gold bracelets on his arm rattled as he rubbed his crinkled brow. He could feel his bottom lip drying over his upper lip.

"Will ye have some water?"

Droplets tickled onto the boy's painted chest, as Lonso stooped down with a ladle full of water. "Fresh out of the barrel," he added, his knees cracking as he squatted down.

Pedro drank thirstily, and Lonso offered him another.

The cabin boy took a deep breath and got ready for the verbal assault. Strangely enough it never came.

"I'm thinkin' ye might need to hoist yerself up and move about a bit, lad. Might help them aches." Lonso chuckled and rubbed his back. "I oughta know; I has 'em most every mornin'."

The pilot's strong hands lifted the boy under his arms. "There now, steady as she goes."

The pain from Pedro's right foot was excruciating. "Oww," he moaned, wincing. He looked down at the fresh gauze bandage around his foot, and up at Lonso, his eyebrows raised.

"We cleaned it early this mornin'," the pilot explained. "The wound ain't too bad. At least, ye're not gonna lose yer foot."

"Like I've lost everything else?" Pedro moaned.

"Ye ain't lost *nothin'*, lad. I'm still here, and so's the Admiral. And I don't think God has gone anywhere."

"God?" Pedro spun around and snarled, "*God?* What kind of God lets such terrible things happen? Tell me that, Lonso! I wrecked our ship and got mauled by a serpent and nearly eaten by cannibals. Just what kind of God allows the likes of that?"

"The steadfast kind whose love endures forever," Lonso replied, softly. "That's what kind."

Pedro nearly lost his balance in the sand. *"Love?* What happened to me was *love?"*

"No, lad, that wasn't love," the pilot replied. "What happened to you was the results of yer own choices. But God took care of you in spite of 'em."

Pedro slumped down on a long wooden plank. His foot hurt. His head hurt. His body hurt. His whole life hurt.

"Think about a few things, young fella. Think about that big river serpent, and then all them Carib natives who had their hearts set on eating you. Who do you think spoiled their dinner plans?"

Pedro said nothing.

"The same God that put it on the Admiral's heart to lead a search party to find—and save—the lad who had wrecked his ship."

Pedro opened his mouth to speak, but no words came.

"You think you're tired? None of us slept last night, 'cause we were out looking for you. And the night before, too."

Pedro felt badly now about his former attitude and wanted to say so, but Lonso wasn't finished.

"One more thing for you to think about: Who do you think led us to where you were? We had no idea where to look. You'd disappeared into the jungle without a trace. But me and the Admiral prayed and trusted God, and He sped us up with those drums, and then gave us our final bearing with that conch shell. We saw the fire, and—you know the rest."

So, Pedro thought, he hadn't been alone, after all. Not really. His shipmates had been searching all along. The Admiral. Lonso. The others. And God had led them straight to him.

"I . . . I don't know what to say."

Lonso laughed. "Well, now, ain't that a blessing for all mankind!" he teased. "C'mon, Pedro, let me show you what else God is doing."

He led the boy up from the shore, to where the men were building out of trimmed logs, what appeared to be a fort, complete with a main gate and battlements.

"What *is* this?" asked Pedro, deeply impressed.

"The first fortified Spanish colony in the Indies, lad!"

Pedro could see it all. Sailors were heaving tall posts into deep holes already dug in the ground. Others used sharp saws to cut the thick timbers from the flagship to size, or banged square iron nails into log planks. Pedro even recognized Chachu's complaining voice, as he worked alongside two others, barely visible in the earthen depths of a new well. Located just inland off the beach, the coastal stockade was to be the first fortified place of defense for Spain off the coast of China.

The date in the *Niña*'s log read December 29th. Pedro had been gone since Christmas morning. In four short days a miracle had taken place inside the barrier reef on the coast of the island of Española. Lonso tossed the boy a worn cap. "I think this is yers."

Pedro could hardly believe his eyes. All this because of the wreck. "The Admiral's not mad at me?" he asked, the cap now in his lap.

"Not anymore. He's seen what God's true intent was. So have the rest of us. It's over, boy. Let it go."

Pedro's sigh was deep and long. With cap in hand, he hobbled along slowly beside Lonso toward the settlement.

"Where did these huts come from?" he asked, referring to the native huts that weren't there, when he'd left.

"Guacanagari," the pilot replied. "He came to our aid. See? There he is, over there."

Sure enough, the grand cacique was directing the men from a bamboo chair that was so wide it could have held two people. Outlined by an odd blend of bright pointy feathers and stringy gray locks, his white face was seasoned with wrinkles. Gold necklaces adorned his neck, and his bare stomach folded over his thighs, making him look very much like the drawing of a Buddha in Marco Polo's book.

"The natives dismantled two of their own huts and brought them out here," Lonso explained.

"Where is their village?" Pedro asked.

"Beyond the mangrove swamps."

Pedro chuckled at the irony of that. He had thought he could escape and be free forever on the island. The truth was the whole crew had been out combing the island for him, and the Taino village was only a swamp away. Lonso went on, "We rescued almost everything from the flagship. Much of it is still on the beach."

Sure enough, wide coils of hemp rope and round wooden barrels stretched along the shore near some canoes, one of which still held the flagship's tiller. Heavy sailcloth and ratlines had been strewn in two large piles away from the tide. The Admiral's three personal trunks were angled up the beach alongside his chair and desk, now dusted with white sand. On top of the desk sat the tiny glass *ampoletta*, its bottom chamber full of sand. Stashed in a huge palmetto frond basket beside the desk were the rolled sheepskins Pedro knew to be the Admiral's valuable sea charts.

"And we didn't lose yer drawings either, Pedro." He handed them to the boy. "Here they are."

Pedro had almost forgotten about these. The nappy burlap satchel brought back good memories of Father Antonio and the monastery. "*Gracias, amigo,*" he told his friend. "*Muchos gracias.*"

There was one more relationship he had to get right. And this would be the most difficult of all. He had been putting it off, but fate was about to take matters into its own hands. Here came the Admiral, and there was no avoiding him.

35

"I FORGIVE YOU"

As Pedro watched the Admiral of the Ocean Sea approaching, he was again struck by his almost regal bearing. Even here on the beach, surrounded by the salvaged remains of his destroyed flagship, dressed only in a white shirt and dark breeches, his once red hair now almost completely white and hanging loose to his shoulders, he still had the grace and natural authority of a nobleman. This made what he was about to do even harder. He had to beg his forgiveness.

He was trembling, as the Admiral came up to him. "Sir, I . . ." Words failed him. Tears came to his eyes.

Seeing them, the Admiral smiled and nodded. And put his arm around his cabin boy's shoulders. "Pedro, it wasn't your fault. I forgive you."

The boy wept harder now, his grief mingled with relief. The Admiral did not hold him responsible. He looked up at the man who was more like a father than any man he'd ever known. "Thank you for saving my life!"

Don Cristóbal became serious for a moment. "I never sail without *all* my men." Then he smiled. "It's good to have you back."

"It's good to *be* back, sir!" exclaimed Pedro, overjoyed.

But now he felt compelled to tell the Admiral the whole truth. "I ran away, sir, because I was so ashamed," the words came tumbling out. "I didn't know how to live with what I did. And," Pedro indicated the gold bracelets on his arms, "these aren't mine. This one was given to me," he pointed to the one on his right arm, "but these three I simply took . . . from a boy who didn't want to give them to me."

The Admiral nodded gravely. "I said you could keep the one given you by your Arawak friend. These others I will give to Guacanagari. He will know which boy they belong to." He thought for a moment. "No, I'll offer him this, in exchange for them." He tapped the jeweled dagger at his waist. "If he accepts, we'll add the bracelets to the Sovereigns' treasure chest. If not . . . ," he shrugged and smiled. "There's already enough gold in there to please them." Then he chuckled. "Turns out, this island has a gold mine on it—with enough gold in it to enable the Sovereigns to take back Jerusalem."

He expected Pedro to be lifted by this news, but the boy was somber. His confession was not finished. "Forgive me, for being a thief. And also for being a liar, because I wasn't going to tell you about them." He paused. "I've learned my lesson."

"And what exactly have you learned, lad?"

"I've learned that greed poisons the soul, sir. And that doing the right thing is always best, no matter how hard it might be." The cabin boy twisted his cap in his hands. "And I learned something about God."

Don Cristóbal raised his eyebrows. "What?"

"That He cares for us, even when we don't know it. Even when we don't deserve it."

The Admiral smiled. "How right you are, boy. And how blessed to have learned this at such a young age. Mind you, don't let the world make you forget it."

By Sunday, the first day in the Year of our Lord 1493, the fort was completed. Together, the Taino and Spaniards had erected a storage building and a sentry station beside the two huts, which would be living quarters for the thirty-nine men, including Chachu, who had volunteered to stay behind. A new well, along with barrels of water and fresh food would get them started. Huge earthenware mounds of wet sand and dirt made a barricade around the perimeter. The *Santa Maria*'s boat remained behind, along with numerous oil jars for collecting gold. The Admiral had instructed the men to trade with the Indians and pan for gold until he returned, which would be as soon as he could mount another expedition, perhaps within the year.

While Pedro was alone on the beach, awaiting the Admiral's instructions, De la Cosa came up to him. He pointed to the wreck of the *Santa Maria*. "That was my ship. I lost her, 'cause of *you*." In his dirty right hand, he was fondling two gold nuggets like they were marbles. Now he slipped them into a pocket of his breeches. "And don't judge me, you little snot," he added. "You lost me my ship. This gold's mine!"

Pedro decided to say nothing, and De la Cosa tromped off. For the first time, he actually felt sorry for the man. Juan De la Cosa's bitterness and greed were going to eat him alive. He blamed Pedro for what happened on Christmas Eve, but he himself had been the officer of the watch. He had chosen to sleep that night, and as Pedro had so recently and so painfully learned, choices had consequences.

On Wednesday, as part of their farewell ceremony, the Admiral arranged a surprise for Guacanagari. To honor him and perhaps impress the natives with the firepower of the Lombard cannon that would be part of the new fort's defenses, Don Cristóbal fired off a round from the beach. With a loud report, it smashed through the remains of the *Santa Maria's* hull, sending pieces of wood flying everywhere.

The grand cacique, startled, pleased, and obviously impressed, bowed with respect to the Admiral. The two men embraced, and Cristóbal stepped into the *Niña's* boat.

It was time to head home, at last.

Continuing soft winds ushered them through the treacherous shoals around the islands on a northwest tack out to the open sea. The lookout kept a keen eye for dark water indicating depth. By noon on Sunday, the winds had finally blown up fresh and full, and the crosses on the *Niña's* three sails billowed out with the delight that only the freedom of the open sea could offer.

The tiny caravel was crowded, to say the least. She was carrying forty-eight sailors, double the crew she had on the outbound voyage, in addition to all her normal sailing equipment. And now she was laden with fresh water and provisions, bamboo cages of feathered parrots, an armadillo, and live jungle rats that lined the port side just under the forecastle. On the starboard side were bushels of exotic fruit, corn, and yucca.

In addition, the six Arawak natives huddled in the back, looking wide-eyed at the sights and sounds, having never been this far out to sea before in any vessel, much less a sailing ship this large.

Finally, there was the Sovereigns' treasure chest, filled with gold jewelry and masks, and pearls, which had been stowed, safe and secure, deep in the ship's hold.

Perched on the slender steps up to the little forecastle, Pedro could hear the dirty bilge water sloshing down in the hold. Today, it didn't smell so bad. In fact, nothing about today was bad. Their voyage of destiny, which had basically accomplished what Cristóbal had set out to do—discover a western trade route to Japan and China—was homeward bound. This was all that mattered.

The breeze jostled the loose black strands of the boy's clean hair. While it had taken some serious sand scrubbing, only a few paint splotches remained on the boy's back, as physical reminders of what happened.

Pedro was happy. The lesson of faith, built on the truth of what happened, filled his heart as wide as the canvas above him. He was back at sea, doing what he loved. It felt good.

Really good.

He watched the sailors scurrying up and down the ratlines, yelling to one another. Just then, Captain Vicente Pinzón stepped around the wooden bilge pump and pushed some overhead ropes out of his way. His face looked worried.

"Sir," he addressed the Admiral, "I'm concerned about sailing back alone."

Don Cristobál did not shift his gaze from the sea in front of the ship. "There's nothing we can do, Vicente," he replied calmly. "We're in God's hands now."

All of a sudden, the lookout's voice bellowed from above. "Sail, ho! Upwind, aft of us! It's the *Pinta!*"

36

"IT WAS THE GOLD, MARTÍN"

All day long the sister caravels sailed as close to one another, as safety would allow. And always, the *Pinta* copied whatever course correction the *Niña* made, as if her captain were anxious to demonstrate his loyalty and his respect for the Admiral's authority.

Pedro, however, was not impressed by this show of subservience, and neither, he suspected, was the Admiral. He was pretty sure that gold fever had gotten to Martín Pinzón—just as it had gotten to him.

Pinzón had, in fact, requested a meeting with the Admiral, and with the setting of the sun, the wind died away enough to allow the *Pinta*'s boat to ferry him to the *Niña*.

There was no captain's cabin aboard the little caravel, and Pedro noted Captain Pinzón's obvious discomfort at having to talk with the Admiral out in public, where anyone nearby could hear what was being said.

The Admiral took pity on him and invited him up on the small top deck in the stern, the stern-castle, where there was room for only the two of them. The breeze would carry their voices away from any curious ears. Pedro, however, was told to sit on the steps, in case the Admiral needed him for anything.

The boy was humbled and grateful. It was a position of trust. It meant that the Admiral knew he would keep anything he overheard strictly to himself.

No sooner were they alone up there, than Martín Pinzón, clutching his wool cap, insisted, "Don Cristobál, my goal was not disloyalty. I was looking for gold, just as you were."

"No, Martín, it was *not* the same," replied the Admiral quietly but firmly. "The gold we found is all going to the Sovereigns. Whatever you found, you intended to keep for yourself, and perhaps share it with your crew, the way pirates share the booty they steal. You're no better than a pirate!"

"Sir, I cannot—I *will* not—accept that!" His voice was growing louder, so that it could be overheard, despite the Admiral's consideration in having their meeting up there.

"It was greed, Martín, *and you know it!*" The Admiral insisted through clenched teeth, while still managing to keep his voice down. "And it is clear to me that you intended to find gold on your own and be the first back to Spain for the glory. You just didn't expect to run into us on your return trip."

At that moment Pedro understood. Gold tainted people. It changed them. It consumed them with greed. Had he himself not fallen victim to its lure? It had even infected the Admiral, who had become preoccupied with finding the source of the gold the Indians wore, instead of concentrating on finding the Chinese mainland. Love of money was indeed the root of all evil. It divided men, and in this instance it had nearly destroyed the entire expedition.

"I believed you were going the wrong way," Pinzón went on lamely.

"I'm sorry, Martín, but I cannot accept that. You knew *exactly* what I was doing and what I intended to do. Your brother certainly understood that."

Pinzón had no counter. He glared sullenly at Cristobál.

"It was the gold, Martín," said the Admiral softly, almost pleading with him to just admit it.

"We certainly found it!" exclaimed Pinzón, brightening. "On one of the islands we went to, we found it glistening in an upcountry river. We have several sacks of it."

Seeing that the Admiral was unimpressed, he tried another tack. "When we heard from the Indians about what had happened to the *Santa Maria*, we came back to see if we could help you, but you had already left."

The Admiral tilted his head. "No, this is what I think happened: As soon as you had enough gold to impress the Sovereigns and satisfy your crew, you headed for home. You never expected to see us, but once your lookout spotted our sail, you had to assume that our lookout had spotted yours. And as we are the only two ships on this side of the world, you caught up with us, as quickly as you could, matched our course, and fabricated this story."

Pinzón seemed shocked. For a moment, he was without words. Then he repeated his story, insisting that it was true. "You've got to believe me, Don Cristobál!"

He's right about that, thought Pedro. *Pinzón's reputation is finished, if the Admiral doesn't bend here. Because what he did is worse than insubordination—it's nothing less than mutiny!*

And, as for turning back to be of assistance, Pedro didn't believe him for an instant. But there was no way to know for sure. Pinzón's officers, if interrogated, would back their captain's version. And the only way to know for sure would be to go back and ask the Indians themselves. But that would have to wait until another voyage, as they were not about to turn around now.

Pedro bit his lower lip. The Admiral's response now could make all the difference. If he accepted Pinzón's excuses, the two captains could sail together on the homeward passage. That would create a much safer scenario for the voyage back across the Atlantic, to be sure.

If he did not accept them, Pinzón would be considered a mutineer and would be subject to the laws of mutiny on the high seas. Pedro knew that meant chains, imprisonment, and a court martial, once they returned to Spain.

But what if Pinzón's crew refused to turn their captain over to the Admiral, for him to be put in irons? That was highly unlikely, as they, too, would be in trouble for attempting to keep the gold for themselves. If their captain were to be tried for mutiny, they would all be considered to be part of it! And Vicente Pinzón might well side with his brother as well, and his crew with him . . .

Pedro shuddered. Obviously such thoughts were going through the heads of the *Pinta*'s crew right now, as they watched the Admiral and their captain on the *Niña*'s stern-castle.

"God," Pedro prayed, under his breath, "You're real, You're here, and You answer prayer. I don't know what to pray, except—have Your way in all of this."

37

LEAKS!

The Admiral took a deep breath—and smiled. "Martín, you've been a great support to this mission. You're a master mariner with great wisdom borne of great experience. I am not willing to let the devil undermine this voyage, any more than he already has. I shall overlook your disloyal conduct on two conditions: I expect your full cooperation during our trip back. And all the gold you collected belongs to the Sovereigns."

All eyes were on Martín Pinzón as he weighed his options. While the crews might not have heard what was said, they were well aware that their fate—and the fate of the expedition—was hanging in the balance.

Martín Alonso Pinzón relaxed and smiled. "Home it shall be, sir, and here is my hand upon it."

As they shook hands, Pedro could almost hear the collective sigh of relief from the watching crews of both ships.

Don Cristobál looked him in the eye and lightly said, "What, sir, are you doing still aboard my ship? Should you not be returning to your own ship, to crowd on all sail for home?"

"Aye, aye, sir. Your word is my command!" and with that, to the cheers of all men aboard both ships, he descended to the main deck and into the *Pinta*'s boat.

As he went to the little ship's fogon in the cooking area to fetch the Admiral some hot water, Pedro pondered on what he had just witnessed. They had been at the brink of disaster. Had either captain made the opposite choice . . . . But God had prevailed, and forgiveness had been the key.

The heavens favored the Spaniards with brilliant sun, as they continued tacking to the northeast. Their goal was to reach the latitude of southern Spain, so that they could sail due east and take advantage of the prevailing Westerlies, which would blow them all the way home. Meantime, heeling well over as she sailed close to the wind, the *Niña* hummed along on the radiant sea, rising on its swell and leaving a white wake behind her.

With his elbows on the rail, Pedro watched the sea run by. The spray felt cool against his bare arms.

"The Admiral should've court-martialed his hide!" whispered Emilio, plunking his hands down on the rail right beside Pedro and drumming his fingers. "Everyone knows Pinzón sailed off for the gold. I reckon he's got a whole bunch of it stashed away on the *Pinta* and has no intention of giving it back."

Cupping his chin in the palms of his hands, Pedro sighed. "That may be, Emilio, but he'll have to live with it. Funny thing is, I always thought of the Pinzón family as a kind of nobility. Captain Martín didn't act very noble. He acted greedy."

"Aye, lads, that he did," said a voice behind them. It was Lonso. "Greed does strange things to a man."

"I could stand a bit of that gold, m'self," Emilio murmured. "T'would make life a whole lot easier."

Pedro thought about this. Riches might make life easier in some ways, but they couldn't protect you from harm. No amount of gold would have stopped those Caribs from their horrible cannibal practices. Besides, the natives in the Indies didn't even care about gold. It had no particular value to them at all.

He shook his head. The world was a strange place, indeed.

He turned to the old pilot. "The Admiral forgave him. I don't know if I could have done that, in his place. I'd be really mad."

"The Admiral *was* mad, Pedro. But anger, even righteous anger, isn't always the answer." Lonso gazed out over the sea. "Justice is what makes the world right, lads, but forgiveness is what gives us the strength to move on."

"What do you mean?" asked Emilio, slipping his broad hands into the pockets of his tattered britches.

"In forgiving, we let go," the old mariner mused. "In a sense, we let God be in control. God will ultimately deal with Martín Pinzón's treacherous ways, should he choose not to change them. Time will tell."

Pedro shook his head. "All I know is, Pinzón may be from a famous family, but he acted like a coward, running off the way he did." He frowned. "Why should we treat him with respect now? He doesn't deserve it."

"True," Lonso replied. "A man won't be treated like a man, unless he acts like one. The trouble is, not all of us end up becoming the men we once thought we'd be."

That night, as the caravels anchored in one of Española's small bays, Pedro slept on the wet curved deck and dreamed of La Rábida. He was starting to feel a longing for home now. He had been gone nearly five months. These five months had altered his life forever and would soon change the lives of many others. Neither the friars at the monastery nor the people of Palos had any idea where the sailors had been or when—or if—they'd ever return.

Pedro wished there was some way to send a homing pigeon across the sea, some way to communicate with others so far away. For now, the only way was prayer. The boy remembered that Father Antonio had promised to pray for him. Tonight Pedro prayed that God would bless Father Antonio.

A vague concern tiptoed into the back of his brain about their return voyage. It would be a second great feat of seamanship, sailing back across the Ocean Sea during the winter. The Admiral would soon set course due east for Spain. Was he right about the winds? Would his secret knowledge prove true once again? Would the winds to the north propel them home, like the trade winds had escorted them over?

"Father in heaven," he whispered, "the Admiral needs Your help again. We all do. You've brought us this far. I pray You will see us safely home. Oh, and would You tell Father Antonio that I'm all right? Thank you. Amen."

For the next four days, the caravels made little progress against head winds and strong currents, tacking back and forth along the northeast coast of Española, loaded to capacity with the extra crewmen and the treasures for their Majesties.

On the afternoon of the fourth day they had still not left Española in their wake, and they were facing their first real challenge of the homeward voyage.

"Sir, she's still takin' on too much water," Emilio reported wearily to Lonso.

The old pilot took off his cap and scratched his neck. "If it ain't ship-worms been chewin' holes in 'er, we might be able to fix it," he said wearily. "She's leakin' heavy now."

The crews of both ships had been manning the bilge pumps more often than usual, ever since they'd set sail for home.

Emilio's arm muscles bulged, as he thrust the wooden plunger down the middle of the tube and heaved it back up again. The smelly brown liquid that usually poured onto the deck had changed to fairly clean seawater. A bad sign. A *very* bad sign.

Within a few minutes, everyone knew the dread truth. The wooden hull of the *Niña* had somehow sprung a leak.

38

DESTINED FOR GREATNESS

It was one thing to open your eyes in the fresh water of the Rio Tinto, but quite another to do it in *salt* water. And Pedro was the only sailor aboard who could swim well enough to dive in the deep and stay down long enough to work. At that moment he almost wished the Admiral's diver, Manuel, hadn't taken sick just before the trip.

What bothered Pedro even more was that he'd never repaired the hull of a ship before and wasn't sure how he was going to do it now—under *salt* water, with his eyes open.

"Feel yer way," Lonso advised. "Use your fingers. It's possible we've only lost some of the iron nail-heads. They dissolve in salt water and drop off sometimes."

That might be true, but it didn't make Pedro feel any better.

The Admiral stood close by. "If it's a true hole, son, the job will take you some time. Take it one step at a time. We're depending on you."

Talk about pressure! Pedro was aware that every eye was on him. Yet, he also sensed that this was his chance to begin to redeem the loss of the *Santa Maria*.

With a safety rope around his waist and the other end in the hands of Lonso, he held his nose and jumped in, feet first. The water enveloped him like a huge glove, and suddenly the only sound he could hear was the hollowness of the water's depths.

Pedro had entered a turquoise world all its own. The visibility was astounding; he could even see the heavy black anchor lying on the sandy bottom in the distance.

It was breathtakingly beautiful, except that Pedro wasn't about to take a breath. At least not yet. Deep red aquatic plants gyrated gently with the water's movement along with huge patches of spiky green sea grass growing along the white sandy bottom. Two orange and yellow fish resembling frogs silently nuzzled their way along a deep coral reef not far from a pair of black-and-white jackknife fish sniffing the crevices for food.

It was a lazy place, one that made Pedro wish he could linger and explore. Vase-like sponges of purple and red and brown gleamed on the limestone in the diffused light. A black-and-yellow eel enjoyed a cleaning by a spindly long-legged crablike creature crawling on him. And Pedro's favorite creatures, three longsnout orange sea horses, swayed with the sea as if to assure him that all was well.

As he felt his way along the hull, the air bubbles coming out of his nose helped relieve the pressure in his ears. Within seconds, a school of tropical reef fish had appeared out of nowhere to surround his bare calves and tickle his feet. He would enjoy this under other circumstances.

He surfaced, took a fresh breath, and went under again. He could feel the sailors' eyes on him, even underwater. He took his time now, looking for tell-tale bubbles emanating from the hull, relying on his fingers as much as his eyes.

On the third dive, he found it. There was a hole on the starboard side, five feet below the waterline. It had been caulked before, and the old caulking had worked loose. Surfacing again, he called for an iron hook and was given one. Going back down, he worked on scraping away the rest of the old caulking. Patching the hull was really an art, especially underwater. Once the hole was clean, he would have to re-pack it with pitch. They had plenty of it on board. Before they had left Española the sailors had made charcoal for the fogons on the way home. When they burned the logs, both tar and pitch had oozed out, and they had carefully collected the gummy black stuff because it was invaluable for patching leaks and sealing the frayed ends of ropes.

Before he had jumped into the water, Pedro had watched the men heating the pitch and placing it in a container with a long snout—a *jarra*, or pitcher, they called it. It had been invented to hold pitch.

Surfacing again, he told Lonso the situation, indicating the size of the hole with his thumb and forefinger. While the men were preparing handfuls of the pitch for him, Pedro systematically checked the rest of the hull for other holes. He found two more—smaller, but deeper—on the port side, just forward of the rudder.

The crews of both ships stood at the rails and watched, because if the hull of the *Niña* couldn't be repaired, the two Spanish caravels would have to return to La Navidad.

When the pitch was ready for Pedro, he took it down, and with nimble fingers packed the warm substance in the first hole, as quickly as he could. Then he came back up and grabbed handfuls for the other holes.

Finally, the cabin boy broke the surface of the water with one hand waving. He had done it!

The *Niña* was safe.

Amidst the clapping and cheering of his sea mates in both ships, the exhausted boy clambered up the rope ladder and flopped on the solid deck.

The whole job had taken almost two turns of the *ampoletta*, but it was successful. Now, the bilge water could return to its nasty and smelly—but welcome—murky brown.

Pedro hardly heard the cheers of his mates, as he flopped on the deck and fell asleep. He was exhausted.

"She's definitely more seaworthy, I must say," the Admiral remarked to Captain Vicente the following morning. "Her mainsail is holding these winds well."

The *Niña*'s captain nodded without reply. And Pedro, seeing his dark expression, understood why. No ship needed two captains, and the Admiral outranked the ship's captain. He also wondered how Vicente really felt about the Admiral publicly reprimanding his brother. Blood was, after all, thicker than water.

Still Vicente held his tongue and appeared polite, at least on the surface. "I agree, Don Cristobál," he replied somewhat stiffly. "She's been quite adept the entire trip."

The Admiral smiled. "Not as sluggish as the flagship, and more nimble."

Vicente nodded, with just the hint of a smile at the corners of his mouth.

Just then, Cristobál seemed to remember his cabin boy. "Pedro?" he called, looking around. "Now where have you gone to?"

"Right here, sir." The muscles in Pedro's shoulders still ached from his ordeal of yesterday, as he got to his feet and saluted.

"Let's talk a bit." The Admiral led the way to the stern-castle, buttoning the top brass button of his dark blue wool cloak against the coolness of the rising wind.

This was the first time in a long time that the Admiral had invited Pedro to join him in conversation. It brought back memories of his favorite times on the flagship, learning to make point or estimate with dead reckoning. Those were the times that put the desire in his heart to become a sea captain himself, one day.

"Shall I fetch the quadrant, sir?"

"A bit later." Don Cristobál tucked his hands inside his cloak for warmth. "Lad, I'm proud of you. Proud of what you did yesterday."

At first, Pedro could not believe his ears. Then he had to fight back tears. No one had ever spoken of being proud of him.

"I know how hard the loss of the flagship was for you," the Admiral went on. "It was hard for all of us. But," he sighed, "some things can't be helped. Once again, God taught us all a lesson." He smiled ruefully. "He always has a better plan than we imagine."

Pedro wasn't sure where this conversation was going. He shifted from one foot to the other, not to compensate for the ship's rolling, but to ease a growing uneasiness.

"Forgiving ourselves for making mistakes is a key, lad," the Admiral said. "I'm not sure why, but it's sometimes easier to believe God will forgive us, than it is for us to forgive ourselves."

Pedro wondered if any of the snoring bodies now strewn about the deck below were able to hear the Admiral's words. He didn't feel comfortable, being this open about God.

Don Cristobál came to the point. "We all make mistakes, Pedro. The temptation of greed reaches each one of us with its evil tentacles at some point in our lives."

With a shiver, he fastened the rest of the buttons on his cloak. "You showed everyone today how much you really care about this voyage and this ship," he said, drawing to a close. "God gave you a chance to redeem yourself, and you took it."

He looked Pedro in the eye. "Now, I want you to do something else for me: I want you to make sure you've forgiven yourself for what happened back on Española. And then I want you to do something for yourself: I'd like you to consider giving your life totally to God, as I have and as Lonso has."

Pedro winced. There it was, right out in the open, for everyone to hear! He wanted to crawl down into the hold and hide among the ballast of kegs and stones. The gold bracelet around his wrist felt especially cold, right now.

The Admiral seemed oblivious to his reaction—or lack of it. "Without the Almighty's hand to guide you, my son," his voice had dropped almost to a whisper, "you'll wind up just another sea captain." He looked to the horizon. "I don't think that is what God wants. I think He has much more in mind for you." He chuckled. "Indeed, you may be destined for greatness."

39

GALE WINDS

My, ain't we a sorry sight this morning," Lonso quipped wryly, as Pedro yawned and greeted the day. The cabin boy—with no cabin to tend—glumly nodded; he'd had to sleep sitting up last night. There was not enough room to lie down, even when they took turns.

The voyage home was turning out to be far different than the trip across. When a sailor wasn't stepping over a mate, he was trying to navigate his way around the barrels and ropes, or simply hanging on to the ratlines for lack of anywhere else to go. Cargo jammed the main deck, as well as the hold. The six Indians huddled together under the half deck toward the stern, not far from the bamboo cages of smelly wild rats and squawking island birds.

Pedro helped wherever he could and was always at the beck and call of the Admiral. He even did one or two drawings of their cramped quarters, working on the smooth top of a wooden crate, when it was not being used as a chart table.

But the thing he enjoyed the most was practicing his skill at navigation and dead reckoning, as well as over-all seamanship. To his surprise, the Admiral paid much more attention to him on the way home than he had on the way over. Don Cristobál patiently explained why they did each thing the way they did, and actually let him mark their course on the chart. Whenever they altered course, he would make sure Pedro understood why the sails were re-set as they were. He even had him take turns at the tiller, so that he could get a feel for the harmony of sail and rudder working together.

Why the Admiral was giving him all this care baffled Pedro, but he was deeply grateful. With each passing day, he was gaining confidence and began to believe he could actually become a master mariner—one day.

But Lonso was still his closest friend and confidant.

"I heard the Admiral talkin' to you the other night, lad," the old pilot said, as he popped a sardine into his mouth. "You should listen to what he said to you."

Pedro grimaced, as he recalled their conversation about giving his whole life to God. He was afraid that someone had overheard, though Lonso was the one person he wouldn't mind talking about it with. But not now. "I don't want to talk about it," he retorted."

"Have it like ye will, boy. But rest assured, God ain't done with you yet." He smiled. "He has a way of asking for every piece of us."

What in the world did *that* mean? Pedro didn't want to think about that, either.

So, he didn't.

January ebbed into February, and the weeks blurred together, as the two tiny caravels sailed ever further east, toward Europe. Each day followed the same maritime routine. The *ampoletta* turned to the familiar tunes of the grommets' ditties. Each four-hour watch brought duties such as scrubbing the decks, pumping the bilge, and mending sails. In the evening, the sounds of a wooden flute or sailors grumbling together in a card game following Vespers offered their own security on the high seas.

Pedro was sick of the food. All that was left of the provisions they had brought on board at Española was bread, water, and sweet potatoes. What he wouldn't give for one taste of the fruits they had discovered on the islands. At least they occasionally had fresh fish caught by the sailors.

Gone were the balmy, tropical days of Juana and Española! The January air on the *Niña*'s open deck in the midst of the Atlantic Ocean was frigid, even on sunny days. More than once, while standing night watches, Pedro had been soaked by the bone-chilling ocean spray.

But those most affected by the meager diet and plummeting temperatures were the Arawak Indians. Pedro noted that they became more and more miserable, and ate less and less. One by one, they began to die, until there were only two left. After each death the body was slid off planks into the sea, following a brief prayer by the Admiral.

"*Why*, Lonso?" Pedro asked, after the fourth burial at sea. "Why are they dying?"

The old sailor tugged his wool cap lower over his ears.

"Hard to tell, lad. Probably homesickness more than anything else."

"What a terrible way to die! Taken captive against their wills, and torn away from their homes and families."

"I agree, lad," the old sailor responded. "A dreadful waste of human life."

By the morning of February 12th, the two ships were approaching the Azores, a group of nine islands about eight hundred miles west of Portugal in the Atlantic.

"The gale's blowin' across the waves now," Emilio announced, as he jumped onto the main deck from a ratline. "Storm coming, and this one's gonna be a lion."

"A lion?" Pedro finished tying down the last animal cage, so it wouldn't blow overboard.

Emilio was visibly shaken. "*Sí.* This storm's approachin' like a lion. I ain't been through many, but I been through enough to know we're gonna be lucky to survive this one! I . . ." The rest of his sentence was torn away by the rising wind.

Low black thunderheads were rolling quickly across the daytime sky, turning it into a dark, ominous gray. Sailors were ordered up the ratlines to furl and tie all sails except the main, before they were torn off the masts. Pedro could smell the rain coming, as gale winds from the southwest quickly built up twenty-foot waves that were already crashing into the stern of the ship. He could barely hear the helmsman yelling something, when a huge following wave swamped the rudder port.

Rain pelted the young seaman's face, as he peered to starboard, to see how the *Pinta* was faring. The Admiral had given him one assignment: to keep their sister ship in sight, and keep him apprised of how it was going with her. It was not going well. Green-water waves were smothering her bow, as she rolled and pitched through enormous swells.

Then, even as he watched, she lost one of her smaller sails. Her crew had not gotten it furled in time, and now it was torn from its yardarm and streamed out in front of her like a sad banner in the wind.

The Admiral and Martin Pinzón had agreed that they would use lighted torches to keep sight of each other in the event of a bad storm, but Pinzón's ship was being blown away from the *Niña,* and it was getting more difficult for Pedro to see the *Pinta's* light.

This he reported to the Admiral, who just shook his head, and cried, "Pray for her, lad! And you better pray for us, too, while you're about it! It'll be the grace of God if any of us survive this storm!"

Pedro double-knotted the line holding him to the port rail and gripped it with all his might. They were no longer steering by the compasses. The only way to survive a winter storm like this was to let the ship be driven by the gale force winds and scud through the waves.

Though it was actually afternoon, it was growing darker by the minute. Pedro strained to catch a glimpse of the *Pinta*, but she had become so small in the distance that now he wasn't sure that he was still seeing her at all.

Meanwhile, the *Niña* was having her own struggles. Somewhere ahead of them contrary winds from the North were creating a cross sea—the waves started coming simultaneously at the ship from different directions! The Admiral and Vicente Pinzón, standing side by side on the half-deck, were yelling new commands to the helmsman with each wave, trying to find the best angles by which to meet them. The waves were strong and high, and relentlessly pounded the small caravel.

The wind was building to a gale. So, the Admiral ordered the sailors aloft to take in the mainsail and set only the foresail. As soon as that was done, he yelled for all hands to join him on the main deck. Raising his voice to be heard over the shrieking of the wind, he prayed to God, promising that if He would spare them from perishing in this storm that they would all make a pilgrimage together to the first church they came to on land.

But the storm continued with the same intensity.

Pedro was scared. More scared than he could ever remember.

Again he looked for the *Pinta*, but he could not see her anymore.

"Admiral," he cried, "the *Pinta* is gone!"

"Keep praying," he called back, without taking his eyes off the sea ahead.

A short while later, he gave Pedro a new assignment: "Lad, when I get these ready, I want you to pitch them over the side."

The Admiral clutched some parchment sheets, wrapped in oilcloth to protect them. Pedro recognized them. They were his charts and his description of their voyage.

"Now find a small cask, put these in it, seal it, and cast it into the sea."

Pedro didn't have to ask why. He knew. Cristobál wanted at least one account of the voyage to survive, no matter what happened to them.

Where would he find a cask? With the oilcloth package tucked tightly under his arm, he made his way aft across the pitching deck to the ship's supply area. There he found what he was looking for—a small cask, half full of precious iron nails. Not finding anything to put the nails in, he took off his hat and put them in that. He would figure out later what to do with them.

There was a top on the cask, but how to seal it? The idea came to him to use pitch. There was enough left from the hull repair, and that way the cask wouldn't leak.

After sealing the cask and re-tying himself to the port rail, he said a prayer. "God, if this is to be the only record of our voyage, if tonight our souls are coming to you, make sure this gets into the right hands."

He cast it into the sea and watched as it bobbed away into the darkness.

The storm assailed the little vessel, but by the mercy of God, their souls were not required of them that night. Or the next night. Or the next.

Finally, at sunset on February 14th, the wind moderated, and the sea began to calm down.

"Land ho!" came shortly after sunrise the next day. But, due to contrary winds, it would be three more days until they reached Santa María, the southernmost and smallest island of the Azores, about nine hundred miles off the coast of Portugal.

The first thing the crew did when they got ashore was to accompany the Admiral to the nearest church to give thanks to God for sparing their lives. Then they set about to reprovision for the last leg of their journey home to Palos.

Four days later, they embarked, leaving a note for the *Pinta*. No one really believed that their mates had survived, but it comforted them to leave the note, anyway.

Foul weather greeted them, as they left the harbor, and stayed with them day after day. Just when Pedro thought things couldn't possibly get as bad as the last storm, they did. This time the ship's log read February 28, 1493.

"Wind's shifted to the southeast, sir," called Lonso to the Admiral, who was up on the stern-castle. "Looks like another bad one. We're already makin' eleven knots!"

"Get those sails in, Señor Niño. Hurry! All hands aloft. You know what to do."

Yes, thought Pedro. *We all know what to do.*

He and the other grommets tied themselves to the railings and braced for the worst.

"Batten down the hatch!" roared Vicente Pinzón.

"Rig lifelines fore and aft!" the boatswain yelled.

As before, the sky darkened, only now there were streaks of lightning, arrowing down to the water. Pedro had seen lightning, of course, but not at sea in a violent storm. He'd heard of lightning somehow being drawn to the top of a mainmast and running down it like a fireball, electrifying everyone in the rigging that descended from the crow's nest.

"God!" he cried into the teeth of the raging gale. "It's Pedro, again! Have mercy on us and save our souls like You did the last time!"

A tremendous cracking peal of thunder seemed to break right over their heads, as a triple bolt of lightning shot down into the water just off their port bow.

But it did not hit them.

The cold front was bearing down on them without mercy. And fast. The sailors knew what to do, but would they have the time? Pedro watched as dozens of sailors scurried up the riggings and yards like monkeys, scrambling to find any bit of sail that was not tightly lashed down.

But the cold was working against them. Men's fingers were so cold, they were not working properly. They started losing their grip. One fell a short distance, then another, barely catching himself before being swept over the side. The Admiral called to Lonso to get the men down quickly, before somebody broke their neck. If they lost a sail or two, so be it.

All of a sudden, a screaming blast of wind attacked the ship with such fury that it tore the lower sail from its yardarm and stripped it away. Then, before anyone could do anything, it dug at a second sail, almost like it had fingers, and successfully clawed it out of its gasket. Incredibly, in the next few moments all her sails were stripped from the yardarms.

For the next hour the *Niña* clawed her way through frigid waves that surrounded them like ravenous wolves.

Normally, the *Niña* rode only five or six feet out of the water. But now, with the following sea pushing water in through the tiller hole and waves breaking on her main deck, and her heavy load of men and cargo, she was riding even lower in the water. Pedro had heard of ships caught in hurricanes that turned turtle, completely upside down, with their masts pointing to the bottom. They filled so quickly that no one could escape, and they went down with all hands on board.

Now the *Niña* was fighting for her life, as she had never fought before.

And the fight went on and on—one day, two days, three. Thirty-foot waves lifted her without mercy high on their swells and then flung her into the depths of their troughs. At night the lightning served to illuminate the monstrous waves that towered over them, and crashed down from above.

Each time Pedro looked up at one of them, he was certain it was the last thing he would ever see in his mortal body.

And each time, somehow they survived.

By March 3rd, deep lines of fatigue were etched into the Admiral's visage. Pedro, trying to protect himself from the icy water that still came over them from both sides, waited for any order the Admiral might have for him. He could barely feel his fingers and toes.

"Sir, she keeps falling off course!" Captain Vicente shouted.

"Just keep as close to the wind, as you can. We can't do any more than that, except pray."

Would they be able to stay afloat much longer? Pedro wasn't the only one wondering. Even the most seasoned sailors knew they were in God's hands now. No ship this small could keep taking this punishment and stay afloat. The *Niña* was exhausted and so were her men.

More than once, Pedro had seen the Admiral praying. And now, he was praying, too, and so was everyone else.

But it seemed that heaven had closed its ears.

40

IN THE EYE OF THE STORM

For two more long miserable days and nights, the tattered ship was driven northeast under bare masts. No one slept. Nor did they eat—even the most seasoned sailors were seasick. The ship's bilge pump, the only device they had to get rid of the water on board, was slowly losing the race. The angry sea continued to wash in through the rudder port, soaking the helmsman and taxing his muscles to hold the giant tiller steady. Even the two wooden cogs holding the rudder to the tiller were now straining to hold the tiller tight.

On the evening of the fifth day of this seemingly endless ordeal, something strange occurred.

"What's happening?" Pedro directed his question to Emilio, who was holding onto a rope ladder and scanning the strange sky like everyone else. Without warning, the winds had suddenly died down, and the thick carpet of dark clouds was beginning to part. The light of a winter moon quietly crept across a calming sea and onto the deck of the tiny caravel.

"Could be the answer to your prayers," Emilio replied, mocking but half serious.

"Maybe heaven's listening, after all," Pedro hoped aloud.

"Sir, do you see it?" called Captain Vicente from the forecastle. "Over there!" He pointed to port.

The clouds had been swept aside, and as the little ship rocked with the waves, Pedro's eyes slowly adjusted to the moonlight. At first, he could detect only the outline, but then he could see it. The dark line of land on the horizon was coming into view. Soon, his ears detected a familiar sound, the sound of surf crashing against rocks.

"What do you make of it, sir?" Vicente's voice broke the silence gripping the ship.

"It may be that God has swept away the clouds, so we could see, that we are much closer to land than we imagined," the Admiral replied from the main deck. "By my reckoning, we're off the coast of Portugal, and that break over there," he pointed to a depression in the landmass, just to the south of them, "is the mouth of the River of Lisbon."

Pedro—and everyone else—waited for him to explain its significance.

"That river has a deep-water harbor in its mouth, a safe haven for any poor souls caught in the living hell that we have been through."

"Señor Lonso!" the Admiral abruptly yelled to his trusted pilot. "Have we any sails left?"

"Only one, sir. A small foresail."

"Then get it set quickly, Lonso, while it's calm."

As the sailors raced aloft to set the small sail on the foremast, the Admiral muttered to Pedro: "That sail is not much help, but we must try to make way with it. This quiet is merely the eye of the storm. If we had no canvas at all, when this wind resumed, we'd be driven on the rocks for certain. At least now we have a ghost of a chance."

To those within earshot he announced, "Men, we have a chance to get in there!" The confidence in his voice inspired all of them.

But the glance that he and Lonso privately exchanged told Pedro how slender the chance was. The west coast of Portugal was renowned for its rocky coastline, treacherous to anyone sailing along it under adverse conditions. It was a graveyard for ships like theirs, unable to use their sails and driven on the rocks. Being dashed against the massive boulders, the Admiral assured him, was every bit as unpleasant as drowning at sea.

"Sir, exactly how good are our chances?" Pedro asked him.

He was silent for a moment. "We are now north of the river. When the storm comes back, the winds will be west and northwest. If they build to the same fury as before, we will be driven hard by them and a following sea toward the rocks on either side of the river mouth."

He paused. "Our small sail will be of little use. At best, it will help us stay off the rocks. Most of the work will have to be done with the tiller. We will have to come hard to port at just the right moment to get into the river. And, if God has mercy on us we just might be able to make it."

"I believe He will help you, sir."

A faint smile played across the Admiral's lips. Pedro sensed that he was actually looking forward to this ultimate challenge to his seamanship.

"Don't stop praying, Pedro. But, it will be harder than trying to spear a brass ring from the back of a galloping horse."

Abruptly the clear sky vanished and the wind picked up. The storm roared back with a vengeance.

"Here it comes, sir!" Lonso screamed. But the words were torn from his mouth by the wind.

Suddenly a rogue following wave, bigger than any they'd encountered, lifted her stern and then smashed it down hard.

Immediately the helmsman shouted from below: "She's lost her way, sir! I can't control her!"

"*What?*" the Admiral whirled around.

"I fear she's jumped her gudgeons, sir!"

From what the helmsman had taught him, Pedro knew what that meant. The rudder operated on a hinge that connected it to the stern. On the forward edge of the rudder were two great iron pins, called pintles, that rotated in two sockets fixed to the stern, called gudgeons. What had just happened was that the wave that had lifted their stern and dropped it, had caused the pins to come out of their sockets. The only thing still holding the rudder to the ship was the long tiller.

This meant they now had no means of controlling their direction. And even the slimmest chance of avoiding the rocks was now gone. They were looking at certain death.

Pedro clutched his jacket shut against the cold. The events going on around him seemed to slow down and recede, and his mind drifted off to the events of the past months: the voyage across the sea . . . the Arawaks . . . the Tainos . . . the Caribs . . . the voyage back home . . . the cost of his disobedience . . . the cost of his greed . . . his kidnapping and rescue . . .

And, the mercy and forgiveness and faithfulness of God—*his* God.

Amidst the swirling chaos around him, the past eight months were somehow coming together into this one moment. Now he knew why he had come, why he was on this ship.

He'd not gone through those experiences for nothing. While he didn't understand everything that had happened to him, he knew for certain that God had spared his life for a reason. God had a purpose for his life. And somehow, right then, the young Spaniard realized who he was, in a way he had never understood before.

"I can do it, sir." At first, he didn't recognize his own voice. His words grew louder. "I'm a good swimmer. I can guide the pintles back into the gudgeons."

Through the pounding rain, Don Cristobál looked at the boy with a frown, almost as if he couldn't understand what Pedro was saying.

"Let me go over the side," the lad explained, "and repair it."

The storm tried to whip his words away, as if it were furious at what was being suggested.

"It's sure death if you stay very long in that icy water."

Pedro nodded. "It's sure death for all of us, sir, if I don't try."

For a long second the Admiral stared at him.

"Very well," he declared quietly, "proceed."

Lonso tied a rope lifeline to Pedro's waist, and then called for two men to stand by at the stern with thicker ropes. These they would pass over the stern, and Pedro would position them under the rudder. When they were in place, he would give two pulls of the lifeline. That would be the signal for the crew to start heaving on the ropes. Another double-pull would signal that the rudder was in approximate position. Then it was up to Pedro, to guide the pintles back into their gudgeons, and signal them to lower the rudder into place.

When all was ready, Pedro swung a leg over the rail and prepared to jump into the sea.

"All right, lad," Lonso coached him, "work as fast as you can! A few minutes in that icy water, and your fingers won't respond."

With calm resolution the Admiral cried, "God be with you, boy."

The shock of the cold water hit his chest and face like a hammer. Taking a deep breath, he swam alongside the ship to the stern. He came up for another breath and then affixed the heavy ropes under the rudder, giving the double-pull signal.

Topside, the crew heaved on the ropes, gradually lifting the rudder up to the proper position.

Then another following wave hit them hard and undid all of their work.

Patiently Pedro began again. He was shaking violently with cold, and as Lonso had warned him, his fingers were stiffening; he had to will them to do what he wanted them to do.

Again, they raised the rudder, until they had it at the right height. Then Pedro took a great breath and dived down into the murky water, to guide the pins back to the holes. He had to do it as much by touch, as by sight, and he was losing all the feeling in his fingers. He would have to get it right, the first time.

With God's help, he could do it.

Grabbing a pin with each hand, he wrenched and twisted them, to get them properly aligned with the holes. The sea was fighting him. Each time they were almost there, another wave would take them out of alignment.

His lungs were screaming for fresh air, so he came up again. His legs were numb. The pins would not stay lined up.

Back under the water he grimaced wryly. This was like trying to spear *two* brass rings from the back of a galloping horse!

I can't do it, he thought. But just as he was about to let go of the pins and give the double-pull signal on the lifeline for them to haul him out, one more surging wave came. And this one, instead of pushing the pintles askew, plunked them back into the gudgeons, where they belonged.

He gave the signal. They hauled him out. Everyone was cheering. Lonso wrapped him in blankets. The Admiral hugged him.

But Pedro knew that precious little of it was his doing.

There was no time for celebration—the ship was still in mortal danger. The *Niña* was now so close to the shore that they could hear the great waves crashing on the huge boulders.

"Sir!" the lookout screamed to the Admiral, "the rocks! We're almost on them!"

Now it was the Admiral's turn to face the impossible. With the rudder back in place and Lonso and the helmsman both manning the tiller, he took over the command from Vicente Pinzón up on the stern-castle, where he had an unobstructed view of what was coming at them.

Pedro, huddling and shivering below with three blankets wrapped around him, could see what the Admiral was trying to do. As the wind and sea were driving them toward the rocky coast, he was gauging each wave as it came under the ship, positioning them to take advantage of whatever thrust it might have.

He called down an unbroken stream of commands to Lonso and the helmsman. "Come to starboard . . . a little more . . . that's it . . . now hold her there . . . all right, fall off just a bit . . . good . . . good . . . now starboard a little more . . . more . . . steady as she goes . . . steady . . . *Now! Hard a port!* Push her all the way over, mate! And hold her there!"

With the thrust of a great white-capped wave on her starboard quarter, the *Niña* swerved to the left, heeling so far over that crewmen screamed, convinced she was going to capsize. But at the last instant, she righted and practically flew past the rocks into the mouth of the river!

The crew was in shock. Then suddenly they all realized at the same time that they were not going to die after all—they were going to live! They were safe!

A great rattling cheer went up, mixed with praises to God on high, for His deliverance.

Lonso emerged from the helm with tears in his eyes. "There's not another man alive who could have brought us in!" he exclaimed to Pedro, his voice breaking. "Not another man with God's hand on him like you just saw."

41

BARCELONA

April in Barcelona—1493. The winter court of the Spanish Sovereigns, King Ferdinand and Queen Isabella, on the eastern Mediterranean seacoast of Spain. It was a breathtaking sight, one which Pedro would one day describe to his grandchildren.

As their grand procession passed by, the people lining the streets cheered. There were more people than Pedro had ever seen in his life, and they cheered so loudly that they drowned out the sounds of clinking spurs and snorting horses. Indeed, Pedro could barely hear the screeching of the caged parrot he carried in his hands—a bird that was creating quite a stir all by itself. Children perched atop their fathers' shoulders pointed toward them, shouting "*Pájaro!* Bird! Bird!"

Dazzled, Pedro gazed up at upper balconies and windows of adobe houses, where dark-eyed *senoritas* waved colorful capes and showered them with orange and yellow rose petals. Women smiled at them behind fans, while men doffed their caps and bowed at the waist.

A band of drummers and pipers led the way, playing stirring martial music, while a mounted escort followed close behind. Their flags and banners unfurled in the breeze, just above the Admiral's head. Don Cristóbal was astride a magnificent black stallion, a few paces ahead of Pedro and the rest of the expedition.

The Admiral was the reason for the parade; everyone wanted to catch a glimpse of Don Cristóbal Colón, the resplendent Admiral of the Ocean Sea, entering the city of Barcelona in triumph. He was the hero of all Spain, including Pedro whose sense of pride at that moment was greater than anything he had ever known. To have been part of this epic, history-making journey—a voyage of destiny that Pedro was sure would change all of Europe—was more than a dream.

It was a miracle.

The Admiral sat tall and straight in the saddle, like royalty, with a new navy blue cloak flung over his broad shoulders. He rode with his left hand holding the reins, and his right resting on his hip. The wisps of curly white hair that peeked out from the back of his matching navy-blue velvet cap, had been freshly trimmed. Every so often he would acknowledge the cheering, raising his right hand in a broad wave of salute.

This was the happiest day of the Admiral's life, Pedro realized—and it was the happiest day of his own, as well. Best of all, they were about to have an audience with the King and Queen!

The officers and sailors walking beside Pedro were feeling the same way. Vicente Pinzón smiled despite the absence of his brother, Martín, whose caravel had been blown all the way to Africa during the first storm. Freshly shaved faces, new shirts and sailors' trousers, and new sandals gave everyone a clean, crisp appearance, matching what they were feeling on the inside.

Pedro de Torreros felt it, too. He was no longer a seaman apprentice. He had proved himself an able seaman. He had learned good seamanship and navigation, had survived a perilous voyage, survived capture and imminent death at the hands of savages, and helped to save the ship on the way home. He might be younger than most sailors, but he had sailed farther than men twice his age. Any captain would be glad to have this young able seamen on his crew.

Today Pedro felt more like a man than a boy. If only his grandfather, or Father Antonio or Father Peréz, could have been here! To see him introduced to the Monarchs of Spain, as one of the sailors who changed the course of history. Following in his father's footsteps, by the grace of God, he would carry on the family name now and bring it honor, not shame.

Sitting on a regal chair, on a raised dais at the back of the grand throne room, Queen Isabella was the most beautiful woman Pedro had ever seen. Her long brocade dress was turquoise and flowed down below her matching silk slippers onto the marble steps beneath her. Her black curly hair had been swept up into two buns, each adorned with fresh flowers. A fur cape was draped over one arm of her chair. Her brown almond eyes held a certain kindness that Pedro had not expected. Every inch of her being announced royalty.

Pedro liked her instantly.

On her right was King Ferdinand. He had more of the aristocratic air Pedro associated with royalty. His dark, Aragonian bloodline was evident, both in his skin tone and his hair color. Bushy eyebrows overshadowed two large black eyes, creating dark circles. Ferdinand's long lean frame bent slightly toward the queen, as he whispered something in her right ear.

After he finished, he smoothed the sleeves of his fur-lined woolen robe and then his graying mustache. Gemstone rings adorned all his fingers but the thumbs.

Mingling on either side of the hall were courtiers—noblemen with elegant dress swords and ladies in coiffed hair and fine silk dresses. Despite the presence of all these people, it was unusually quiet. The only sound came from the heels of new leather boots and flat sandals crossing the black-and-white squares of the marble floor, punctuated by the occasional startling *squawk* of a parrot. Shafts of morning sunlight came down from high clerestory windows, as torches flickered along the walls and warmed the hall.

All at once, there was a collective intake of breath. The Sovereigns were standing up! Even Pedro sensed how rare this was, a courtesy extended only to visiting royalty.

"Don Cristóbal Colón, our Admiral of the Ocean Sea!" King Ferdinand's voice resonated off the stone walls. "We welcome you!"

The Admiral approached the dais, mounted its three steps, then knelt and kissed the king's hand. "Thank you, sire."

"We have heard of your successes," said Queen Isabella with a smile.

"Yes, Your Majesty."

"Please, sit with us." She motioned for a chair to be brought and placed by her side.

There was a murmur on the court. This had *never* happened before!

Every eye watched and every ear listened, as the Admiral related the wondrous tale of his quest for Cipangu and Cathay.

As the Admiral told of crystal blue waters, exotic rain forests, and colorful Asian coral reefs, Pedro's mind traveled back across the Atlantic. The young Spaniard twisted the gold bracelet at his wrist and warmed with the memory of Macu, the Arawak friend who had given it to him.

When Don Cristóbal related the loss of the *Santa Maria*, there was no blame apportioned; in fact, he suggested it may have been God's will, for the magnificent fort of La Navidad came into being, as a result. He anticipated that it was just the first of many Spanish colonies to come, as Spain settled a New World.

"And now, Your Majesties, may I present your gifts?"

With this, the Admiral stepped down from the dais and walked over to his crew. "These men were members of my expedition. They bring you treasures from the Indies."

With great respect, one by one the sailors came forward to place huge palm baskets on the steps. These were stuffed with such novelties as sweet potatoes, Indian corn, and green-leaf tobacco. Two sailors brought forth some wood carvings from the Arawaks. Emilio arranged some wooden spears on the steps. Another sailor laid down two folded hammocks. Pedro displayed the caged parrot for the Sovereigns, while two more sailors carried up cages containing a jungle rat and a dog that could not bark.

Lonso himself, dressed in fresh striped trousers, escorted the two Arawak Indians to the steps. The fresh paint on their faces and long feathers in their hair reminded Pedro of that first morning on the beach. They were shivering, and Pedro realized it had nothing to do with the temperature in the hall; they were overwhelmed by what they were seeing. They felt *here*, as he did *there*, when he first met them. Would they ever be able to return home, as he had?

"Your Majesties, there is one more gift," declared the Admiral, who had saved the best for last. He motioned for the leather-bound chest to be brought forth.

It took four seamen to lift it, and under the Admiral's direction, they placed it on the dais directly in front of the Sovereigns. Then he had them remove the top, so that all might see what it contained.

There was a gasp—from the Sovereigns, as well as the courtiers. The chest was filled to overflowing with gleaming gold artifacts! Masks, necklaces, bracelets, even raw nuggets—all caught the light from the torches and windows and reflected it. There was more pure gold here than any of them, including the Sovereigns, had ever seen.

Whispers escalated into excitement, as the court began to realize and then speculate on what this might mean for Spain, and the world. A crusade to reconquer the Holy Land, a vast fleet of exploration, settlements to the ends of the earth, Spain ascending over all the realms and kingdoms of the known—and unknown—world.

As the excitement died away, the court fell silent. Without warning, the King and Queen suddenly knelt down together, in front of their thrones. The entire court followed their example.

Raising his hands above his head, King Ferdinand's voice boomed to the rafters. "O Lord, You have answered our prayers. We are eternally grateful. You have shown us the sea route to Asia, and opened the way for us to carry Your Word to distant lands. Help us to use these gifts wisely."

With that, the entire hall broke into singing the *Te Deum*. At the last line, Pedro's eyes, like many others, filled with tears.

O Lord,
in Thee have I trusted.
Let me never be put to shame.

What else could there possibly be, Pedro wondered, to add to this moment?

But there was one more thing.

42

THE GIFT

It was a warm spring afternoon, as the two-wheeled cart, driven by Father Antonio and pulled by the monastery's horse, Caballo, creaked past the bronze plaques at the entrance to La Rábida. Pedro breathed a happy sigh. "It's just the same!" He had feared that somehow it might have changed, while he was gone. *He* certainly had!

Father Antonio seemed surprised. "Of course, it's the same! Things don't change very quickly around here."

Waiting for them at the front door was the abbot, Father Peréz. "The Admiral has told me good things about you, young man. Many good things."

Pedro jumped down and ran and hugged him. "It's good to be home, Father!"

"We are grateful to God that He brought you home, Pedro. We prayed for you every day without fail, and the Lord certainly answered our prayers."

"But, this may not be your home for long," the abbot replied, with a mixture of joy and sadness. "The Admiral has been offered a fleet—a *real* fleet—to return to the Indies, and he wants you aboard his flagship, as a navigator."

"What? I can't believe it!" His fondest dream had just come true.

Then, he too, was sad. "But I love it here! I don't want to leave—at least, not right away."

Father Peréz folded his hands in the loose sleeves of his plain brown habit. "I hope what you want is what God wants for you. That is how we have been praying for you."

Pedro sighed. "It is, Father. I just don't want to go, right away. I never realized how much I love it here, until I thought I would never see La Rábida again."

The abbot put a hand on his arm. "Pedro de Torreros, you will always have a home here, for as long as you like. Consider La Rábida your spiritual home."

"As it is mine," came a voice from behind them.

It was the Admiral. "Before we go to Vespers, there is something I want to say to you, Pedro, in private."

He looked at Father Peréz, who ushered them into the little refectory, where they had first met, and excused himself.

When they sat down at the table, Don Cristobál was solemn, and for a long moment his blue eyes were fastened intently on Pedro. Then he slowly drew out the red leather pouch with the Crimson Cross in it, opened it, and put the cross on the table before them.

"You heard the story of this cross, the night we met."

Pedro nodded.

"Do you remember what Father Juan said about what was to happen to the cross next?"

Pedro thought a moment. "He said that it was to become a special sign of God's blessing, reminding each person to whom it was given of their destiny as one of God's servants."

The Admiral was impressed. "Absolutely right, lad!" He paused. "Do you remember what else he said?"

That was more difficult. But it came back to him. "The abbot said that one day God would show you to whom the Crimson Cross was to go next."

"Correct. And He has."

Pedro stared at him, as the reason for this meeting began to dawn on him.

"Pedro de Torreros, God has instructed me to give this cross to you, that it will guide you and encourage you, as it has me. Keep it with you always. Guard it with your life. And someday God will show you to whom you must give it."

As the Admiral passed the cross to him, Pedro was overwhelmed. He traced the outline of the silver-filigreed cross with his finger, his heart full.

As the friary bell sounded, the Admiral looked out the open door to the valley beyond, now filled with the golden haze of late afternoon. With eyes trained for the horizon at sea, he looked far into the distance, almost as if he could see into the future.

"One day," he mused softly, "you will be an admiral yourself. You may even have a procession in your honor."

Pedro was speechless.

"I know it sounds impossible to you now, but you have learned that nothing is impossible to God. And you are sailing for Him now, remember?"

Pedro grinned. "Aye, sir, indeed I am!"

"Good, son." The friary bell rang again. "We'd better hurry, Pedro; you know how Father Juan doesn't like us being late."

They hurried to the chapel and slipped into the last pew, just as the monks were chanting the last of the *Te Deum.*

O Lord,
in Thee have I trusted.
Let me never be put to shame.

HISTORICAL NOTE

The man we know as Christopher Columbus was born and raised in Genoa, Italy, where he was known as Christoforo Colombo. But in gratitude to the Spanish sovereigns, Ferdinand and Isabella, for commissioning his westward voyage to the Indies, he adopted Spain as his native land. Already he had begun referring to himself as Don Cristobál Colón, his name in this book.

While he made four voyages in all, we deal with only the first, the voyage of destiny, which turned out to be one of the greatest adventures of all time. Don Cristobál was widely regarded as the most gifted navigator of his age. He felt that his seamanship was a skill God had given him, to enable him to fulfill his destiny: To bear the light of Christ west to the people of Marco Polo's fabled Indies, where riches would be discovered that would finance the recovery of the Holy Land for Christendom, and the rebuilding of Solomon's Temple in Jerusalem.

The abbot of the Franciscan monastery known as La Rábida was Father Juan Peréz. At one time he had been a chaplain to Queen Isabella, and after she at first rejected Columbus's project, Father Peréz did write her a note asking her to reconsider. Had it not been for Peréz, Columbus might never have sailed to the New World.

From the crew manifest of the Santa Maria, we know that Columbus had a cabin boy named Pedro. We made up his background and early years at La Rábida, but he did, in fact, sail with Columbus on all four voyages to the New World. Chachu, Peralonso Niño, and Juan De la Cosa are likewise drawn from life, as are Captains Martín and Vicente Pinzón. The other members of the crew are fictional.

The first voyage is as accurate as we can make it. The sailors' mutiny nearly happened and was narrowly averted. The little flotilla traveled the last three days at breakneck speed before they reached the island Columbus gratefully named San Salvador (Holy Savior).

At first, relations between the Spaniards and the Arawak natives who greeted them could not have been friendlier. The Arawaks, whom Columbus called Indians (being convinced he had reached the Indies), greeted these white men as their deliverers, come to protect them from the larger warlike tribe of cannibals known as Caribs.

Continued references in the book to Cathay (China) and Cipangu (Japan), even after Columbus had reached the Carribean Islands, are due to his mistaken belief that he was in Asian waters.

The temptation that turned Columbus from his path of missionary exploration was gold. Trinkets and ornaments of the precious metal, worn by the innocent natives, changed everything.

The wreck of the Santa Maria happened as we describe it. Pedro was at the helm and was devastated by what had happened. He learned well from this tragedy, however, and in later years went on to become an admiral in the Spanish navy, in command of five ships. But his adventures immediately after that fateful night, as well as what occurred subsequently between him and Columbus, are the work of fiction.

Columbus's masterful feat of seamanship, bringing the stricken Niña into the safety of the River of Lisbon under bare poles, is exactly as it happened, as was the triumphant reception of Don Cristobál Colón, Admiral of the Ocean Sea, at the court of Ferdinand and Isabella.

Old Europe had discovered the New World, and nothing would ever be the same.

The **CRIMSON CROSS** juvenile fiction series
by best-selling authors
Peter Marshall and David Manuel
(*The Light and the Glory* and *From Sea to Shining Sea*).

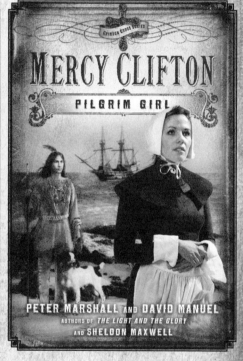

Nate Donovan: Revolutionary Spy
Marshall, Manuel, Maxwell, $9.99
ISBN-13: 978-0-8054-4394-3
ISBN-10: 0-8054-4394-0

Mercy Clifton: Pilgrim Girl
Marshall, Manuel, Maxwell, $9.99
ISBN-13: 978-0-8054-4395-0
ISBN-10: 0-8054-4395-9

To access interactive quizzes, historical time
lines, puzzles, and exclusive videos of the books,
visit the official Crimson Cross Web site at
www.crimsoncrossbooks.com.

Pure Enjoyment™